❖ ❖ ❖ *A Town Called Hope · Book 2* ❖ ❖ ❖

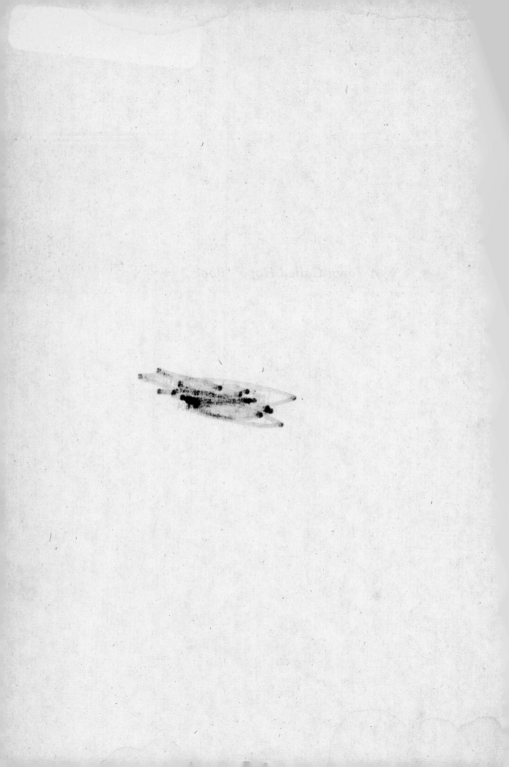

Prairie Fire

CATHERINE PALMER

TYNDALE HOUSE PUBLISHERS, INC.
CAROL STREAM, ILLINOIS

Visit Tyndale's exciting Web site at www.tyndale.com

TYNDALE and Tyndale's quill logo are registered trademarks of Tyndale House Publishers, Inc.

Prairie Fire

Designed by Rule 29

Edited by Kathryn S. Olson

Unless otherwise indicated, all Scripture quotations are taken from *The Holy Bible*, King James Version.

Scripture quotations marked NLT are taken from the *Holy Bible*, New Living Translation, copyright © 1996. Used by permission of Tyndale House Publishers, Inc., Carol Stream, Illinois 60188. All rights reserved.

Library of Congress Cataloging-in-Publication Data

Palmer, Catherine, date
   Prairie fire / Catherine Palmer.
     p. cm. — (A town called Hope ; #2)
    ISBN 0-8423-7057-9 (softcover)
    I. Title. II. Series: Palmer, Catherine, date   Town called Hope ; #2.
   PS3566.A495P65 1998
   813'.54—dc21   98-19977

New repackage first published in 2009 under ISBN 978-1-4143-3158-4.

Printed in the United States of America

15 14 13 12 11 10 09
7   6   5   4   3   2   1

For Sharon Buchanan-McClure,

my friend

᠎

I have come to bring fire to the earth. . . . From now on families will be split apart, three in favor of me, and two against—or the other way around. There will be a division between father and son, mother and daughter, mother-in-law and daughter-in-law.
Luke 12:49, 52-53, NLT

When you walk through the fire of oppression, you will not be burned up; the flames will not consume you. For I am the Lord, your God. . . . You are precious to me. You are honored, and I love you.   Isaiah 43:2-4, NLT

CHAPTER 1

Hope, Kansas
October 1865

T HERE'S not a good heart among those folks," Jack Cornwall
muttered as he led his horse across the bridge away from
Hope. "Not a one."

With icy claws of pain gripping his wounded shoulder, Jack
staggered down the road that would take him to Topeka. A chill
wind whistled eastward across the Kansas prairie. He swung
around and glared into the night, as if by sheer willpower he could
intimidate the coming storm into retreat. Heedless, a frigid gust
whipped beneath his lapels and ballooned his battered leather
jacket.

Gritting his teeth, Jack stopped and bent over, fighting nausea.
The stallion edged forward to nuzzle his master's neck with a
velvet nose. A low snuffling conveyed the creature's unease at
this midnight journey. Jack ran a hand down the coarse mane as
he fought the reality that assailed him.

He had lost everything he'd ever fought for, everything he'd
ever loved. His home. The Cornwall family farm. His sister Mary.
Five of the men in his battalion—including his closest friend. The
Confederacy and its goal of a new and vital nation. And now his
little nephew, Chipper.

The darkness surrounding the man swirled through his
thoughts. Hunger twisted his stomach. Thirst parched his tongue.

If he blacked out now—here—far from warmth, he might never make it back to his parents' home in Missouri. He tugged on Scratch's reins. The horse needed shelter from the autumn wind. They both craved decent food and a place to rest. But where?

The prairie dwellers who had dug their homes out of the Kansas sod despised Jack, and even now he tasted their hatred in the blood on his tongue. Earlier that evening the residents of Hope had gathered to cheer their neighbor Seth Hunter in the fistfight. The outcome ended any chance Jack had of taking Chipper back to Missouri. With his jaw nearly busted and his shoulder half-torn apart, Jack had been forced to surrender. The crowd had parted, watched him pass, and then clamored around Seth with whoops of victory.

"Ah, forget the whole confounded bunch of 'em," Jack snarled. Then he gave a bitter laugh. "*Hope.* Yeah, sure."

A short distance down the road, a soddy formed a low hump in the endless, bleak stretch of tall prairie grass. Jack knew from hearsay that the homesteaders Jimmy O'Toole and his wife, Sheena, were his enemy Hunter's close friends, and this evening they were away at the dance. He doubted they would permit him to spend a night at their place. Not only were they loyal to their neighbor, but the O'Tooles lived with a passel of kids and relatives in the little soddy. The crowd itself would make a visitor unwelcome.

Jack snorted at the thought of the O'Toole family. Bunch of Irish street rats. Street rats turned prairie dogs. The image amused him, but his grin sent a stabbing pain through his jaw. Had Hunter broken the bone after all? Jack prodded the muscle and sinew beneath his roughly whiskered skin. Nah, it wasn't busted. Bruised, though. He'd be surprised if he didn't lose a tooth or two.

Checking his shoulder, Jack discovered that the bullet wound he'd suffered two months before had torn open during the fistfight. With all the travel he'd been doing, the blasted thing had never had a chance to heal right. Now blood seeped through his shirt and made his fingers sticky.

"Scratch," he said, eyeing the ramshackle barn near the soddy, "like it or not, the O'Tooles are fixing to have company. If you promise to keep quiet, I'll fetch you some fresh water and maybe even a few oats."

It didn't take Jack long to slip into Jimmy O'Toole's barn, tend to the horse, and locate a pile of hay in a back corner. He had half a mind to raid the nearby soddy for food, but he and his Confederate vigilante buddies had already run into trouble with the law. He didn't like the idea of landing himself in a Kansas jail. Bad enough to trespass into somebody's barn—he'd already been doing a good bit of that during the months of tracking his nephew. But busting into their house and taking their food was another matter. Yankee soldiers once had pillaged his home. Jack Cornwall would never sink so low.

He pried off his boots, stretched out on the hay, and shut his eyes. His shoulder burned like fire. If the injury didn't heal right, what would it mean to his dream of starting a blacksmithing business? How would he be able to work . . . take care of his parents . . . take care of Lucy . . . sweet, gray-eyed Lucy . . . ?

"I never saw such a *ballyhooly* in all my life," a woman's voice announced suddenly in the darkness—barely fifteen feet from where Jack lay. "Did you, Erinn? Now tell me the truth."

Jack stiffened and reached for his pistol.

"We all expected the fight." The second voice was much younger. A little girl. "All summer that wicked Jack Cornwall has been trying to make off with Chipper. Mama said Mr. Cornwall followed our Seth and Rosie the whole way from Missouri, so he did."

"Bad as Mr. Cornwall may be," the woman said, "we're to follow the good Lord's example of forgiveness. Jesus spent many hours in the company of the wicked, and his compassion helped them see the error of their ways. He never turned his back on a person, no matter how evil—and neither should we."

"If you turn your back on Jack Cornwall, he's likely to shoot you in it!"

"Aye, I can't deny 'tis a good thing he's gone."

So the O'Tooles had returned from the celebration. Jack had been expecting them, of course, but not in the barn. Not tonight. The family lived so close to the Hunter homestead they could have walked the short distance with ease. So what business did these two females have wandering around in the black night with not even a lantern between them?

"Shall I fetch a lamp from the soddy, Auntie Caitrin?" the younger girl asked. "It's so dark in here."

Jack shook his head. *No. Say no.*

"Yes, indeed," Caitrin said brightly. "I thought the moon would be enough to see by, but that wind has brought in too many clouds. You and I might be out in the barn all night fumbling with the latches on my trunk."

"Aye then, I'll be back in a flash."

"Take care now, Erinn! Don't run!"

Jack heard the child's footsteps on the beaten earth of the barn floor as she dashed toward the soddy. From his position on the hay, he studied the shadowed silhouette moving through the gloom. The woman was tall, straight, and as big around the middle as a freight wagon. It appeared she was expecting twins.

"Too ra loo ra," she sang, her voice meandering between words and humming. She bent over a large square trunk below the barn window, then she straightened again. "Too ra lay . . . now where did I lay that pink bonnet?"

She waddled straight across the floor and stopped in front of the hay pile. Jack held his breath, willing himself to remain motionless. Leaning down, the woman began to grope around in the darkness. Her hand brushed against the toe of his boot, and she jerked backward.

"Oh, my goodness—"

"Don't scream." He caught the hem of her skirt. "I won't hurt you."

"Who-who-who—"

"Nobody. Just a traveler. I need a place to sleep."

"Take your hands off my—"

"Auntie Caitrin?" The child's voice sounded at the barn door. "I've brought the lamp."

"Don't let the girl see me," Jack hissed. "Send her away."

The woman wavered. "But I—"

"Let me rest in your barn tonight," he went on, "and I'll be on my way at dawn. I'm wounded."

He could hear her breath heavy in her throat. "Are you . . . are you that man? That Cornwall?"

"Auntie Caitrin?" the child called again. "Where are you? Even with the lamp, I can't find you."

"Protect me tonight," Jack whispered. "I'll never trouble you again."

Caitrin squared her shoulders. "I'm here, Erinn, my love," she called. "Set the lamp on the shelf there by the barn door, and then you'd better go back to the house. 'Tis so late I've decided to repack the trunk myself. I'll be home in time to hear your papa read the Bible."

"But I wanted to help you."

As the light moved closer, Caitrin suddenly dropped the bulk of her immense girth on top of Jack—a pile of dresses and petticoats! He stared in surprise as a lithe woman danced across the barn and swept the lamp away from the child.

"There now, will you disobey your auntie, Erinn?" Caitrin said. "Scuttle back to the soddy, and tell your mama I'd adore a cup of hot tea before bed. Sure, we'll work on my trunk tomorrow."

"Tomorrow I have chores!"

"We'll look through it right after lunch, so we will. I'll show you all my gowns and hats. I promise." Caitrin set her hands on her hips. "Now to bed with you, my sweet colleen."

"Oh, but you said—"

"Indeed I did, and my word is my vow. I wasn't thinking about the hour." She lowered her voice and cast a glance in the direction of the hay pile and the intruder shrouded in darkness. "What if there's a *pooka* in the barn?"

Erinn threw her arms around her aunt's waist. "Oh, Auntie Caitie! Could it be? I'm terrified of goblins!"

"Now then, I'm only teasing. Of course there's naught to fear. We've the good Lord with us always, and his strength is our shield. But 'tis never wise to wander about in the night. Go set the kettle on the stove to boil—there's a good girl. I'll be home before you can wink twice."

The child detached herself from her aunt and raced out of the barn, pigtails flying behind her. The woman strode to the back of the building and held the lamp aloft, bathing Jack in its soft yellow light.

"Now then, *pooka*," she said. "What do you mean by trespassing into Jimmy O'Toole's barn?"

Clutching his shoulder, Jack struggled to his feet. "Look, I said I wouldn't cause you any trouble."

"No trouble? You're Cornwall himself, are you not? Sure, you're the very devil who caused such a ruction with our Seth tonight. You're the wicked fellow who's been chasing after poor little Chipper and trying to steal him away from his rightful papa."

She held the lamp higher. "Look at you standing there with your rifle and pistol and a knife stuck through your belt. Why then, Mr. Cornwall, you're trouble itself. You're the very man who—" Frowning, she peered at him. "Are you bleeding, sir?"

Jack glanced at his shoulder. "The fistfight tonight. An old wound tore open. A few weeks back your precious Seth Hunter pulled a gun on me. He shot me."

"Of course he did," she retorted. "As I recall the story, you were trying to shoot him first. Oh, this is an abominable situation. How can I go off to my tea and my warm bed if I must leave you out here bleeding? How can I sleep in God's peace tonight if I've abandoned one of his creations to a night of pain? Wicked though you are—and just one glance at your woeful condition confirms it—I can see I'm to play the Good Samaritan. Sit down, Mr. Cornwall."

With a firm shove on his chest, she pushed him down onto a milking stool. Then she hung the lamp on a nail that protruded from one of the barn's rough-hewn beams. Seizing his collar, she ordered, "Take off your jacket, sir. Quickly now, I don't have all evening. If you want Jimmy O'Toole traipsing out here with his shotgun, just dawdle."

Jack had barely begun to struggle out of his jacket when the woman grabbed a lapel and yanked off the garment. She took one look at his tattered shirt and seeping wound, and she clapped her hands against her cheeks. "But this is terrible, sir! Is the ball still in your shoulder?"

"No, it came out the other side."

He bent forward to show her the even greater wound on his back. At the sight, she gasped and sank to the floor, her purple-red silk skirts puffing around her. Covering her face with her hands, she let out a moan.

"Wouldn't you know?" she mumbled. "Papa was a fishmonger, and I nearly swooned every time he gutted one of those poor . . . miserable . . . and now this. Now *you*."

Jack studied the mass of auburn curls gathered at the woman's crown. Her hair was crusted with little trinkets—paste diamonds, silver butterflies, bits of ribbon. A delicate gold necklace hung with a heavy pearl draped around her long white neck. The scent of sweet flowers drifted up from her silk gown. Jack swallowed.

A beautiful woman. Jewels. A dark night. Common sense told him to take advantage of the turn of events. At the very least, he should snap the choker from her neck and ride away on his horse. If it was genuine, the pearl alone would feed him from here to Kansas City.

So why did he want to stroke a hand down the woman's back, whisper reassuring words, fetch her a drink of cool water?

"Ma'am?" he began, reaching out to her.

She pushed his hand away. "No, I can do this. Truly I can. And I will *not* swoon." Getting to her feet, she gathered up the clothing she had dropped earlier. "First I must pack the trunk as I promised Erinn. Then I'll fetch you something. Water. Medicine. Heaven help me," she moaned as she threw her garments into the open trunk, "I am not a nurse. What to do? Sheena would know, but of course I can't—"

"Ma'am," Jack cut into her agonized monologue as he rose to his feet again. "I'm not asking you to do anything for me. Just leave me alone here. Let me rest. I'll be gone at dawn."

She slammed down the lid of her trunk and faced him. "How can I leave you here with such grave injuries? I am Caitrin Murphy. I would never walk away from a person in need."

"Yeah, well I'm Jack Cornwall, and I don't need anything from anybody."

"Don't be ridiculous," she snapped. "Everyone needs *something*. You more than most, I should think. Even if you didn't have that . . . that awful bleeding shoulder . . . you're clearly in need of a good hot meal. Clean clothes. A haircut. A razor."

She took a step closer and looked him up and down. "Mr. Cornwall, if the condition of your flesh is any indication of the state of your soul, you are in need of a thorough cleansing both inside and out."

"What?" he said in disbelief. "Who gave you the say-so to judge me?"

"I always speak my mind. Now sit down." She pushed him back onto the stool. "Wait here."

Lifting her skirts, the woman stalked out of the barn. The scent of her fragrance lingered a moment in the air. Jack drank it in as he reflected on how long he'd been without female company. Too long. During the war, he'd spent months at a time on active duty or living in the woods with his vigilante friends and struggling to keep the Confederate cause alive. Then he had returned to find his home burned and the family farm sold to a Yankee out of failure to pay taxes. Mary was dead, Lucy suffering, and Chipper stolen away by a man who claimed to be his father. There had been no time for courting.

The auburn-haired beauty who had penetrated Jack's solitude stirred something inside him. Women had a certain softness about them, he recalled. A musical sound to their voices. A magic to their walk. He remembered now the whisper of silk skirts against petticoats. The fragility of a single curl at rest against a blushing cheek. The touch of a slender finger to the hollow of an ivory throat.

Miss Caitrin Murphy was certainly among the prettiest women Jack had ever seen. In fact, she might be perfect—except for that tongue of fire. Clearly she was no velvet-petaled flower just waiting to be plucked. The woman had thorns. Sharp, prickly spikes. She had labeled him wicked. Called him trouble. *Sit down, Mr. Cornwall. Wait here, Mr. Cornwall. Don't be ridiculous.* And what was that business about his soul needing a good cleansing?

High and mighty is what she was. Bossy, too. Just the sort of female to avoid.

"Now then, Mr. Cornwall," Caitrin Murphy said as she stepped into the barn, a wicker basket looped over one arm and a pail of water in the other hand. "I shall set you right, as a good Christian woman should. And then I'll rejoice at the sight of your backside heading out of Kansas."

"My pleasure," Jack returned. "I wouldn't live in a place like this for love nor money."

"And we wouldn't want you." She set down the pail and basket. "All the talk in the soddy is about you, so it is. 'That wicked Jack Cornwall attacked our Seth and tried to steal little Chipper,' says Sheena. 'Good riddance to bad rummage,' says Jimmy. You can thank the good Lord there's a flurry of tucking the wee *brablins* into bed or I'd never have made off with this food. Here, I brought you a loaf of bread, some apple cider, and a sausage."

She set the food in Jack's lap and busied herself with the water pail. He stared for a moment in disbelief. He had left home with twelve dollars in his pocket. When that ran out, he had resorted to eating what he could shoot or pick from kitchen gardens. But fresh bread? A whole sausage? And apple cider?

He picked up the loaf and tore off a hunk. The yeasty aroma beckoned, the crisp brown crust crackled, the center was spongy to his touch. He put the chunk in his mouth and closed his eyes. *Bread.*

"You like it?" Caitrin asked.

When he looked up, she was studying him, her head tilted and her eyes shining. Green eyes. Long dark lashes. He took another bite.

"It's good," he said.

"I baked it myself." Her lips curved into an impish smile. "Wouldn't my sister have a fine fit if she knew I was feeding our bread to Jack Cornwall? Sheena and I bake the loaves for sale, you see. There's a little mercantile across Bluestem Creek on the Hunter homestead. Rosie and I market goods to the travelers passing down the road."

"Rosie?"

"Rosie Mills. She's to be Seth's wife, so she is."

"Wife?" Jack frowned, thinking of his sister Mary and how deeply—and foolishly—she had loved Seth Hunter.

"Sure, it happened tonight after the *ballyhooly* died down," Caitrin explained. "Rosie loved Seth all summer, and he loved her, too. But they were both too blind and stubborn to admit it. This evening she tried to leave on the stagecoach, but Seth fetched her back again and announced to everyone that she was to be his wife. So all is well, and in a few weeks' time, Seth will have a lovely wife, and Chipper will have a mama to call his very own."

Jack stiffened. "Chipper's mama—his *one and only* mama—was my sister Mary."

Caitrin wrung out a rag and took a step closer. "Take off your shirt, Mr. Cornwall. And while you do, I trust you will bring to mind the sad circumstance of your sister's death. Seth told us about the loss of his wife and your sister, and I'm sorry for it. But life does not always unfold as we wish."

"What do *you* know about life?"

Her eyes flashed as he shrugged off his shirt and tossed it onto the hay pile. "I know a great deal about life," she said. "Life is about losing, letting go, and moving on. I have lost more than a man like you could ever understand. I have lost love. Hope. Dreams. Everything I had lived for. But I did not go off in a rage of bitterness and revenge as you did, Mr. Cornwall. I am Caitrin Murphy. You destroy. I create."

She pursed her lips and began washing the bloody wound on Jack's shoulder. At the touch of the wet rag, flames of pain tore through his flesh, searing deeply into muscle and bone. He knotted his fists and stared down at the tips of Caitrin Murphy's shiny black slippers. Could this sharp-tongued snippet of a woman possibly be right? Had his life become a path of vengeance and destruction—a path so narrow he could find no room to turn around?

"You're a fiery little thing, you know that?" he said. "Aren't you the least bit afraid of me . . . big ol' blazing Jack Cornwall roaring into town and scaring the living daylights out of everybody?"

She gave a shrug as she began working on his back. "Fiery Caitrin Murphy and blazing Jack Cornwall. Sure, we're a matched pair, the two of us. But where I've given myself to God to be used as his refining fire, you're naught but a swirling, raging, blustering prairie fire bent on destroying everything in sight."

"Fire's fire," Jack hurled back. "I'm a blacksmith by trade, and I know my business. Don't pride yourself, Sparky. One flicker of that refiner's fire can set a prairie aflame."

"Or draw precious gold from raw ore. 'Tis all in how a person chooses to make use of his fiery spirit, Mr. Cornwall. A contained blaze is a good thing, but you're a wildfire out of control. You need taming."

"Fight fire with fire, as they say." He touched the woman's arm. "Maybe you want to try taming me, Miss Murphy?"

"Wicked man. 'Tis no wonder they call you a devil." She pushed his hand away, rinsed the rag, and began to wash again. "This wound is frightful. Sure, you must get yourself to a doctor, Mr. Cornwall. You might lose this arm, and then where will you be with your blacksmithing?"

"I don't need a doctor. Couldn't pay one even if I did."

"You have no money? But what have you been doing all the years before now?"

"Fighting."

"A soldier? Then a doctor will surely see you at no charge. You did battle for the honor and glory of your country."

"I'm a Confederate. I fought to save the South from the aggression of Yankees like Seth Hunter. No Kansas abolitionist doctor will treat the likes of me."

"Well, I've just come from Ireland, and I don't know much about your war and your silly politics." She dropped the stained rag back into the bucket. "But I do know you'll find better medicine at an apothecary than you will on Jimmy O'Toole's homestead. Here's a salve he uses on his sheep when they've got the fly. You must keep it near and use it often. And I brought clean bandages."

Jack studied the pile of lace-edged fabric strips she pulled out of her basket. "These are bandages? They look more like hand-kerchiefs."

"They were once a petticoat stitched by my own hand and edged in fine Irish lace. I could find nothing else to serve the purpose."

She handed Jack a swath of white linen and a crock of salve. "You tore up your petticoat?" he asked.

"'Twas an earthly treasure." With a shrug, she took his elbow and unhooked the lamp. "Come with me, Mr. Cornwall. You must sleep in safe hiding tonight. Perhaps Jimmy will take it into his head to check on his mules. Here's a little storage room the dear man built for me under the loft. We take more goods in trade than we can possibly display in the mercantile, so I use this room to stockpile the surplus. By the by, I shall thank you not to steal any of our inventory tomorrow when you leave. I keep careful records, and I shall know what's missing."

Using the key that hung from a ribbon around her neck, she unlocked the door to a tiny room stacked with bulky flour sacks and tinned goods. After spreading a pallet of quilts on the floor, she arranged a few things beside it. The bandages, salve, sausage, and bread she set into the basket. Then she rummaged around in her storage boxes and took down a comb, a razor, a small hand mirror, and a cake of soap. Finally, she lifted the lid of a square biscuit tin.

"Take this, Mr. Cornwall," she said, bringing out a handful of money and setting it into his palm. "It's my part of the earnings from the mercantile. I haven't much use for it out here on the prairie. Get yourself to a doctor, sir."

Caitrin turned toward the door, but Jack stepped in front of it, blocking her path. A look of dismay crossed her face as she realized he had trapped her inside the room. The light in her green eyes faded . . . to be replaced by a flicker of fear that Jack had seen all too often in his years on the battlefield. He didn't budge.

"Tell me something, Miss Caitrin Murphy," he said. He held up the wad of folded bills. "Why? Why'd you do this?"

"I told you, I . . . I have little use for money."

"I don't believe that." He took a step toward her. "Nobody does something for nothing. What's your motive?"

She swallowed hard. "Mr. Cornwall, I must go. Sheena will be looking for me. If Jimmy finds you—"

"Tell me!" He grabbed her wrist. "Nobody ever gave me anything for free. Now why'd you do it? Tell me."

"Because . . . because I found you here . . . and you'd been injured."

"Pity?"

"Only the weak are to be pitied." As she said the words, a strength seemed to fill her, and she lifted her chin. "I helped you because I am a child of God, and so are you. You were created for good, for a future and a hope. Though you may have burned out of control in your life, you are still precious to the Father. And because of him—with his love—I love you, Mr. Cornwall."

Before he could respond, she slipped around him and squeezed through the door. Jack stood for a moment, stunned, as if a bolt of lightning had shot through his head and come right out his boots. And then he shook off the daze, made a dash across the barn floor, and caught the woman by her arm.

Clapping her hand over her mouth, she stifled a cry. Her eyes widened in fear, and a curl of auburn hair tumbled to her shoulder. Jack didn't care if he scared her. Didn't care what she thought. Didn't care about anything but knowing. Knowing for sure.

"What did you say?" he demanded.

Breathing hard, she searched his face. "I said, you are precious to the Father."

"Not that part. What you said after. Say it."

"With the Father's love, I . . . I love you."

"*Again*."

"Why must I? Surely you've heard those words before!"

He stared at her, tongue-tied, trying to make sense of things. And then her face softened. The tension slipped off her shoulders.

"Oh, Mr. Cornwall," she murmured. Reaching out to him, she touched his injured shoulder with her fingers, and then she ran their tips down the length of his bare arm. Her green eyes softened and filled with a warm light that radiated to the smile on her lips.

"You are precious to the Father, Mr. Cornwall," she said, squeezing his hand. "Hear the words and believe them in your heart. You are precious, and with his love, I love you. *I love you*."

She held the lamp before her as she turned again. Then she moved away from him, out of the barn, out of reach. The golden light faded, and he was left again in darkness.

CHAPTER 2

CAITRIN rolled over on the corn-husk mattress and gathered her niece in her arms. Young Erinn barely stirred. In the same bed, four-year-old Colleen snored softly against her auntie's shoulder, while tiny Jamie lay snuggled at their feet. At two, Jamie was already a bright, clever child, and Caitrin loved him dearly. Resting her cheek against Erinn's bright copper hair, Caitrin gazed out the window at the rising sun.

Jimmy had left the house well before dawn, and Sheena was already outside gathering eggs for breakfast. Will still slept in his parents' bed, but baby Mollie was stirring and beginning to coo. A wonderful family, the O'Tooles. Caitrin felt blessed that her sister had welcomed her into their crowded household after her long journey from Ireland. Busy with the mercantile and consumed by her chores, she had been happy enough . . . until last night.

Her thoughts turned again to the man who had trespassed into Jimmy's barn. Jack Cornwall had evoked the only welling of emotion inside Caitrin since she left Ireland. Moving through life with numb determination had kept her from facing the pain of losing the man she had planned to marry. But Cornwall's intrusion into her safe little world had sparked a conflagration of feelings . . . feelings she didn't want and couldn't seem to stuff away again.

Fear. Oh, he had frightened her. Lying there in the hay, shadowed by darkness, he had scared her half-balmy. And then later, when he caught her arm, blocked her path, and chased after her through the barn, she had known the taste of terror. After all, the man was a criminal. He had shot at Seth Hunter more than once. Rumor had it, he'd even spent time in a Missouri jail.

Aversion. When had she last seen a man so greatly in want of a cake of soap and a tub of hot water? He must have been on the trail for months, with little food, no place to sleep, and the definite lack of a place to wash. Jack Cornwall carried on him the scent of horses, tobacco, and dust. His wound had horrified her, too. She could not imagine how such an injury could heal unless he saw a doctor and agreed to rest. The touch of his blood on her fingertips . . . the scent of his leather jacket . . . the warmth of his calloused hand . . .

Caitrin closed her eyes, remembering. What was that other emotion the man had aroused in her? She could hardly put a name to it. Confusion? Dismay? Fascination? Yes, that was it. He had fascinated her. Intrigued her. His voice was deep and resonant, almost husky coming to her out of the darkness. He spoke of himself with firmness, certainty, even pride. And those shoulders! But of course—he was a blacksmith. Even now, the image of Jack Cornwall's shoulders was planted firmly in her memory. Broad they had been, woven with thick sinew, and as hard as flint. Sure, the man had been blessed with enough muscle for two.

Caitrin opened her eyes and studied the rosy light filtering into the soddy. Jack Cornwall would be long gone by now, far to the east, heading for Missouri and his family. She hoped he would find a doctor. And forgiveness. Hope. Love.

Father, please send Jack Cornwall someone who will love him, she prayed silently as she hugged Erinn's warm little form. *Let him hear the words again and again until his dark, empty heart is filled with the certainty of love. And, Father, may he find you. May he know the taming of your . . .*

"Jack Cornwall's here!" Jimmy shouted, bursting through the

door into the soddy. His hair stood out on his head like a red flame, and his green eyes flicked around the soddy from bed to bed. "Where's Sheena? Gather the children! Caitrin, are you still abed? Get up! Get up, everyone!"

The baby burst into a wail like a banshee. Erinn jerked awake and grabbed Caitrin in a stranglehold about the neck. Colleen tumbled out of bed, hitting the floor with a thud. And then she began to howl.

"Caitrin!" Jimmy hollered over the hubbub. "You must bar the door. Hide the *brablins*. I'm after Sheena."

"Jimmy, wait!" Caitrin struggled out of bed, Erinn still hanging from her neck. "Jack Cornwall walked away from the Hunter homestead after the fistfight last night. Everyone saw the man leave. How can you say he's here?"

"His devil of a horse! 'Tis hobbled out behind the barn, so it is."

"Sure, you must be mistaken." A wash of chills skidded down Caitrin's spine. She swallowed. "Have you searched the barn?"

"That I have, and he's nowhere to be found. Not a sign of the *sherral* but his horse. I fear he's stolen away my Sheena."

"Oh, Papa!" Erinn burst into tears.

"Now then, lass," Caitrin said, prying the child from her neck and looking straight into the pair of fearful green eyes. "If Mr. Cornwall's horse is hobbled behind the barn, he won't have gone away with your mama, will he? You must calm yourself, Erinn." She turned to her brother-in-law. "Jimmy, how can you frighten the children so?"

"Where is Sheena then?"

"She went to fetch eggs for breakfast. Have you looked in the coop?"

"The coop! Sure, I'm a fair *googeen* this morning." Jimmy picked Colleen up off the floor and set her firmly on the bed. "Caitie, bar the door. Will, stand guard with the shotgun."

Jimmy thrust the double-barreled weapon into his son's arms.

Just as quickly, Caitrin grabbed it away. "What can you be thinking, Jimmy O'Toole? The boy is only six!"

"Look, there's Mama!" Erinn cried out, pointing to the soddy window.

Caitrin and Jimmy raced to the window to discover the plump little woman sauntering toward the house, a basket of eggs over her arm and a smile on her lips. The ribbons on her bonnet fluttered in the morning breeze as her skirt danced like a flag. On a whim, she set the basket of eggs on her head and broke into a little Irish jig, her feet deftly picking out a set of jaunty steps.

"Glory be to God, Sheena!" Jimmy roared through the open window. "Get your backside into the house, woman. There's trouble afoot!"

Sheena's head jerked up, and the basket toppled. Caitrin sucked in a breath as it fell . . . but Sheena reached out and caught it before it hit the ground. Clutching her prize to her stomach, she glared at her husband.

"The eggs, you old goat!" she shouted. "I nearly dropped them."

"Jack Cornwall is here. On our farm!"

"Awkk!" Sheena's hands flew up, the basket tumbled, eggs bounced to the ground and broke open. She grabbed her skirts, lifted them knee high, and raced to the soddy. "Cornwall! Lord save us, Cornwall!"

Jimmy threw open the door, pulled his wife inside, and slammed down the heavy oak bar. "His horse is hobbled behind the barn, so it is," he said, taking her by the shoulders. "I had just watered the mules when I rounded the corner, and there it was. Sure, it's a great black devil of a horse, and Cornwall's saddle lay nearby. He can't be far."

"In the barn?"

"No, no. I looked there first. He's nowhere to be found."

"He'll steal the children!" Sheena grabbed the baby from the cradle and wrapped her arms around the infant. "Jimmy, you must go and fetch Seth. Tell Rustemeyer to come, too. The three of you must hunt Cornwall down. Kill him if you can."

"Now then!" Caitrin said, inserting herself between husband and wife. "Sheena, Mr. Cornwall won't be after our wee ones. What good would it do him to make off with a stranger's child? None at all. And, Jimmy, if Cornwall's horse is here, why then it's a sign he spent the night in your barn, so he did. Perhaps he left the animal as a gift."

"A gift!" Jimmy snorted. "The man's a criminal. It wouldn't be in his nature to leave a gift."

"How can you be so certain of his nature? Perhaps Mr. Cornwall is not the fearsome man we all believe. Perhaps he has a . . . a certain longing in his heart, something none of us can truly understand. Perhaps he was lonely last night and was grateful for the shelter."

"There she goes again," Jimmy said, addressing his wife. "Ever takin' the worst and coatin' it in honey. Your sister would insist hell was nothin' more than a warm beach holiday, so she would."

"Jimmy! Watch your tongue in front of the *brablins*," Sheena scolded. "Maybe Caitie's right. If Cornwall stayed the night in our barn, he'd be long gone by now. He must have left his horse behind him."

"And set off for Topeka on foot? Sure, the two of you are a pair of silly, beeheaded—"

"Then where is the man, Mr. Jimmy O'Toole?" Sheena demanded. "If Cornwall wouldn't go off without his horse, where is he?"

As Jimmy and Sheena fussed, Caitrin slipped over to the window again to study the barn. Was it possible? Could Jack Cornwall still be hiding out in her little storage room? He had promised to leave before dawn. Surely he wasn't foolish enough to risk staying in a place where everyone viewed him as the worst kind of villain.

Then another thought dawned, more awful than the first. Jack

Cornwall was dead. Perhaps his wound had filled his blood with contagion. Or the sausage she'd brought him had been too old. Or the salve for flyblown sheep had been poison to humans. Filled with remorse for his wickedness, perhaps he had ended his own life. The cider. The razor. A snake. Any number of things could have killed the man.

Caitrin gulped. First and foremost she must keep everyone away from the barn while she inspected the storage room. She would find a way to manage the consequences of her discovery later.

"Sheena's right, Jimmy," Caitrin said, turning from the window. "You must fetch Seth and Rustemeyer and search your land for Mr. Cornwall. If you don't find him, you will have no choice but to consider the horse a gift. An apology for the trouble he caused us all."

Before he could argue, she went on. "While you search, Sheena, the children, and I must carry on with our chores as usual. Sure, we can't cower in the soddy day and night in fear of a lone, wounded, half-starved man. I am late to the mercantile as it is, and won't Rosie be scalded? Shall I go off without my breakfast, Sister?"

This appalling notion sent Sheena into a flurry of activity. Mourning the loss of the eggs, she barked orders left and right. Jimmy was to fetch a rasher of bacon from the smokehouse. Erinn must wash and dress the wee *brablins*. Will would stir the oatmeal and slice the bread. And Colleen must set the dishes on the table.

Her heart still in her throat, Caitrin quickly dressed and made up the beds, folding blankets and pushing the corn-husk mattresses back into shape. Then she helped Sheena cook the breakfast and serve it up. As the family ate, Jimmy announced that he would ride immediately to Seth's place. The two of them would travel upstream to speak with Rolf Rustemeyer, the big blond German farmer who homesteaded to the north. If they were lucky, other neighbors could be persuaded to assist in the search, and the O'Toole land would be scoured from top to bottom.

"We'll flush out that louse and pack him off to jail," Jimmy said. "If I have anythin' to do with it, the *sherral* will plague us no more."

"Aye," Sheena said, giving her husband a look of admiration. "That's the Jimmy O'Toole I know. Hunt down that blackguard Cornwall. Shoot him if you must. Sure, you'll keep your family safe from evil, won't you, my sweet?"

Caitrin could hardly force a single bite down her dry throat. She took a gulp of water and pushed her chair back from the table. "If you'll excuse me, I must fetch a few tins of oysters from the storage," she said. "Sure, Rosie will be wondering what's become of me."

"The storage room!" Sheena gasped. "Jimmy, did you check it for that Cornish vermin?"

Caitrin held her breath.

"Aye." Jimmy nodded. "The door was locked, of course. Our Caitie's a careful lass, so she is."

Caitrin managed a smile of gratitude. But she *hadn't* locked the storage room door the night before. If she had locked him in, Jack Cornwall couldn't have departed for Kansas at dawn. Then why was Jimmy unable to open it?

Sickeningly certain she knew the answer to that question, Caitrin threw her shawl around her shoulders and tied on her bonnet. After collecting the supply of fresh bread, butter, and cheese for the mercantile, she hurried outside and made for the barn.

Last night's wind had brought a nip to the air. Winter would not be long in coming. The prospect filled Caitrin with dismay. This autumn was to have brought her wedding to Sean O'Casey—a wedding she and the dashing young Irishman had planned in secret. But his father had made other plans, and in the end Sean had not been defiant enough to stand up for the right to marry the woman he truly loved. Though he had wedded the daughter of a wealthy mine owner instead, Sean had sworn he would always love his Caitie. She knew she could never love another.

Trying to push away the pain that gripped her every time she thought of her beloved, Caitrin stepped into the barn. Though her heart would always belong to Sean, he was lost to her now. Ireland was lost. Home was lost.

"'This is the day which the Lord hath made,'" she whispered as she made for the storage room under the loft. "'We will rejoice and be glad in it.'"

Caitrin repeated the verse of Scripture three times more for good measure. She knew she must seek out each day's joy rather than dwelling in its sorrow. God had given her this life and not another. Wishing would not change her lot. Anger would not change it. And certainly bathing herself in misery would never alter the fact that she lived on the Kansas prairie in a one-room dirt house with seven other people . . . and not in the O'Casey family's fine stone cottage on the green sod of Ireland.

This was the day the Lord had made. He was her strength. And no matter what came her way, she would rejoice and be glad.

Lifting her chin, Caitrin knocked on the storage room door. "Mr. Cornwall? Are you there?"

"Depends on who you are."

"I'm Caitrin Murphy."

"Then I'm here."

Relief that he was alive was replaced quickly by irritation. "And did you not promise me you'd be long gone from this place by morning?"

"Yep."

"Then why are you still here?"

The sound of heavy scraping was followed by the storage room door swinging ajar. Jack Cornwall's large frame filled the narrow gap. "Mornin', Sparky," he said.

Caitrin glanced at the barn door to make certain none of the O'Tooles had followed her, and then she slipped inside the storage room. "Don't wish me a good morning, Mr. Cornwall, when you've sent the entire household into a flap by leaving your black horse tied outside in broad daylight. Jimmy fears you'll steal his children away. Sheena dropped the morning's eggs. In short, the mere thought of your presence has thrown everyone helter-skelter."

"What does the thought of my presence mean to *you*, Miss Murphy?" he asked, his voice low. He leaned his good shoulder against a storage cabinet and studied her up and down. "Wish I'd gone?"

"Of course I do." Unwilling to let him see the consternation his appreciative appraisal caused her, Caitrin marched to a corner of the room and began sorting through the stacked tins. "Now you'll have to wait until tonight to make your escape. And what if Sheena decides to have a look in the storage room? Sure, Jimmy O'Toole will string you up from the barn rafters if you're discovered. Even now, he and Seth and Mr. Rustemeyer are joining forces to scour the land for you. *Why* didn't you go?"

She turned to find Jack standing barely a heartbeat away. Catching her breath, she focused on the man's face, truly seeing him for the first time. He had gray eyes—terrible, steely gray eyes, as hard and cold and impenetrable as iron. A strong nose, its bridge slightly bent as though it had been broken once long ago. Cheekbones high and squared. A jaw that might have been carved from solid oak. And a mouth . . . oh, she hadn't expected such a mouth . . .

"Why didn't I go?" he repeated.

She jerked her attention to his eyes. "Yes, why? You've caused so much trouble."

"No one knows I'm here but you, Miss Murphy." That mouth tipped up at the right corner in a lazy grin. "Do I cause *you* trouble?"

Caitrin hugged her produce basket tightly, willing it to form a protective barrier between them. "You have not answered my question, Mr. Cornwall. Aren't you well enough to travel? Has your shoulder grown worse? Or did you simply fail to wake before dawn?"

"The shoulder's bad," he said. "I need the rest. But that's not why I stayed."

"Well, are you going to give me an explanation, or am I meant to guess and guess like a child at a riddle game?"

He smiled outright at that and seated himself on the lid of the pickle barrel that had prevented Jimmy from opening the door earlier that morning.

"I stayed because of the bandage," Cornwall said simply.

Caitrin glanced down at his bare chest and the white strips of linen wrapped around his shoulder. "The bandage? Are you quite well in the head, Mr. Cornwall? Or shall I write to an asylum and have you put away for a lunatic?"

His face sobered instantly. "An asylum is no place for a lunatic."

"No? Then what am I to make of a man who lingers in a place of danger because of a bandage?"

"Miss Murphy, are you going to listen to what I have to say, or do you intend to carp at me all morning?"

She swallowed down her annoyance. "By all means talk, Mr. Cornwall."

"I'm much obliged." He pointed to the collection of lamps Caitrin would sell later at the mercantile. "Last night after you left I lit one of your lamps and went to work on my shoulder. The salve is good, I think. Ought to help. Anyway, when I unrolled the bandage and started to wrap the wound, I noticed the lace. Fine Irish lace, I think you said?"

Caitrin nodded. "Aye, 'tis bobbin lace. In Ireland women work lace by the fire in the evenings; then we sell our creations to a laceman, who peddles them in the city. But that lace was a new pattern. I liked it, so I decided not to sell it. What does my lace have to do with your failure to leave this property as you promised?"

"I studied the stitches you'd used to sew the petticoat," he said, ignoring the question. "Tiny stitches. Even my mother would approve . . . and not much gets past her." He gave a low chuckle. "She's particular. My sister Mary always used to say . . ."

He paused and reflected a moment. When he spoke again, his voice was rough. "Been a long time since I saw fine lace on a lady's petticoat hem. Long time since I thought about a fireplace with a woman stitching beside it. Long time since anybody said to me the things you said last night. In fact, the more I turned your words over, the more I knew I hadn't ever heard such notions. I decided you were something different, Miss Murphy. So, that's why I made up my mind to stay awhile."

"Stay?" Caitrin snapped out of the daze his words had evoked. "Sure, you can't stay here another night, Mr. Cornwall! Not in the storage room. I'm not a nursemaid, and I won't be fetching and running for you. I've my own work to be after, so I have. I'm busy sunup to sundown. And what if you're discovered? I'd bear the blame of it, so I would—harboring a criminal, sheltering the enemy. I'd be labeled a traitor to the whole town of Hope and everybody who loves Seth Hunter. Jimmy and Sheena would have every right to pack me off to Ireland, and I can't go back to Ireland. I *can't*."

"Nobody's going to find me. Lock the door when you leave. I'll read a few of those books on the shelf. Sleep a little. Rest my shoulder. Clean my guns. Get things back in shape. When I'm better, I'll leave."

"But you can't stay! I won't allow it."

"Are you planning to rat on me?" He crossed his arms over his chest and appraised her. "I didn't think you would. You're too blasted spunky to run crying for help. Fiery Caitrin Murphy and Blazin' Jack Cornwall, that's us."

"I'm *nothing* like you."

"No? All my life I've aimed to do something worthwhile,

something that matters. I'll fight anybody to right a wrong and see that justice gets done. If I want something to happen, I do it myself. I'm bullheaded, contentious, and tough as nails. Are you any different?"

Caitrin clutched the handle of her basket, and the blood drained from her knuckles. "It terrifies me to see how the fire inside you matches that in my own soul, Jack Cornwall," she said in a low voice. "Sure, we're a pair of candles burning brightly. Never have I known a man like you, a man whose flame will not flicker out at the slightest gust. But what can become of people like us out on this windswept prairie? Why will you linger here? What is it you want?"

"I want to watch you turn raw ore into gold."

"Only God can perform such a miracle." She met his eyes, determined to have the upper hand. "You cannot stay."

"I reckon I will."

"I'll lock you up and leave you to die."

"No, you won't."

"Sheena will find you."

"You'll keep her away."

"I'll tell Jimmy."

"Nope." He stood and held the door open for her. "I'm *precious*, remember? What was that you said about me last night? Oh yes. You *love* me."

"Turn my words against me, then. Make light of what I said to you in honest Christian charity." She squared her shoulders. "You *are* as wicked as they say, Mr. Cornwall. Though the good Lord commands me to love all men, I certainly don't like you. Not in the least. You are rude and stubborn and selfish. Sure, I rue the moment I laid eyes on you."

Aware she must hurry to the mercantile or someone would come searching for her, Caitrin stepped past Cornwall. Relief at escaping him had just begun to seep into her when he caught her elbow. Her heartbeat skidded to a halt. Would she never be able to get away from the man without his barricading and accosting her?

She spoke through gritted teeth. "What is it *now?*"

"I wrote a letter to my parents last night." He pulled an envelope from the hip pocket of his blue denim trousers. "I understand you run a post office at that mercantile of yours. Suppose you could mail this for me?"

"Give me one good reason why I should do anything for a man like you."

"All right. A fellow I ran with at the end of the war has been searching for me. He thinks maybe I can pull our old bunch out of some hot water they got themselves into. My folks need to be on the lookout for this man."

Caitrin snatched the letter and stuffed it into her apron pocket. "Anything else I can assist you with, Mr. Cornwall?"

He smiled. "The key. You wanted to lock your storage room, remember?"

"Take it," she said, tugging the ribbon necklace over her head. "Lock the door yourself from the inside. And if my prayers are answered, you'll use that key to let yourself out tonight and leave us all in peace."

She whirled away from the man before he could capture her again. As she raced for the barn door, she heard his voice ring out behind her. "Good-bye, Sparky. Don't work your pretty little hands too hard."

Mortified, Caitrin turned on her heel. "*Whisht!* Be quiet, you great rogue!"

Jack Cornwall was standing in plain view, his broad shoulders gleaming in a patch of morning sunlight and his brown hair ruffling in the breeze from an open window. If not for the blood-stained bandage on his shoulder, he would have passed for the finest specimen of a man Caitrin had ever seen. He wasn't handsome and elegant like Sean O'Casey. His face was rough-hewn.

His form was lean—all flesh and muscle without the hint of softness. His clothes were worn, dusty, faded. But he filled up the barn with a powerful presence that froze her breath in her throat and turned her feet into blocks of wood.

Clutching her shawl at her throat, Caitrin stared at the man. Outlined in sunshine, he stood calm and unafraid, studying her across the open space. And she understood.

Jack Cornwall was not staying in Jimmy O'Toole's barn in order to heal his shoulder. Nor to hide out from his enemies. Nor to filch himself a few free meals. In fact, he wouldn't care much if someone discovered him.

He was staying because of her. Because she fascinated him . . . just as he fascinated her. Fiery Caitrin Murphy and Blazin' Jack Cornwall, a matched pair.

"Auntie Caitie!" Erinn's high voice sang out just beyond the barn door. "Are you there, Auntie Caitie?"

Unnerved, Caitrin lifted her skirts and turned away. "I'm here, Erinn! Will you go with me to the mercantile this morning?"

The little girl danced into view, her pigtails bouncing at her shoulders. "Oh yes, I'll go with you! And after lunch may we open your trunk and look at your dresses?"

"Aye, that we shall." Caitrin glanced back over her shoulder as she left the barn. Jack Cornwall was gone.

CHAPTER 3

CAITRIN set her basket of tinned oysters on the glass display case and looked around in search of Rosie Mills. Evidence of the previous night's harvest celebration littered the large room that had begun as Seth Hunter's barn and had been transformed by Rosie and Caitrin into the Hope Mercantile and Post Office. Planks set on sawhorses still held stacks of plates and tin cups. A half-empty crock of apple cider sat beside a dish of stale popcorn. Lanterns, their wicks burned low, hung from nails around the room.

Caitrin frowned. It wasn't like Rosie to leave such a mess. It wasn't like her to be late to work, either. At that moment Caitrin spotted two figures framed by the door in the wall that divided the front of the mercantile from the barn at the back. Rose was caught up in Seth's arms as the man tenderly kissed her. Chagrined to have interrupted such a private moment, Caitrin quickly ushered Erinn back out of the mercantile, and then she called softly from the doorway. "Rosie? Rose Mills?"

A flushed face framed by a bright yellow bonnet emerged into the light. "Caitrin?" Rosie said. "Oh, it's you."

"Aye, and how are you this fine morning, lass?"

"I'm wonderful," Rosie murmured as Seth Hunter's tall frame emerged to stand behind his fiancée.

"Miss Murphy," he said, tipping his hat. "Good morning."

31

Caitrin noted the bright twinkle in Seth's blue eyes, and she smiled. "Finely and poorly, as we say in Ireland," she returned. "But I believe the pair of you have seen the day off to a better start than I. Now if you'll excuse me, I shall send Erinn to the creek to fetch water."

Grabbing her niece by the hand, Caitrin marched the protesting child through the mercantile door. "But, Auntie Caitie, I wanted to fold the bolts of fabric this morning. You promised I could."

"Aye, that I did." Caitrin handed the girl a pail. "But we must scrub and mop first. The mail coach from Manhattan will be here soon. Shall we have our customers thinking we run a pigsty instead of a tidy shop?"

Scowling, Erinn headed for the creek, the tin bucket creaking as it swung on its handle. In a moment Seth's son, Chipper, burst from the nearby soddy and raced his dog toward the water to greet their visitor. Caitrin folded her arms and studied the children for a moment. Then she lifted an eyebrow at the mercantile.

Seth had emerged in the barnyard, whistling as he saddled one of his mules. "Jimmy was by here a few minutes ago," he called. "He has reason to believe Jack Cornwall spent the night in his barn. He's gone to round up Rustemeyer so we can search his land."

"The best of luck to you," Caitrin said. And she added under her breath, "You'll need it."

After allowing Rosie a moment to compose herself, she walked back toward the building. Caitrin was proud of the establishment and all it had come to mean to the growing community of Hope. Thanks largely to her initiative, the rough board siding wore a coat of bright red paint, a large lettered sign hung from chains over the door, and bright glass cases lined the walls. The mercantile itself was stocked to the rafters with everything a traveler could need on a journey west to the wild frontier or east toward the safety of cities and towns.

Caitrin peered around the doorframe and gave Rosie a knowing grin. "Is it all right to come in now?"

"Don't be silly," the younger woman protested, her cheeks suffusing a bright pink all over again. "Why wouldn't it be all right?"

"Well . . . you and Seth . . . a pair soon to be married . . ." Caitrin gave a shrug.

"If you must know, Seth had just given me a good-morning kiss," Rosie said, stuffing a strand of wayward brown hair back into her bun. "I was upstairs in my little loft bedroom, and after I dressed, I came down the ladder to start cleaning the mercantile. Then Seth walked into the barn from the back, and when he saw me, he said, 'Good morning, my sweet prairie rose,' and I said, 'Good morning, Seth.' And then he kissed me—just like any man might kiss his future wife, which I didn't think was wrong in the least. Do you?"

Caitrin laughed. When she was flustered, Rosie Mills's tongue wagged faster than a dog's tail. "No, 'twasn't wrong," Caitrin said, laying a soothing hand on her friend's arm, "I think a good-morning kiss was exactly right."

"Yes, it was," Rosie whispered. "It was perfect." Then she flung her arms around Caitrin's shoulders. "Oh, Caitie, I'm so happy! So, so happy! I never believed I would see the day when Seth and I would marry. I was prepared to let him go. I was sure God meant for me to head back to the orphanage in Kansas City."

Caitrin smoothed a hand over Rosie's hair as her friend hugged her. "Sure, I knew Seth would never let you get away from him," she said softly. "He loves you so much, Rosie. He loves you with all his heart."

"Yes, he does!" Rosie pulled away and spun around in circles again. "He loves me, Caitie. Seth Hunter loves me. All night long I repeated it to myself. Seth Hunter loves me. He wouldn't let me go. Not even one mile! He rode after me and claimed me as his very own. Oh, and, Caitie, we're going to be married very soon!"

"Really? And when might the happy day be?" Caitrin began picking up dirty plates and stacking them one atop the other. Though her heart rejoiced for her friend, a hard knot had formed at the bottom of her stomach.

"The wedding is Sunday next, barely ten days from now," Rosie sang out, her voice musical. "Seth said he's going to round up a preacher if he has to ride all the way to Topeka. He doesn't think it's proper that I continue to live on his homestead. Seth says he wants to honor God and keep my reputation pure. He's going to ask Sheena if I can stay with your family the next ten days. I know it will be a terrible crush with all the children, and I told him I'd sleep in the barn."

"In the barn?" Caitrin looked up from the chin-high stack of plates, and her heart stumbled. "Oh, I don't think that's necessary. Jimmy's barn is nothing like Seth's."

"They're identical, Caitie. Except for the front of Seth's barn being a mercantile, they're exactly the same. If I could sleep in Seth's loft for an entire summer, why shouldn't I sleep just as well in Jimmy's?"

"It's dirty, that's why." Caitrin dumped the plates in the tub of water that had been used for apple bobbing. Instead of soiled dishes, all she could see was the image of Jack Cornwall standing in Jimmy O'Toole's barn. If he was discovered, everyone would know how he came to be staying in the storage room.

But Caitrin had to admit to herself that her concern for her own reputation was only half the problem. She didn't want anyone to find Cornwall because his life might be threatened. True, he was a dangerous man with those wicked gray eyes and that cocky grin. But she had unexpectedly formed a connection with him. Despite all his boldness, she sensed something vulnerable in the man. He was *human*, and he didn't deserve to die for it.

"We've cleaned Seth's barn," Caitrin said, praying she could keep Rosie away from Cornwall until she had convinced the man

34

to leave. "It's tidy, and it smells decent. Jimmy's barn has those dreadful mules inside. The pig wanders in and out. And the goats! Have you ever smelled what a goat can do to a barn, Rosie?"

"I don't care how Jimmy's barn smells," Rosie said. "Anyway, it won't be for long."

"Well, I won't allow it." Caitrin feverishly scrubbed at the sticky debris of caramel apples and popcorn. "You can't stay in Jimmy's barn. A bride must have better."

"But there's no room for me in the O'Tooles' soddy."

"Indeed there is. You'll sleep beside me, so you will. We can move Colleen into Sheena's bed for the time."

"I would never do that."

"You'll do as I say!" Caitrin announced, standing and waving a dripping fork at her friend. "You'll sleep in the soddy, Rosie Mills, and that's all there is to it."

A look of concern crossed Rosie's pretty face. "Caitrin? You're shouting at me." She paused a moment before crossing to the tub and draping an arm around the Irishwoman. "Oh, Caitie, I'm so sorry. I didn't stop to think how you must feel about all this. Here I am rambling on and on about my own wedding and all my dreams, completely forgetting that not so long ago you were planning to marry your beloved John."

"Sean."

"That's right, and the wedding would have taken place this autumn. But now you're all alone. I never once gave a thought to the terrible pain in your heart. Can you forgive me?"

Caitrin dropped the fork back into the tub and let out a breath. "Never mind about Sean O'Casey, Rosie. I hardly think of him more than four or five times a day anyhow, and then I realize there's nothing I can do to change what has happened. Sean is married, and I live in Kansas. My love for him will never die, yet I know I must not look back. If I do, I'll begin to wonder . . . to wonder . . ."

When she couldn't go on, Rosie spoke softly. "You'll wonder how it would have been to marry the man you love. You'll wonder about the children you might have borne. You'll wonder about the happy years you might have spent in his arms."

Caitrin shook her head. *No,* she wanted to say. *I'll wonder why Sean didn't come after me as Seth came after you. I'll wonder why he didn't stop me from leaving Ireland. Why he didn't put his love for me above all else. Why he let me go.*

"I'm so sorry, Caitie," Rosie whispered, holding her friend tight. "I'll try my best not to jabber about Seth."

Caitrin squared her shoulders and tugged on the bow of Rosie's yellow bonnet. "Never you mind, Miss Rose Mills and soon-to-be Mrs. Seth Hunter. You will talk about Seth as much as you like, and I shall enjoy hearing every word of it. If you'll permit me, I'll help you plan the finest and most elegant wedding Hope, Kansas, has ever seen."

Rosie beamed. "Hope has never seen a wedding. Ours will be the first."

"And the best." Caitrin watched as young Erinn entered the mercantile carrying a heavy bucket of water. "We must order ribbon from Topeka, Rosie. What color would you like? I love purple, so I do, but I believe you have a special place in your heart for yellow."

"Yellow ribbons!" Rosie whirled away, her gingham skirt billowing around her ankles. "Yellow ribbons and sunflowers! Oh, I wish Hope had a real church. We could put ribbons everywhere, Caitie. I'm going to sew Seth a new shirt, did I tell you? And Chipper will have brand-new shoes and a new hat from Topeka. But what should I wear for the ceremony? I love my blue gingham dress, but maybe I should think about spending a little of the money I've saved from the mercantile and the bridge tolls. I really love that bolt of pale blue cotton with sprays of roses everywhere. You know the one I mean? There it is, Erinn; can you see it?

Climb onto the ladder and take it down from the shelf for me, will you please? And what about that pink there with the tiny dots all over it? Do you like that one, Erinn? . . ."

Caitrin sank back to the floor and the pile of dirty dishes. *Father, I love Rosie,* she prayed as she scrubbed. *I love her so much, and Seth, too. Help me to share in their joy and not for one moment dwell on my own sorrow. I don't want to grow into a bitter, angry woman eaten up by jealousy. And help me . . . please help me to put away all my memories of Sean.*

Oh, Sean. Caitrin's thoughts drifted away from her prayer. The young man's name evoked a blissful image of her handsome suitor marching up the hill to the Murphys' thatch-roofed cottage by the sea. Aye, but Caitrin had been proud to walk the streets alongside such a dashing man. With his dark curly hair and fine mustache, he had been the grandest-looking gentleman in the county. And how Sean could dance! Never had a pair of feet moved so fast and with such perfection. When Sean O'Casey took Caitrin Murphy into his arms, a whole crowd gathered around to watch. How many years had he courted her? Four? Or was it five?

"It's the mail coach from Manhattan!" Rosie shouted, shattering Caitrin's reverie. "It's crossing the bridge, and look at this place. Erinn, grab the broom. Caitie, please help me put this fabric away. Oh, what if Mr. Dunham has brought passengers? They won't buy a thing!"

Caitrin leapt up and shoved the tub of water behind one of the makeshift tables. As she headed for Rosie and the swaths of calico piled on the counter, she spotted Jack Cornwall's letter lying on the floor in a puddle of water. Realizing it must have slipped out of her pocket, she swept it up and pressed it against her skirt. Blotting the paper did little good. The ink on the envelope had run, and the letter inside would be a sheet of soggy pulp.

"Hurry, hurry!" Rosie called. "Caitie, where did we hide the strongbox yesterday? And just look at this floor! Erinn, leave the sawdust alone and sweep up that popcorn over by the coffee mill."

Caitrin pushed the damp letter into her pocket and hurried to help. With only three of the fabric bolts folded and the floor still littered with remnants of the party, Mr. Dunham, the mail-coach driver, walked into the mercantile. Two fur trappers and a couple of soldiers followed him. They'd seen worse, Caitrin realized.

Rosie welcomed them and made excuses for the state of the floor. Mr. Dunham was more interested in hearing about the exciting events of the previous night. She was deep into the tale of Seth's chasing down her stagecoach when Chipper and his dog, Stubby, bounded into the mercantile. A moment later Seth, Jimmy, and Rolf Rustemeyer walked in. When they started telling the trappers and soldiers about the mysterious appearance of Jack Cornwall's black horse, Caitrin spied her opportunity.

She took out the letter, grabbed two sheets of blotting paper and a new envelope, and went to work at a back table. Cornwall's message must get to his parents—and as soon as possible. Certainly they should be warned about the troublemaker searching for their son, who was in enough hot water himself. They deserved to know about Chipper's decision to stay in Kansas with his father. They needed to understand that Seth Hunter had laid his memories of their daughter to rest and was planning to marry again. And they should be told of their son's injury. If Caitrin couldn't budge Cornwall from the storage room, perhaps a letter from his parents would.

Working quickly, she opened the envelope and took out the sodden page. She unfolded it and laid it between the sheets of blotting paper. Then she copied the address onto the dry envelope.

"Caitrin?" Rosie called from the front of the store. "Do we have any oysters?"

She barely glanced up. "In the basket on the counter. I brought some tins from storage this morning."

Caitrin peeled off the blotting paper and began to refold the letter. As she turned up the bottom of the page, she scanned the faded blue ink. She knew it was wrong to read Cornwall's words. Very wrong. But as surely as the blotting paper had soaked up the water, her eyes absorbed his words.

. . . *Keep a sharp lookout for Bill Hermann. He included my name when he testified, and he's hoping to implicate me in the Easton lynching. Don't tell him I'm holed up hurt. He'll come after me.*

Caitrin swallowed and folded up the bottom third of the letter. Mr. Cornwall's troubles were not her concern. All the same, she did wonder if he had mentioned anything about Jimmy's barn and the woman who had discovered him there in the darkness. She skimmed the letter for her name.

. . . *a Miss Murphy is looking after me here. She's about as Irish as they come—red hair, rosy cheeks, and a brogue so thick you could cut it with a knife. Don't have a fit of apoplexy about her being Irish, Ma. She's stubborn and mouthy. . . .*

Caitrin looked up and frowned. The very idea! How dare Cornwall call her mouthy? What else did he say about his rescuer? She glanced at the letter again.

. . . *How is Lucy? I know she misses me, and I don't like to think about her there alone. Please tell her I'm coming after her soon. Tell her she'll be with me the rest of her life, and I'll make sure she's the happiest woman on earth. Tell Lucy my heart is always with her. . . .*

Chagrined, Caitrin creased the last fold of the letter and slipped it into the envelope. So, there was a woman in Jack Cornwall's life. A woman he loved and intended to marry.

Good. A man so uncontrolled and ruthless ought to marry and be tamed by a loving wife. Best wishes to Jack Cornwall and his Lucy. May they live happily ever after.

Caitrin dropped the letter into the basket of outgoing mail. She didn't care in the least that Mr. Cornwall was engaged to be married. As for herself, she had too much work to do to ponder such matters. And besides, what gave him the right to label her *mouthy*? Certainly she spoke her mind, as any creature with a backbone ought. She held to her opinions, and she didn't mind sharing them if the situation called for it. She had a brain in her head, after all, and what good was a brain if a woman couldn't use it?

As she wiped the counters, she pondered the man's words. Why would Cornwall's mother have a fit to learn his caretaker was Irish? There was nothing wrong with Ireland and nothing wrong with Caitrin's manner of speech. *A brogue so thick you could cut it with a knife?* Of all the impudent, disrespectful—

"Caitie!" Rosie called. "Bring the mail over here, please. The stage is leaving."

Caitrin grabbed the basket and marched to the front of the mercantile. She dumped the letters into the driver's open canvas satchel, dusted off her hands, and stalked away. *There, Mr. Jack Cornwall,* she thought. *And may you be gone as swiftly as your letter.*

As the others walked out of the mercantile, she swept popcorn into a pile and pushed it toward the door. The chickens would like pecking at it, and she didn't suppose a little salt would kill them. In a moment she would finish the dusting. Then she could set to work measuring the front of the mercantile for its new windows. Rosie would certainly be surprised to hear how Caitrin had worked a miracle of persuasion at the harvest dance. The next time Mr. LeBlanc hauled a load of flour from his mill to sell in Topeka, he would return to Hope with a set of large glass windowpanes.

Floors. Shelves. Windows. Caitrin Murphy had more than enough work to fill her days. There simply wasn't time to mourn Sean O'Casey. As for Rosie and Seth, their wedding preparations would be her focus. If Rosie wanted to daydream and gush all day long, so be it. But Caitrin had more important things to do.

And Jack Cornwall? Well, he could rot away in the storage room for all she cared. She couldn't spare a second thought for a man with a cruel tongue, a troubled past, and a fiancée languishing after him. So much for the notion that he had lingered in Kansas out of fascination for Caitrin Murphy. That was a grand joke on her, but she was the better for learning the truth.

Whisking the popcorn out the front door, Caitrin straightened and leaned on the broom handle a moment. At the edge of the barnyard, Seth held Rosie in a farewell embrace. Oblivious to the two waiting men, he tenderly kissed her lips. Then he whispered against her ear, and she nodded eagerly in response. Reaching up, she touched the side of his face and straightened his hat. He kissed her on the cheek before mounting his mule. And then—as if he couldn't bear the thought of a single minute away from her—he leaned over, took her hand, and kissed her fingers.

Caitrin watched as Rosie stood on tiptoe to wave good-bye. Seth turned half around in the saddle, letting his mule follow the others across the pontoon bridge. As the men headed off, Rosie hugged herself, hardly able to contain her joy. Then she lifted her skirts, raced across the barnyard, grabbed up Chipper and swung him around and around.

Caitrin turned away. There was work to be done.

Jack Cornwall sat on the pickle barrel trying to read the text of *The Pilgrim's Progress* by lamplight and wondering if Caitrin Murphy would come. He had heard her in the barn just after noon that day. She and the little girl had opened a big wooden trunk and sorted through dresses, hats, and gloves until Jack thought he was going to climb the walls of the tiny storage room.

Their chatter about voile, tulle, satin, and silk hadn't bothered him. He didn't mind the endless discussion of fringe, ribbon, and lace. And he even held up under the lengthy debate about which kind of sleeves were the most flattering—flared, tiered, puffed, or capped. In fact, he could now declare himself a veritable encyclopedia of ladies' fashions. As if such knowledge were worth a plugged nickel.

No, it wasn't the female babble that had stretched his nerves. It was Caitrin Murphy's voice. Musical, it sang in his ears and sent his heartbeat stumbling like a dancer with two left feet. He craved the sound—the roll of the *r*'s, the hint of laughter in every word, the lilt that made each sentence she spoke like the verse of a song.

Risking discovery, Jack had knocked out the center of a knot-hole and peered out at the two. Caitrin Murphy glowed in the dingy barn like a stained-glass window in a darkened church. Her hair flamed in shades of rust, cinnamon, and copper. Against the conflagration of auburn curls, her skin was as white and pure as snow. And her emerald green dress swished and swayed around her hips until Jack's head spun.

The image of the woman had burned in his thoughts all afternoon. Certain his decision to stay at the O'Toole place to recuperate had been wise, he spent the silent hours washing, shaving, and cleaning up. He focused his attention on medicating his shoulder and exercising the stiff joint. During the weeks of pursuing his nephew, Jack had tried to ignore the wound. But now he knew his recovery was crucial. If Bill Hermann found him, he'd need his wits and his strength. And a job in blacksmithing promised the only hope he had of caring for his parents and Lucy in the years to come.

Moving his arm in circles, he stared at the words on the book in his lap. *I would advise thee, then, that thou with all speed get thyself rid of thy burden; for thou wilt never be settled in thy mind till then. . . .*

Jack slammed the book shut. Thee, then, that, thou? What kind of garbage writing was this supposed to be? The only *wilt* he knew anything about was a piece of soggy lettuce—and it never settled anybody's mind or stomach either.

He glowered at the book's green cover. Where was Caitrin? Was she going to leave him out here to starve? He glanced at the shelves stacked high with jars of apple jelly, beef and venison jerky, and dried apricots. Okay, maybe he wouldn't starve. But didn't she want to see him? Wasn't she even curious about whether he'd left yet?

He was curious about Caitrin Murphy. So curious his brain fairly itched. What had brought a woman with so much life in her all the way from Ireland to the barren Kansas prairie? What spurred the ambition that drove her to tend a mercantile day after day? Where had she come up with the notion that God considered any man precious? The first battlefield skirmish he'd witnessed had taught Jack that human life was as fragile as a cobweb. If God thought people were precious, why did he let them die so easily? And what had possessed Caitrin to utter those amazing words— words that fluttered around in Jack's head like crazy butterflies? *I love you. I love you.*

"So, you're still here, *pooka*," Caitrin's musical voice said in the semidarkness.

Jack jerked upright. The woman was standing a pace away just outside the storeroom door. "I didn't hear you come in."

"Sure, you were too busy reading that book. What is it?" She leaned across him and studied the cover. "*The Pilgrim's Progress.* Good, perhaps it will scare some religion into you."

"What makes you so sure I don't have religion already?" Jack stood, hoping to catch another whiff of the sweet scent that had drifted up from her hair a moment before. "Maybe I'm a preacher in disguise."

"A devil more like." She shoved a basket into his stomach. "Here, *pooka*. It's all I could gather without the others taking notice. There's a chicken leg for you and some corn. I trust you won't mind eating it off the cob in the American fashion—you being such a fine citizen of this country, while I'm merely Irish."

She brushed past him and went to her money jar. Jack watched in amazement as she emptied her pockets and refilled her stash.

Obviously it would be a simple matter for him to steal everything she'd earned that day and add it to the cash she had given him earlier. Either she didn't care about money at all . . . or she trusted him. An odd thought.

"The Irish don't eat corn on the cob?"

She swung around. "We eat potatoes, don't you know? We dance little jigs and search behind every bush for leprechauns with their pots of gold. We're *Irish*."

Bemused at the hostile tone in Caitrin's voice, Jack studied the woman in silence. She was arranging and dusting her shelves with enough steam to power a locomotive. He knew he should try to figure out what might have set her off, but his attention wandered to the more interesting fact that a single tendril of fiery hair had escaped her topknot and drifted down onto her long white neck. What was the scent in her hair? Some kind of flower, but he couldn't put a name to it. He took a step closer.

"I trust your shoulder's healing, Mr. Cornwall," Caitrin said, stacking and restacking small paper sacks filled with coffee beans. "Perhaps you're well enough to be off tonight. We've Rosie Mills living with us now, and it was all I could do to keep her from spending the night in that very loft above your head. She'll be staying here with the O'Tooles until her wedding, and if you think I can stop her from having a look in this room, you're wrong. If anyone is stubborn, it's her. In fact, I'd wager Rosie Mills is a great deal more mouthy—"

Caitrin caught her breath, and her hands paused on the coffee sacks. "A great deal more what?" Jack asked, wondering whether that auburn curl would feel silky or coarse to the touch.

"Talkative," Caitrin finished. "She talks a good bit more than I do."

"I don't mind your talk."

"Don't you?" She whirled around. "I suppose now you'll tell me you have all manner of fine opinions about me."

"I might." He took the tendril between his thumb and fore-finger. "I've been thinking all manner of fine things about this particular curl."

Silky. He stroked down the length of the tress until his fingers touched the bare skin at her nape. "As a matter of fact, I'd have to say that this is the finest curl I've ever seen on a woman. And it smells nice. What is that scent, Miss Murphy?" He bent his head and traced the side of her neck with his breath. "Flowers. Roses?"

"Lily of the valley," she whispered, her voice barely audible.

He could feel the tension emanating from her as she stood motionless, barely breathing. But she didn't run. Didn't protest. So he took the tendril and feathered it against her earlobe. "This is a fine ear, Miss Murphy. A perfect ear. And as for your neck . . ." He trailed his fingertip down her velvet skin to the high collar of her dress. "It's a fine neck you have, Miss Murphy. What you said a minute ago was right. I believe I do have all manner of fine opinions about you."

"No," she managed. "No, you don't, and may the good Lord forgive you for your wicked lies."

Her green eyes assessed his, and her voice grew in strength as she faced him. "Though we both may be fiery of spirit," she continued, "you and I could not be more different in the way we have chosen to live our lives. You are a treacherous man, Mr. Cornwall, and I have great compassion for the poor woman who trusts you with her heart. You are not worthy of Jimmy O'Toole's sheltering barn. You do not deserve one kernel of the kindness I have shown you. From this moment, I shall pray that you will mount your black horse and ride as far from this place as possible. Your words disgust me. Your touch repels me. And though you may wither away in this room, you will never see me again."

Caitrin marched past Jack with her jaw set. He let her get as far as the storeroom door. "What was it you told me last night, Miss High-and-Mighty?" he said. "Those three little words?"

She stopped and faced him. "You'll be fortunate to ever know the honest love of a good woman. If you don't rid yourself of your burden of wickedness, you'll never receive the great blessings of our Father in heaven. And for those two losses, sir, I give you *these* three words: I pity you."

Caitrin was gone as quickly as she had come. Jack stared after her into the darkness. *Pity?* He clenched his fists, torn between desire for the woman whose scent still lingered in the room and fury at her bold rejection. She had labeled him a treacherous, wicked liar. What did she know about Jack Cornwall?

He yanked up his book and hunkered down on the pickle barrel again. Nobody was perfect, and Jack had his fair share of flaws. Sure, he possessed a lightning-quick temper, and he'd rather settle a score with a gunfight than a debate. He could hold a grudge better than any man he knew. He liked to do his work well, and he wouldn't tolerate imperfection in himself or anybody else. And he didn't have a lot of patience for nonsense.

Maybe he hadn't set foot in a church for years—but that didn't make him some kind of sinner condemned to the everlasting flames, did it? He'd sure prayed plenty of times on the battlefield. Caitrin had referred to his burden of wickedness. What did she know of the burdens he carried?

With a snort of disgust, he opened his book and took up where he'd left off. "'Get thyself rid of thy burden,'" he read aloud. "'For thou wilt never be settled in thy mind till then; nor canst thou enjoy the benefits of the blessing which God hath bestowed upon thee till then.'"

As the words sank in, Jack flung the book across the room. The movement tore through his injured shoulder like wildfire. Standing, he clamped a hand over his wound and stalked out of the room. Enough was enough. It was time to get on with life.

CHAPTER 4

"HAS JIMMY accepted the notion that Jack Cornwall has finally gone?" Rosie asked as she sat stitching beside the O'Tooles' warm stove with Sheena and Caitrin. "I noticed he went out after supper tonight to check on the black horse."

Sheena grunted. "Aye, after the men found no sign of the villain the other day, Jimmy vowed to keep combing the land. But he gave up on it today. The horse is ours, though we have no desire for it."

"No desire for a good horse, Sheena?" Caitrin asked, looking up from a wool sock she was darning. Any talk of Jack Cornwall made her uncomfortable. She had kept her word and stayed away from the storage room the past five days, but she couldn't seem to stop fretting about him. Though his horse remained, surely without fresh food or water the man himself had gone.

"Why wouldn't Jimmy want a fine horse like that?" she wondered aloud. "'Tis better than a mule, so it is, and there's no reason to hate the horse just because its owner was rotten. The trouble over little Chipper is ended. Cornwall must have surrendered the boy to Seth and Rosie and gone on his way. I can't think the horse is anything but a gift."

"A gift from a Cornishman?" Sheena spat out a snippet of thread. "I'd prefer a wheelbarrow full of rotten potatoes from a friend over a fine horse from a Cornishman."

Rosie looked up from stitching her wedding dress—a pale yellow gown with a row of pearly buttons down the bodice. "How do you know Chipper's uncle is a Cornishman, Sheena? Did Jimmy speak to him?"

"His name is Cornwall, isn't it? I should think that settles the matter."

"Cornwall is a county in England," Caitrin explained. "It lies along the western coast. A rough place, so it is."

"What's wrong with Cornishmen?" Rosie asked.

"The Cornish are the very pestilence of the earth," Sheena spoke up. "Tell her, Caitie."

Caitrin sighed. "Here we are in Kansas, Sister, and half a world away from the shores of Ireland. What use is it to hate the Cornish?"

"What use? For a start, Jack Cornwall's behavior toward us shows the very reason the Cornish are such a wicked people. They're a greedy, selfish lot. They'll lie and cheat an honest person into utter poverty if given half a chance. Tell Rosie about the Cornish, Caitie. Go on."

"The troubles go back hundreds of years," Caitrin said, unwilling to dispute the elder sister she always had loved so dearly. "The Cornish are a Celtic people, as are we Irish. They're clannish and warlike, and their tales of King Arthur are as ancient as our legends of Bran the Blessed. Sure, the beloved green sod lies but a few miles from the coast of Cornwall, divided only by the Irish Sea."

"And there's half the trouble," Sheena cut in. "Fishing."

"The Irish claim certain fishing grounds, and the Cornish claim others. But it's never quite settled which is which and whose is whose. We've battled over fishing rights for centuries."

"Tell Rosie about the mining, Caitie."

"Tin mining," Caitrin explained wearily. She could hardly believe the scarlet hue that had risen to her sister's cheeks over this discussion of a trouble so far removed. "Ireland has few precious things to dig out of the ground beyond peat and tin. We burn the peat, but we can sell the tin for a profit." She thought for a moment about Sean O'Casey and his new wife, the daughter of a wealthy mine owner. "A man with an interest in a tin mine can earn himself a fair measure of riches."

"And those wicked Cornishmen are tinners, too," Sheena said, tucking pins into her unruly red hair. "Sure, they try to undersell us, don't they, Caitie? They set their prices just a tad lower than ours, and all the market races after Cornish tin. Ooh, they're a scheming, nasty lot, those snakes. I knew Jack Cornwall was as wicked as the rest of them, so I did, the very moment I heard his name. 'Twould be just like a Cornishman to chase after a poor, wee child and try to steal him away from his rightful papa. Viper! I do believe if I ever clap eyes on Jack Cornwall or any of his breed, I'll wring their necks with my bare hands, so I will."

"Sheena!" Caitrin jabbed her needle into the toe of the sock. "Would you be so cruel yourself, now? And you here in Kansas without a mackerel or a tin mine in sight?"

"A Cornishman is a Cornishman is a Cornishman," Sheena said. "Take one of them out of Cornwall and put him in the middle of a desert—and he'll try to cheat you out of the very sand you're standing on."

At that moment Jimmy stepped into the soddy and tugged off his boots. Caitrin eyed him in silence. She had no desire to continue this ridiculous discussion. Good or bad, a man should have the chance to prove himself by his own actions . . . and not be judged by the entire history of his race.

Jack Cornwall, of course, *had* shown himself a liar.

In his letter he had called Caitrin mouthy and stubborn. But fancying himself at an advantage in the barn, he had tried to woo her with all manner of pretty words. And then he had touched her. Caitrin shut her eyes, willing away the memory of the man's fingers against her skin. Every time she thought of that moment, a shiver ran straight down to the tips of her toes. But Jack Cornwall had promised his life to another woman, a creature who even now sat waiting for him to come and make her a wife. How cruel of him to use two innocents for his own pleasure.

No, the man had proven himself unworthy—not because he was Cornish—but by his selfishness and troublemaking in both Missouri and Kansas. And *why* couldn't Caitrin remember those things, instead of the tingling caress of his fingertips sliding down her neck . . . and the way his broad shoulders gleamed in the lamplight . . . and the look in his gray eyes when he spoke to her . . . ?

"You left a lamp burning in the storage room, Caitrin," Jimmy said, crossing in front of the stove. "I spied it when I was seeing to that horse."

"A lamp?" Caitrin swallowed and glanced out the window.

"No fear. I went in and blew it out." He settled down on a stool with his pipe. "You'd left the door unlocked."

"Caitie, that's unlike you," Sheena said. "You always lock the storeroom."

"She's been working too hard on my wedding," Rosie put in. "You must be exhausted, Caitie. I'll go lock up for you. Where's the key?"

"No!" Caitrin stood quickly, almost knocking over her own stool. "I'll do it. I . . . I want the fresh air."

Jimmy gave a chuckle. "Fresh air? Sure, it's cold enough to freeze your lungs out there. I'm expecting snowfall any moment. Leave the storage door unlocked tonight, Caitie. Nobody's going to steal your precious supplies."

"No, no. I'd better see to it." Before the others could try to dissuade her, Caitrin grabbed her shawl, pushed open the soddy door, and hurried outside.

As she raced across the open yard toward the barn, her heart beat out a frantic prayer. *Oh, Father, what shall I do if Jack is still here?*

How can I make him go away? And why does the merest thought of him leap into my soul on wings of hope and joy? He's not a good man. He's caused so much trouble for everyone. Father, I pray . . . oh, I beg of you . . . don't let my loneliness blind me! Show me the man as he truly is!

The barn was pitch-black inside, but Caitrin flew across the dirt floor without a thought for roosting chickens or clumps of hay that might trip her feet. Gasping for breath in the frigid air, she forced her steps to slow as she approached the storage room. She could see the faint outline of the open door, and she pushed it open with one hand.

"Mr. Cornwall?" she whispered. "Are you here?"

The little room was cloaked in silence. As she calmed, a chill crept up her bare arms. She stepped inside and peered around, but it was too black to see. "Mr. Cornwall?" she said a little louder. "'Tis Caitrin Murphy. Where are you?"

Again, nothing. Fumbling in the dark, she found the lamp on a shelf. She managed to light it and take it down. The faint yellow glow revealed an empty room. The pallet of quilts lay folded in one corner. The pickle barrel was shoved up against a wall. A stack of books sat beside it along with the crock of salve. The bandages lay in a heap on the ground.

So he had gone away tonight, just a little before Jimmy came in to blow out the lamp. Or perhaps Jimmy's near-discovery had caused him to flee. Perhaps even at this moment, he was riding his black horse toward Missouri and the man who wanted to hunt him down. Swallowing, Caitrin picked up the length of bloodstained fabric and studied the delicate lace edging. *Been a long time since I saw fine lace on a lady's petticoat hem.* Jack's deep voice drifted through her thoughts. *I decided you were something different, Miss Murphy. Something I've been needing a touch of.*

Why had he needed her? She reflected on their conversation, and the answer was obvious. Jack Cornwall had needed Caitrin Murphy because of the three words she spoke on their first meeting . . . words he confessed he had never heard in his life. *I love you.* So simple, so easy to say. He had asked those words of her again and again. Yet she had not deigned to speak them to him a second time.

Despite his poor opinion of her in the letter to his parents, Jack had expressed a need. But she had been too proud . . . too high and mighty . . . to fill the empty place in him. Because he thought her stubborn and mouthy and because he had trifled and flirted with her while intending to marry another woman, she had railed out at him. Called him wicked, treacherous, a liar.

The Lord Jesus would never have done such a thing. Though Christ stood in righteous judgment of the unrepentant wicked, he also loved them so deeply he came to earth to give his very life for them. Aye, he dined with tax collectors, forgave thieves, and protected wanton women. "He that is without sin among you, let him first cast a stone at her," the Master had said. "All things whatsoever ye would that men should do to you, do ye even so to them."

Oh, but the haughty Caitrin Murphy had been wounded. Too miffed to see beyond herself to Jack Cornwall's need for true love—the love of God—she had spurned the man. And now he was gone.

Caitrin carried the lamp to the door. Who was the more wicked of the two? She knew very well the Light of Life, yet she had snuffed out that holy glow in the face of a man who had never heard a word of love spoken to him.

Shivering in misery, she pulled the door shut and glanced at the empty keyhole. Jack had gone off with the key. And that was all he had taken from this place—a little food, a few days rest, a head full of harsh words, and a key.

Remorse forming a lump in her throat, Caitrin set the lamp on a nail keg and fell to her knees beside the pile of hay on which she had first discovered Jack Cornwall. Clasping her hands together, she bent over and poured out her heart.

"Forgive my pride," she whispered, "forgive my cruel words, and forgive my selfishness . . . my jealousy. . . . Oh, Father, that was it. I was jealous of her, that woman in the letter. It was Sean and the miner's daughter all over again, and I was the one abandoned. Forgive me, please forgive me—"

A loud thump sent hay scattering across Caitrin's lap. "Who's Sean?"

Her eyes flew open to find Jack Cornwall himself crouched on the hay in front of her. Shirtless and smiling, he was the picture of vigor. For a moment, her mind reeled. Had God dropped the man from the sky? Was he an apparition to which she must beg forgiveness in person? She stared, unable to speak.

"Sean and the miner's daughter," Jack said. "Anybody I would know?"

Caitrin squinted up at the barn's rafters. Then she focused on him again. "Where did you come from?"

"The loft. I exercise my shoulder up there at night." In demonstration, he leapt up, grabbed a low wooden beam, and swung himself onto the loft ladder. From there, he seized a support beam with both hands and pulled up and down, his chin meeting the top of the bar as his muscles strained with the effort. Three, four, five, six. On the seventh, he let go and dropped down onto the hay again.

"I reckon I'm just about as good as new," he said, breathing hard. "Take a look at the shoulder."

Her tongue still tied in a knot, Caitrin studied the mound of hard sinew with its visible scar. Indeed, the wound had closed in front and back. Though the mark the bullet had left remained thick and tight, his shoulder obviously was flexible. Powerful. Massive.

"So, tell me about this Sean fellow," Jack said. He squatted on the hay across from her and draped his arms across his knees. "Somebody back in Ireland?"

Caitrin blinked and focused on his face. Shaggy brown hair, squared cheekbones, silver eyes. Her heartbeat faltered. "I thought—I thought you had gone away."

"Tomorrow. I wanted to get back in shape for the journey in case I run into trouble. Long way to Cape Girardeau. After I'm there, I'll need to find a job. The work I do takes a good arm." He looked her up and down. "Didn't expect to see *you* again."

"Jimmy said—"

"The lamp. I know. I watched until he'd gone into the soddy before I lit it, but he came back out to check on Scratch—my horse. He must have seen the light while I was up in the loft. I reckoned I was done for, but he just blew out the lamp and walked away."

"He assumed I'd left it lit."

Jack nodded. "So you came out to see if that wicked, lying scoundrel was still in your storeroom."

"The door . . ." She gestured vaguely in that direction. "I needed to lock it."

"Figured I'd finally gone, huh?"

"Oh, Mr. Cornwall, I must tell you how sorry I am for my harsh words," Caitrin burst out. "You have every right to think me mouthy and stubborn, for that is exactly what I am. And even though your dear mother believes ill of the Irish, she's no worse than my sister, Sheena, who holds a poor opinion of the Cornish—never mind how vigorously I dispute her. I should not have spoken so cruelly to you, for you are indeed precious to God and—"

"Hold on a minute. How do you know what my mother thinks of the Irish?"

Caitrin trembled in the cold, but she knew she must confess. "Your letter. It fell into a puddle at the mercantile, and while it dried, I read it. Not all, but some. More than I should. It was truly bad of me, and I implore your pardon. You see, when first we met and spoke here in the barn, our words together were heated and lively and full of spirit. I began to think of us as truly a pair of candles burning bright . . . as though we were alike in purpose and in heart. I believed we were something of a match, you and I, and a measure of my loneliness faded in the hope of a kindred soul. But then I read your letter. It was the knowledge of your beloved Lucy that provoked me so. When you spoke words of admiration for me the other evening, sure, I could only think of poor Lucy waiting for your return and the day you would make her your wife."

"My wife?"

"Aye, and what you did was so like Sean O'Casey, you see. He declared his undying devotion to me, yet all the while he knew he would marry that miner's daughter. Instead of accepting you as a man like Sean—capable of wooing one woman while another waited in assurance of marriage—I expected better somehow. I always expect the best of people, and so often I'm disappointed. But I never learn, do I? Sure, Sean spoke all manner of fine words and tender nothings until I was no better than butter in his hands. And when I heard your flattery—"

"Did you melt?"

She swallowed at the implication behind his question. "Your words put me in mind of Sean O'Casey and the miner's daughter. All the while you were speaking to me, I knew about your Lucy waiting at home. Aye, but I momentarily forgot what a wicked man you are, and that is where I made my error. Rather than hear you out and forgive you as a Christian ought, I grew angry at you for toying with me while Lucy sat in expectation of becoming your wife."

Jack shook his head as an odd grin tilted one corner of his mouth. "Miss Murphy, you're a wonder. A miracle. A flame-haired, green-eyed marvel."

Wariness stole over her. "What do you mean?"

"You've forgiven me for the sin of turning you into a puddle of melted butter. And all for the sake of Lucy. Lucy Cornwall—my pretty little sister."

Sudden heat raced into Caitrin's cheeks. "Your *sister*? But the letter said—"

"What was it I put in that letter meant only for my parents' eyes? Could you refresh my memory?"

"Please forgive me for reading it."

"Me forgive you? I thought I was the wicked one."

"Sure, I'm wicked, too." She could hardly force out the words. Her face grew hotter as she studied her clasped hands. "You wrote that you would return to Lucy and never leave her. You intended to keep her with you all your life. I never thought—"

"I reckon you didn't." He stood and walked away.

Caitrin bent over and buried her face in her hands. Oh, this was too horrible. She had all but confessed to the man an attraction she couldn't admit even to herself. And she had mistaken his sister for a fiancée. She had to leave! The soddy would be warm and cheerful, and maybe she could put this wretched encounter out of her mind.

"Cold?" Jack's voice spoke behind Caitrin as he draped a thick quilt over her shoulders. "It's starting to snow. They'll come looking for you pretty soon."

"Aye." She sniffled and clutched the quilt at her throat. "I must go."

"Just a minute." He sat down beside her and slipped his arm around her. He had put on his jacket, but she could feel the bulk and strength of his arm through the fabric.

When he spoke again, his words were rough. "I'm going to tell you about Lucy. Maybe after I explain things, you'll see past my so-called wickedness to the man I really am. Maybe you'll understand why I went after Chipper the way I did. For years my parents have been embarrassed to speak Lucy's name beyond the walls of our house. I'm not sure Mary even told Seth Hunter about her. But I'm not ashamed of my sister, and I don't mind that you read the letter. You see, Chipper meant everything to my parents. My sister

Mary had died, and I was a grown man making my own way. In their minds, Chipper was all they had left of a real family."

"But what about Lucy?" Caitrin asked. "Why don't your parents claim her?"

"Never mind what they do or don't do—*I* claim her. Lucy is my sister, and she'll be my family long after the rest of them have passed on. Chipper already chose to stay here with Seth Hunter. My father isn't well, and he'll be gone soon. Ma won't be long after him. But Lucy is young. And she's . . ." He lowered his head for a moment. "Well, she's troubled. But I'm going to take care of her, I swear it. I plan to take a job in a livery and hammer horseshoes from dawn till dusk if that's what it takes."

"Your purpose in life is to care for your sister?"

"Protect her. I'll use my blacksmithing to provide for her. I learned my skills in the army. One day I'll have my own smithy. But now—Cape Girardeau—I'll work for somebody else to look after Lucy and my folks. I'll save what I can. Buy some land. Put up a house."

"Then you're a builder after all, Mr. Cornwall." Caitrin let out a shaky breath, finally beginning to relax in the warmth of his embrace. "I said you weren't, but you are."

"Maybe I am."

She ventured a glance at the man beside her. His face was so close she could see the texture of his skin. He smelled of shaving soap. Staring into a mist through which she couldn't see, his gray eyes were depthless.

"Your sister," Caitrin whispered. "What is the nature of her trouble?"

Jack looked at her, and she read the pain in his face. Clearly he was assessing her, weighing whether this mouthy, unforgiving, judgmental woman had the capacity to understand the sorrow that wracked him. Humiliated at the pride that had formed such a barrier between them, she reached out from between the edges of the quilt and laid her hand over his. Slipping her fingers through his, she became aware of firm sinew, callus, and a breadth that dwarfed her clasp.

"This is a hand that can protect a dear sister," she said softly. "You will bring healing to your Lucy."

"No." His jaw clenched tight, he shook his head. "No. Nobody can fix her troubles."

"What problem could hold a woman prisoner all her life . . . and offer no hope of solution?"

Jack was silent, but Caitrin could feel his heartbeat hammering against her shoulder. Finally he pulled away from her, the muscle in his jaw working hard. He looked up at the rafters of the loft. "Lunatic Lucy, they call her," he ground out angrily. "Touched in the head. Crazy as a coot—"

"Stop." Caitrin grabbed his arm. "Jack, you mustn't—"

"People throw rocks at her. Taunt her. And now, for her protection, we have no choice but to keep her confined. My parents can't manage her, but I can. And if anyone tries to interfere—if anyone hurts Lucy ever again . . ."

Beneath Caitrin's hand, the muscle in his arm bulged and hardened into solid granite. She laid her cheek against it, praying for the words to calm him. "You'll save your Lucy. I'm sure of it."

"Yeah, like I saved Chipper from the clutches of Seth Hunter."

"Chipper belongs with Seth. They love each other."

He grunted. "*Love.*"

"Aye, and your love will save Lucy from her troubles."

"Nothing will save Lucy." His eyes hard, he scrutinized her. "What is it with you? You don't back away from me like I have smallpox. Don't you know I'm Loony Lucy's brother? You know what people say—maybe it's a family disease, and you'll catch it from me. Or maybe my wicked, lying ways brought Lucy's calamity on us. Maybe it's the punishment for my sins."

"Stop it, now." She covered his mouth with her hand. "Nothing you've done has brought this calamity on your sister. All of us have sinned in one way or another."

"I don't stand a chance of forgiveness for what I'm feeling right now, Caitrin Murphy, and I can't make myself repent." He pressed her hand hard against his lips. "The need you bring out in me burns like a fire inside. I think about you day and night, wanting a taste of those sweet lips . . ." He covered her mouth with his and pulled her roughly against him. His fingers slid into her hair, dislodging pins and combs. "Caitrin, hold me. Hold me tight. I've had the scent of your hair racing through my head like a cyclone whirling out of control."

For a moment Caitrin hung motionless as his mouth ignited a blaze across her lips. Shock captured her breath in her throat. Pleasure reeled through her, sending tingles dancing down her spine and shivers skipping into the base of her stomach as she arched into his kiss. And then truth tore through her heart.

"Jack," she said, clutching his shirt and pushing him away. "Sure, you must not be so bold with me."

"Don't tell me that look in your green eyes isn't desire."

She shook her head. "I won't lie to you, Jack Cornwall. You're the first man since Sean to fill my thoughts for even a moment. Aye, I'm a woman, and inside me . . . there's also a need . . ." She bit her lip. "There's a longing in my heart that only the true love of a man can fill. But the Bible says—"

"Don't preach at me, Caitrin," he growled.

"No, but if you would possess my lips, then you must take my mind and spirit, too." She struggled to her feet and tugged him up to stand beside her. "I'm more than a creature with flaming hair, Jack. I've a brain, so I do, and you know precious little of what's inside it. I've a heart, too. The Spirit that dwells in my heart is not my own. Sure, it's the very presence of God himself. You've a good face and strong arms, but I know nothing of your mind and heart.

Indeed, you and I might find pleasure together. But pleasure lasts no longer than a season. And then what?"

Jack searched her eyes, and Caitrin refused to lower them in modesty. *Let him see that I meant what I said. Let him understand. And, dear God, please let my heart stop aching for another kiss from his lips.*

"It's time for me to go," he said. "Say the words, Caitrin. Say them to me before I leave. I want to hear them one last time."

Oh, Father, make them your words! she breathed upward in prayer. *Make them words of the Spirit. Let them come from you and not from me. Not from my heart.*

"Say the words," he repeated, gripping her shoulders.

She reached out again from her protective quilt and laid her fingertips against the side of his face. "You are precious to the Father, Jack Cornwall," she whispered. "You are precious. And with the Father's love, I love you."

"Caitrin Murphy." With a groan wrenched from deep inside him, he folded her into his embrace. "Please don't tremble. I won't hurt you."

"Aye, but you will."

"No, I swear it. I know I'm rough and bullheaded. I've done wrong in my life. And sometimes I don't think things through from start to finish before I act." His arms tightened around her. "But I'd never hurt you. You're something different, Caitrin. Every time you talk, little pieces of you get twisted around my heart. I don't understand the way you think. We're a matched pair, all right, but I don't understand that God who holds you so tight and keeps you apart from me. I need—" he paused and she could feel him searching—"I need . . . something from you. I don't know what it is."

"Maybe 'tis the three words. Not the ones you keep after me to say. Those others." She stood on tiptoe and whispered into his ear. *"You are precious.* Just think of it, Jack. You are precious to the Father—"

"Caitrin?" Rosie Mills's voice rose to a note just short of a shriek. She was striding across the barn floor, a lantern hanging from her hand. "Caitie, what are you doing? Who's that with you?"

Caitrin jumped, but Jack pulled her close again. "It's all right, Miss Mills," he said. "Caitrin's been out here talking to me."

Rosie's eyes widened as they darted from one face to the other. Then her mouth fell open. "Caitie!" she gasped. "That's Jack Cornwall!"

CHAPTER 5

I DON'T believe we've been introduced," Jack said, assessing the astonished young woman who stood before him. He could feel Caitrin quaking in his arms, and he tucked her hand inside his to reassure her. "Name's John Michael Cornwall, but most folks call me Jack. I'm Chipper's uncle. And you must be Miss Rose Mills."

"You-you-you—" Rosie stammered, pointing a finger—"you tried to kidnap Chipper! Y-you grabbed me at the party. You shot at Seth."

"All true. But not until after Seth had kidnapped my nephew from the only family he'd ever known."

"You're a Confederate!"

"Well now, that's a different matter entirely."

"Turn Caitrin loose!" she shouted. "You'll never get your grimy hands on Chipper this way. Let her go, you—you *Cornish snake*!"

"As I hear tell, Cornwall is not heavily populated with snakes, Miss Mills," Jack said, working to hold back a grin. "And I'm not inclined to turn loose of a good-looking woman who wants to be held." He bent to brush a kiss across her cheek.

"Caitrin Murphy!" Rosie gasped and clapped her hand over her mouth.

At that, Caitrin shrank into herself, mortified at his boldness. Jack was momentarily surprised at her response, but reality quickly became apparent. Fiery and stubborn Caitrin might be, but her loyalty to the O'Toole family proved she was no rebel. It wasn't likely she would fight them for the right to choose the man who would court her. And she would never defend a man with Jack Cornwall's reputation in the town of Hope.

The moment he'd been dreading had come. It was time to go, and he had made up his mind to leave with all the gallantry he could muster. If he could protect Caitrin from the hostility she would face over having cared for him in secret, he would do it. He loosened his embrace and stepped aside.

"Go ahead with your friend, Miss Murphy," he said. "I apologize for the inconvenience I've caused you."

"Inconvenience?" The flame in Caitrin's eyes roared to life as she turned on him. "You have caused me more misery—more *agony*—than you can ever imagine! Sure, you've tilted me topsy-turvy, Mr. Cornwall. First you settle yourself in my storeroom and refuse to budge. And just when I think you've finally gone away, I begin to dread the thought of your leaving. You call me mouthy and stubborn—but the very next moment I'm your flame-haired Irish beauty. You try to kill my friend and steal his son, yet you treat me with a gentleness I've never known from a man. You command me not to preach at you, yet you beg to know what it is that makes me different."

She squeezed both her fists together and shook them at him. "A full half of my heart is praying for the moment you walk out of this barn and leave me in peace," she said. "And the other half can't—can't bear the thought of never seeing you again! After all the havoc you've caused, will you simply stand aside and wish me away with Rosie—as though I'm the merest of acquaintances?"

Jack stood rooted, absorbing her words and trying to make sense of the storm crashing around inside him. "Do you think I'm having an easy time here, Caitrin? I wandered into this barn broken and defeated. And then you came along with your lace petticoat and your red hair. You called me a villain, but you treated me like a man. You trusted me. You healed me. I don't know how, but you gave me hope. I should have left this godforsaken prairie days ago, but—"

"Now just a minute there, you smooth-talking scoundrel," Rosie cut in. Taking a step forward, she jabbed Jack in the chest with her finger. "This prairie is not godforsaken. I'll have you know a better class of people lives here than you'll ever be good enough to join! We take care of each other. We defend each other. And as for Caitrin—I don't know what kind of deceitful flattery you've tried to pull on her—but you can just take your black horse and ride straight out of here, because Seth and Jimmy won't abide your presence for a minute. Not a single, solitary minute!"

"Rosie, please," Caitrin said. "You don't understand."

"Oh, don't I? He's been toying with your heart. If he can't destroy us by stealing Chipper, he'll just ruin the prettiest, sweetest woman in our town. He's trying to sully you, Caitrin, but somehow you're blind to it. If he can't lure you into sin right here and now, he'll probably bamboozle you into running off with him."

"That's ridiculous," Jack spat out. "Caitrin has a mind of her own."

"Yes, she does," Rosie said. "And a home of her own, too. Caitrin, don't think for one second about leaving with this man. We love you, and you belong with us. Seth has planned a wonderful gift for you. I was supposed to keep it a secret until the wedding, but I'll just tell you the truth right now. This winter Seth is going to build us a brand-new house and barn—and he's giving *you* his soddy, Caitrin. Think of it. Your own house, a store to help manage, a town full of people who care about you. And if it's a husband you want, well, there's always Rolf Rustemeyer."

"Rolf?" Caitrin said.

"Who's Rolf Rustemeyer?" Jack demanded.

"He's a wonderful, upstanding, hardworking gentleman," Rosie said. "He would never steal children. He would never fight for slavery. And he would never seduce a poor, innocent woman in a dark barn. More than once Rolf has told me he would like to court you, Caitrin. So there! Your life is settled and perfect . . . and don't you listen to this man for one more minute. Now come with me before Jimmy walks out here and starts shooting."

Rosie reached for Caitrin's arm, but Jack blocked her. "Not so fast, Miss Mills. You seem to be forgetting that this poor, innocent woman you *love* so much has a right to her own opinions. As far as I'm concerned, Caitrin can choose where she wants to live, what she wants to do, and who she wants nearby. If she ever works her way through the tangle and chooses to have me at her side, you can bet your last dollar I'll treat her right. I'll protect her. And I'll fight any man who tries to come between us. Count on it."

Stamping her foot, Rosie glared at him. "I am not a betting woman!" she said. Then she swung around and faced her friend. "Fine, then, Caitrin. Choose."

"*Not yet,*" Jack pronounced slowly and carefully in Rosie's face. "I have to go back to Missouri and take care of a little trouble that's been following me around. Besides that, I have people to look after. Responsibilities." Then he straightened and met Caitrin's green eyes. The look of bewilderment in them softened his fury. "I may not understand everything about you, Caitrin," he said. "But I respect you. You're something special. Something I've been needing. Maybe it's those three words, huh? What do you think?"

"Sure, I don't know, Jack," she whispered.

"I don't know either, but I'll find out. You can depend on that. And now, if you ladies will excuse me, I'll get my stuff and head out before someone in this friendly little town starts shooting at me again."

He strode across to the storeroom, grabbed his shirt, his guns, and the bag of supplies he'd been accumulating, and headed for his horse. As Jack bridled Scratch, the stallion tossed his head, eager for some exercise. Jimmy had put the saddle on a sawhorse nearby. "Okay, boy," Jack murmured as he fastened the cinch. "Easy, now."

Both women were standing just where he'd left them, stock-still and staring after him as he led Scratch out of the barn. It was all he could do to walk away from Caitrin Murphy, but he wouldn't cause her any more trouble than he already had.

Jack mounted and set off, peering through the swirling flakes of the now heavy snow in search of the trail that led to the road. The sky was black, as black as it had been the night he'd come to this place. But he felt none of the defeat that had burdened him then. The flame of Caitrin Murphy burned brightly inside him. So did the words she had spoken . . . those three little words. *You are precious.*

He threw back his head and stared up into the dizzying flurries, but the calm in his heart held firm. *You are precious to the Father,* her words echoed. *Precious to the Father.*

"Hey, God," he shouted upward. "Jack Cornwall here. I've been looking for you."

Watching the snow fly, he drank in a deep breath of chill air. *And I've been looking for you,* a voice answered softly.

⁊

Caitrin hurried across the barnyard toward the soddy, praying fervently to escape Rosie's questions. She had almost reached the door when her friend laid a hand on her arm.

"Caitrin?" Rosie asked. "What on earth have you done?"

Pausing, Caitrin took a breath and turned. "I know you want an explanation for what you saw tonight, Rosie, but I don't have one that will satisfy." She spoke quickly, hoping to put an end to the conversation. "Sure, I found the man lying in Jimmy's barn the night of the harvest party. After his fistfight with Seth, the bullet wound in his shoulder was torn open and bleeding. I gave him a little salve and some food, as a Good Samaritan should. He was in no condition to defend himself, so I put him in the storeroom to keep Jimmy from finding him that night . . . then he refused to go away. But now he has, and that's that."

"Jack Cornwall kissed you," Rosie said, her eyes crackling beneath her yellow bonnet. "I saw it."

"He's not like we thought . . . not wicked through and through. Aye, he carries guns and rides a big black horse and shoots at people now and again. But only for a good reason. He *does* have his reasons, Rosie. You must believe that."

"I'll never believe anything that man says as long as I live. He's just like the serpent in the Garden of Eden, hiding in places where he doesn't belong and tricking innocent women with sly words."

"And what do you know of the words that passed between Jack and me?"

"Jack? You call him Jack?"

"He's a human being, Rosie, not a serpent. His name is Jack, and he has a heart far more tender than you could ever imagine. The wrong he did to Seth was done on behalf of his dear parents, so it was. Chipper is all they have of a family, except for—"

Caitrin caught herself. If she told Rosie about Lucy Cornwall, her friend's anger would surely soften. But that would betray the secret pain Jack had shared with her. If he wanted others to know of his sister and her burdens, he would tell them himself.

"Jack is loyal to his family," Caitrin continued. "He has said he would fight to protect those he loves, and that is exactly what he did in riding after Chipper. Does that make him evil?"

"Jack Cornwall also said he'd fight any man who tried to come between the two of you. Are *you* among those he loves, Caitie?"

Caitrin sucked in a breath. "Of course not. He hardly knows me. We spoke together but a few times, and never in the light of day. Jack has been away at war, and I'm likely the first woman he's met in a long time. I put a bandage on him and fed him some sausage. Sure, he won't have found love in that."

"Do you love him?"

"Rosie!" Caitrin jerked the quilt up higher on her shoulders. "How can you ask such a silly question? As I've said a hundred times, I love Sean O'Casey as much today as I did the day I left Ireland, and even though he wed the mine owner's daughter, I shall never love another man as long as I live. But I won't brand Jack Cornwall a villain. I caught a glimpse of the true man that he is, and my eyes were opened."

"I think your heart was, too."

Caitrin looked away. "Think what you will, Rosie. He's gone away now. He'll be riding for his home in Missouri and the family who needs him. Work calls him, and responsibility, too. He won't trouble us again, you can be sure of that."

"After what I saw in the barn tonight, I'm not sure of anything," Rosie said. "For your sake, I pray he never comes back."

Caitrin's eyes filled with sudden, unexpected tears. "If you wish to pray about Jack, Rosie, pray for his soul," she choked out. "Pray that the Spirit of God will fill his heart. Pray for the troubled family who depends upon him. Pray for his safety from those who pursue him. Pray that he may find a good woman who has the courage to love him as he deserves. For my own part, I shall pray that if Jack Cornwall's name is ever spoken again in the town of Hope, you will remember that he is a man and not a snake. Perhaps then the Holy Spirit will direct your tongue to defend him with words of kindness, truth . . . and forgiveness."

Wiping a hand across her damp cheek, Caitrin pushed open the door and stepped into the soddy. Jimmy was snoring beside the fire. All the children were asleep. Sheena glanced up from her mending.

"Ah, Caitrin, there you are," she said. "Poor Rosie was in kinks of worry over you. You've been away such a long time. Are the stores all in place?"

"Aye, Sheena." Caitrin picked up her darning and sat down on the low stool. Behind her, she heard Rosie slip into the room. "All is as it should be."

"I'm glad to hear it," Sheena said. "With devils like Jack Cornwall roving about the place—"

"I'm sure Jack Cornwall is no more a devil than you or I, Sheena." Rosie spoke firmly as she took her place beside the fire and spread her wedding dress over her knees. "Caitrin, what do you think of this row of ruffles? Maybe I should take it off. I'm not really the ruffly kind of girl, am I?"

Caitrin blinked back the tears that threatened. "You're the good kind of girl, Rosie Mills," she said. "And ruffles or not, you will look beautiful on your wedding day."

>—

"I do wish Hope had a real church," Sheena said as she and Caitrin slipped onto a bench near the front door of the mercantile. "A wedding should be held inside a proper sanctuary. Nothing else seems quite right."

"The real church is the body of Christ—everyone who believes in him," Caitrin said. "And with all of us collected here today, the Hope Mercantile is as fine a place as any for Rosie's wedding."

Caitrin surveyed the decorations inside the wood frame building and tried to take joy in her handiwork. Sprays of winter wheat tied in huge yellow bows hung on the mercantile's walls. Sunflowers with nodding brown faces and bright golden petals clustered in vases, bottles, and jars around the room. Every counter wore a length of sunny yellow calico or gingham topped with plates piled high with cupcakes and cookies. Seth had built a little pulpit, and it stood on the rough dirt floor facing the gathered crowd. Near it, hands clasped behind his back, waited a bald-headed little minister. The man had been imported all the way from Topeka just for the occasion.

As the community's motley band began to play on fiddles,

accordions, and mouth harps, Caitrin let out a deep breath. Well, she hoped Rosie and Seth would enjoy their wedding day. She had done all she could to make the surroundings beautiful. The good Lord himself had melted away every flake of the early snow that had fallen. He'd arranged for a sky the color of chicory blossoms and an afternoon sun in the exact buttery shade of Rosie's wedding dress. Caitrin had no doubt that the union established this day would be wreathed in happiness.

As for herself, all contentment had walked out of her life with Jack Cornwall. For the past few days she had been a tangle of nerves. Snappish, impatient words slipped from her tongue. She could find no pleasure in her neat rows of merchandise and the eager customers who stopped at the mercantile to buy. She could not even delight in Sheena's little brood. They vexed her, tried her patience, and made so much noise it was all she could do not to scream at them. Jack had stolen nothing from her—nothing but the very joy of living.

Against her own best intentions, Caitrin checked the barn storeroom at least three times a day. But of course, he was never there. When she tried to sleep at night, his words ran in dizzy circles around her brain. Worst of all, every time she thought about the years stretching ahead, she saw nothing but bleak isolation.

The prospect of owning Seth's soddy only served to remind her that she would spend the rest of her days alone. Always alone. *Was that such a terrible thing?* she asked herself time and again. It should not be. The apostle Paul himself had chosen the single life, better to dedicate himself to the Lord's work. Surely Caitrin could adopt such a holy attitude.

But no. The rapture in Rosie's eyes plunged a knife of agony into her heart. And she despised herself all the more for it.

Caitrin dug into her pocket for a handkerchief. Was every man who barely touched her soul bound to abandon her? First Sean

O'Casey. Then Jack Cornwall. Who would be next? *No one*, for she would never dare let another man near enough to hurt her. Caitrin sniffled. She could only pray that people would assume her tears were borne of happiness for dear Rosie . . . and never suspect that she wept out of vain, wretched pity for herself. Oh, could God ever forgive her for such a sin? And could she ever find a way out of this maze of misery?

A tap on her shoulder halted her recriminations for an instant. Jack? She looked over her shoulder to find a pair of warm gray eyes crinkling at the corners, a thatch of shaggy blond hair, and a smile as bright as heaven itself.

"*Ist* beautiful, the mercantile," Rolf Rustemeyer said, his words thick with German accent. The huge, solidly built farmer leaned closer and patted her arm with his heavy, work-worn hand. "You maken fery pretty, Fraulein Murphy. You maken happy day *für* Rosie *und* Seth."

Rolf's determined effort to communicate softened Caitrin's dismay. She gave him a warm smile. "Thank you, Mr. Rustemeyer. It is a lovely day."

"*Ja.*" He nodded. "Goot day *für* vedding. Zoon Rolf Rustemeyer vill builden big *Kirche. Kirche. Für* veddings, peoples dying."

Caitrin frowned. What on earth was he talking about? "*Kirche?*" she repeated. "What is that?"

"*Ach.*" He slapped his knee in frustration. "*Kirche.* Is *Gott's Haus.*"

Caitrin used her knowledge of the Gaelic tongue to decipher the message. "A *Kirche* is like a *kirk*? A church. You're going to build a church for the town of Hope, are you?"

"*Ja, ja, ja!*" Rolf beamed.

The band began to play louder, and Caitrin glanced toward the mercantile door. Seth Hunter—straight, tall, and handsome—entered with little Chipper holding tightly to his hand. The proud father's new white shirt fairly gleamed, and his son all but danced in his shiny new shoes. Aye, but they were a fine pair, the boy a mirror image of his papa. Rosie had made herself a wonderful match indeed.

"Fery zoon, I vill *Kirche* builden," Rolf whispered, tapping Caitrin's shoulder again. "Here I builden. Near mercantile. You vill zee me on daytime. All days, *ja?*"

Caitrin's smile froze as the significance of his words sank in. Rosie had told her that Rolf would like to court her. Perhaps he would even want to marry her. To Rosie, that would be a wonderful solution to Caitrin's loneliness. And if Rolf spent day after day building a church near the mercantile, she would have no choice but to acknowledge him.

Caitrin studied the big man, all brawn and hardy good humor. Though his reputation in the community was spotless, Caitrin viewed Rolf more as a potential project than as a suitor. He needed a good haircut. A cake of strong lye soap would do wonders with the dirt embedded in his hands. And a few more English lessons would serve him well socially. Just as Caitrin had helped transform a barn into a mercantile, she might change a rough-hewn farmer into a gentleman. But to put her future into those large hands? To give her heart to Rolf Rustemeyer? Oh, heavens!

"'Tis the bride!" Sheena whispered, elbowing Caitrin.

Everyone stood as Rosie stepped into the mercantile. She was a vision . . . her yellow dress lit up the room, her brown hair gleamed, and her smile could have lit a thousand lamps. Seth looked as if he might burst with pride as she came to stand at his side. Love fairly poured out of the man's blue eyes. Rosie bent to kiss Chipper's cheek, and the little boy threw his arms around her neck.

"Hi, Rosie," he cried out. "We're gonna get married now!"

The nervous excitement in the room broke, and everyone chuckled as the happy threesome moved to stand before the preacher. When the familiar words of the wedding ceremony filtered through the room, Jimmy took Sheena's hand. It was a perfect moment, Caitrin thought. Two hearts joined as man and wife. One little soul given a brand-new mama.

The women in the congregation dabbed their eyes. Children sat transfixed. Men turned their hat brims in their laps and grinned with satisfaction. Chipper's gangly puppy, Stubby, wandered into the mercantile and lay down at Rosie's feet, his big tail thumping up puffs of dust.

"Seth, you may now kiss your wife," the minister said at last.

For a moment, silence hung in the room. Then Seth folded Rosie in his arms and gave her a kiss that was warm, tender . . . and much too long. The children giggled. One of the men called out, "Save it for later, Seth!" and everyone burst into laughter.

As the congregation rose, Caitrin stuffed her handkerchief into her pocket, determined to make a joyful occasion of the event. Rosie and Seth turned to walk out of the mercantile, and everyone rushed to engulf the couple. Caitrin worked her way through the throng until she was able to give the bride a warm hug.

"God's richest blessings upon you, Rosie," she whispered. "I wish you every happiness in the world."

"And you, too, Caitrin!" Rosie said. "I pray that you'll find as perfect a man for you as Seth is for me."

Seth leaned through the crowd and laid a warm hand on Caitrin's shoulder. "Thank you, Miss Murphy. The place looks great."

And then the couple were whirled away . . . out into the fresh air where tables and benches had been set up to feed everyone. Caitrin squared her shoulders against the tide of melancholy that threatened once again, and she headed for the serving line. Rolf Rustemeyer and Casimir Laski had been roasting a pig since dawn. Neighboring women had brought dishes filled with steaming corn, green beans, and black-eyed peas. There were bowls of mashed potatoes and crocks of brown gravy. And the fresh rolls piled in baskets almost could have fed the biblical five thousand without a miracle.

Caitrin rolled up her sleeves and took charge of the potatoes and gravy. By the time she had dished out a dollop for every visitor, her arms were aching. She filled her own plate and headed for a table near the barn.

"Caitrin, come over here!" Rosie called, beckoning from the heavily festooned central table. "Sit with us!"

Obedient, Caitrin turned and set her plate beside Chipper's. The little boy had fed half his pork to Stubby, who was licking his chops for more. "A grand day this is for you, Chipper," she said. "Sure, I never saw a pair of shoes so fine."

"Yeah," Chipper managed around a mouthful of bread. "Papa bought 'em for me. I gots a mama *an'* a papa now, Caitrin. Rosie's gonna live with us in the soddy, did you know? An' Papa's gonna build us a new house this winter. A wood one."

"Truly? Not a sod house?"

"Nope. Wood." Chipper swallowed the bite. "Papa told me that Rosie might have a baby brother or sister for me one of these days. You need to get yourself a daddy, Caitrin. That way you can have babies."

"Now, Chipper," Seth said sternly.

But Rosie was laughing. "You're exactly right about our babies, sweetheart. I'm going to pray that you'll have lots and lots of brothers and sisters. And then won't we all have fun?"

"I sure do wish Gram an' Gramps could be here now," Chipper said. "Uncle Jack, too. I miss 'em. Maybe they could all get married to us, an' live with us, an' then we'd be one family."

There was a moment of awkward silence, but Caitrin finally found her tongue. "What a big family that would be, Chipper," she said. "I think you and your new mama must want a family as big as the O'Tooles'. And where is poor Will O'Toole today? In all the excitement, have you forgotten your best friend?"

"Look down there at the end of the table," the child said, pointing. "There's Will with Erinn an' Colleen. They watched Rosie get married to Papa an' me today. Will says Rosie will be a good mama. Why don't *you* want to be a mama, Caitrin?"

"Oh, look, Chipper," Rosie cut in. "Jimmy's going to make a speech."

The gangly Irishman rose and lifted his mug of hot apple cider. "'Tis a fine day for our good friend Seth Hunter, and as fine a day for the rest of us here to have the pleasure of rejoicin' in his wedding. Sure, there never was a man as good, honest, and hard-workin' as our Seth. Nor was there ever as pretty and lovin' a woman as dear Rosie—save my own sweet Sheena, of course. And if I didn't say that I'd be sleepin' in the barn tonight."

Jimmy paused amid the chuckles. "So, here's to the happy pair," he continued. "Seth and Rosie, may you live long, grow rich, and bear more wee *brablins* than you can count in a day!"

A chorus of hurrahs followed the toast. Caitrin glanced around, wondering who would stand up for Rosie. Sheena—though happy to speak her mind in private—would never have the courage to make a public pronouncement. And then Caitrin noticed that everyone's eyes were trained on *her*. Flushing, she realized that she was Rosie's close friend, and by all good grace she should offer a toast.

She stood, lifted her mug, and prayed hard for words to form on her tongue. "Rosie has brought the light of happiness to many here on the prairie," she began. "And I count myself blessed to be among those her life has touched. Not only is she good and kind, but she bears witness to the joy of Christian love that flows from her heart. In marrying Seth, our Rosie has found a partner . . . a friend . . . a true love . . ."

Caitrin squeezed her eyes shut and took a deep breath. "Rosie has found all the happiness she so richly deserves," she finished quickly. "Rosie and Seth, may your marriage be one of tenderness and everlasting love from this moment forward."

Sinking onto the bench, Caitrin buried her nose in her mug and took a deep drink. Oh, it had been a poor toast . . . unplanned and awkwardly spoken. Just when she meant to be strong, her own silly woes had swarmed out to engulf her. She *must* move past this self-pity. She *must* stop dwelling on a man who had been barely a flicker in her life. And she would. Truly, she would. God help her!

"Me now!" Chipper cried, climbing up onto the wobbly bench. "Who's gonna talk about me?"

The child looked around the crowd. Caitrin's heart went out to him. Perhaps Will would stand up for his little friend. She glanced down to the end of the table to find Sheena's son deep into a slice of cherry pie.

Chipper turned in a circle on his bench. "Does anybody have a speech about me? 'Cause I gots a new mama today, an'—" He paused and his face lit up. "Oh, look everybody! Here comes somebody to talk about me. It's Uncle Jack!"

CHAPTER 6

JACK rode his horse to within five paces of the nearest table, and the crowd broke into screams of terror. Women covered their children's heads. Men threw protective arms around their wives. A blond giant of a fellow leapt to his feet and came at the intruder. Heart hammering, Jack jumped to the ground and held up both hands.

"I'm unarmed!" he shouted over the roar. "I come in peace."

Head down, shoulder butted forward, the giant kept coming. Jack kept his hands up as long as he could. When he realized the fellow meant business, he went for the shotgun in his saddle scabbard.

"Stop, Rolf!" a woman's voice cried out. "Rolf, no!"

The giant skidded to a halt. Caitrin Murphy materialized at the man's side and grabbed his arm. "No, Rolf!" she said. "Look. Mr. Cornwall holds no weapon. You must let him speak."

Breathing hard, Jack waited in tense silence as the giant assessed the situation. "You not fight Seth?" the man growled, pointing a beefy finger. "Not little boy to take?"

Jack held out his empty hands. "I'm unarmed," he repeated. "I've come in peace."

"What do you want with us, Cornwall?" Seth called across the clearing. One arm clamped around Chipper, he rose from the wedding table. "You know you aren't welcome here."

Jack stepped forward, determined to keep his attention away from Caitrin. "I came to talk to you, Seth," he said. "You and everybody else."

In the wary hush, a child's voice rang out. "Hi, Uncle Jack! Guess what! Me an' Papa an' Rosie got married today."

"Hey there, Chipper." At the sight of the little blue-eyed boy, Jack's defenses faltered. This was his sister's son, the baby he had cuddled on his lap and rocked to sleep a hundred times. *Oh, Mary. If only you could see your child one more time. If only you could hold him . . . sing to him . . .* Jack swallowed at the knot in his throat.

"You know what, Uncle Jack? Nobody made me a speech." Chipper frowned. "Did you come to say a speech about me? Or . . . are you gonna fight Papa again?"

"I didn't come here to fight anybody, Chipper," Jack said, taking another step into the midst of the gathered tables. He searched the child's blue eyes and read the longing in them. "All right, little buddy, I'll make you a speech. How's that?"

"Yeah!" Chipper said, pumping a little fist. "Get a cup."

Aware of the tension racing through the crowd, Jack knew one wrong step could put him in danger. These people didn't trust him . . . and rightly so. He had tried to take the boy. He had disrupted previous gatherings. He had battled Seth Hunter with words, weapons, and fists. Any one of them might choose this moment to exact revenge.

If he had his way, Jack would speak his piece and get out. But Chipper was gazing at him with a plea for reconciliation. Jack glanced to a table in search of a cup.

"Take this, Mr. Cornwall." It was Caitrin's musical voice. Both hands outstretched, she offered a tin mug filled with cider.

Jack met the woman's eyes for an instant. It was all the satisfaction he could permit himself. Even so, the sight of shining green eyes, fiery hair, and lips soft with pleading nearly derailed him. Forcing his focus back to the boy, he lifted the cup.

"I've known Chipper since he was born," he addressed the gathering. "He used to weigh not much more than a sack of dried peas. Yep, he was a wrinkled little thing and about as bald-headed as an old fence post."

"Uncle Jack!" Chipper clamped his hands on his head and squealed in delight.

The crowd murmured, and a few low chuckles gave Jack the encouragement to continue. "Fact is, at the start I could hold Chipper in one hand. Right there in my palm, just like that. When he got bigger, he liked to ride around on my shoulders. Liked to eat mushed-up pawpaws. And he liked to holler, too. That boy could put up quite a squall to get what he wanted."

Chipper giggled, and the party guests began to relax. The blond hulk sat down on a bench next to Caitrin. "My nephew always knew what he wanted," Jack went on, "and not a one of us who loved the little rascal ever had the heart to tell him no. Now Chipper's made up his mind to have himself a papa and a mama."

Jack turned to Seth Hunter—the field hand Jack's father had driven from the Cornwall property, enraged at his Yankee sympathies and his secret courtship of beautiful, golden-haired Mary. Seth stood straight and tall, his hand on his bride's shoulder and his arm around his son. Behind Seth stretched his properties— a house, a barn, and fields that had brought in a good harvest. Around the man sat friends and neighbors who would defend him with their lives.

"The boy chose well," Jack said, lifting his cup to honor the man who had been his enemy for so long. Then he returned to his nephew. "Here's to Chipper. May his days be filled with fishing, swimming, kite flying, and all the joys of boyhood. And may he live a long, happy life in the sheltering arms of his parents . . . Seth and Rosie Hunter."

A stunned pause gripped the wedding guests for a moment. And then they lifted their cups and sang out, "To Chipper!"

Before he could choke on words that had been torn from his gut, Jack tipped up his tin cup and downed the cider. *That's right,* that voice inside him whispered. *Make peace. If you want to win, you have to lose. The last shall be first.*

His stomach churning in rebellion at words that reeked of weakness, Jack leaned over and slammed the tin cup on a table. *No! Fight. Stand up for yourself. Take the boy. Take Caitrin.* Bitterness rose in his throat, threatening to strangle him. From the moment he had ridden away from the woman, he had searched for a way to make her his own. But every scheme he cooked up involved violence and bloodshed. Every plan except this one.

That quiet voice had whispered a different approach. A new way. *Surrender. Let go. The last shall be first.* Jack never even got as far east as Topeka. In the stillness of a night as cold and alone as any he had ever known, he had hunkered down on his knees next to his horse and tried to listen to that voice.

Amid the blackness inside him, his own failings came to him one by one. He heard the clangor of his rebellion, his rage, his deceit. The echoes of his violent rejection of God drifted through the cavern of his empty soul. As he listened to the din of his stormy life, Jack recognized a future as hopeless as his past. Remembering the Jesus Christ to whom Caitrin's soul belonged—that refining fire who could bring gold from raw ore—he surrendered to the Master, begging to be filled with the harmonious melody of forgiveness.

At that moment the raucousness had stopped. Silence reigned. And then a sweet song began inside Jack. Peace filled the cavern. Hope stretched out before him like a bright pathway leading to eternity.

For the next few days after his night of repentance, he had walked on that shining path. He had listened to the music of that quiet voice. Drifting in a sort of daze, he had decided that a return to Hope was the answer he'd been searching for. He would make a public offer of reconciliation with his enemies. Then he would go one step further.

And that's when the buzz of rebellion stirred to life inside him. *Revenge, chaos, hatred,* it screeched, all but drowning the heavenly music in his soul. From that moment, Jack had been engaged in a different sort of battle, a fight that only prayer had seen him through. Gritting his teeth against the torment inside him, he lifted his head and faced his former foe.

"Seth," he said, "I've come to make peace."

Seth's dark eyebrows lifted a fraction. He looked down at Rosie. The woman's face had paled to an ashen white, but she gave her husband a nod of reassurance and gathered Chipper into her lap. Leaving her side, Seth walked around the table to stand in front of Jack.

"You want peace," he said. "Why?"

"For the boy. I don't want him to grow up with the notion that you and I hate each other."

"I'll see to that. I've never been a man of vengeance, Cornwall. The trouble between us doesn't change the fact that you're his uncle, and I'll make sure he always remembers his Gram and Gramps. Rosie and I plan to raise Chipper in a home where godly love is the rule."

Jack nodded. "It's good to know that."

"You didn't need to come back here and interrupt my wedding to get that promise out of me. What is it you want?"

"I reckon I came to put your notion of godly love to the test." Jack drank in a breath. *Say the words. Say them now.* He cleared his throat. "I'm here to ask a favor of you, Hunter."

A ripple of murmurs raced through the crowd. Seth's eyes narrowed. "There's only one thing I've got that you want," he said. "And you can't have him."

"This is not about the boy. I told you I gave him up, and I did.

83

Whether anyone here believes it or not, I'm a man of my word. I won't lay a finger on Chipper."

Seth's blue eyes still were hooded in wariness. "I'm a dirt farmer, Cornwall. What could you possibly want from me?"

"Permission."

"Permission for what?"

"Work." Jack listened to the hubbub that followed his request. He couldn't let the crowd's displeasure derail him. With God's help, he would win over his enemy and make a place for himself. He needed a place like Hope, a place where he could make time to silence the rebellion inside him and listen to the quiet voice. He needed time to learn and grow. He needed hope.

"Like you, Seth, I've been fighting a war," Jack said. "While I was gone, the family home was looted and burned. The farm was stripped. We had to move out. There are folks in Missouri I'd just as soon never lay eyes on again. I need to ply my trade, and I'm asking you for a place to do that."

"On *my* land?"

"That's right."

Some of the men began shouting at Seth, encouraging him to run off the intruder, kick him out on his backside, give him a taste of his own medicine. The blond giant stood to his feet again.

Seth stared at Jack, his face expressionless. "Let me get this straight," Seth said. "Your papa ran me off his farm. You spent the summer doing your dead-level best to steal my son away from me. You shot at me. You stole my rifle. You disrupted every iota of peace we had around here. And now you want me to give you a chunk of my land so you can work it?"

Jack rubbed the back of his neck as the jeers grew in intensity. This wasn't going well. Another minute or two and the whole crowd was liable to string him up. So much for making peace. So much for hope.

Jack settled his hat on his head. "I reckon your godly love

84

doesn't stretch that far," he said. "I don't blame you for it. Well, I guess I'd better head out."

Forcing himself not to look at Caitrin, Jack turned his back on Seth. Any man worth his salt would see this as a great opportunity to run his enemy into the ground. Kick him while he was down, and then spit in his face. Vulnerability made his spine prickle as he started for his horse.

"Hold on a minute, Cornwall," Seth called after him.

Yep, time for the payback. *Help me, Father, please help me here,* Jack prayed. When he turned, he saw that Rosie had raced to her husband's side. Well, this would just about finish things off, he thought. The last time he spoke with the woman, they'd wound up yelling at each other in the O'Tooles' barn. She was liable to spill the beans on him, hurt Caitrin in the process, and turn the hubbub into a hullabaloo.

"Mr. Cornwall," Rosie said, her shoulders squared, "what kind of work do you do?"

The question caught Jack off-balance. "I'm a blacksmith, ma'am."

"A blacksmith," she repeated. She glanced over in Caitrin's direction and seemed to draw courage. "Well, I guess we don't have any blacksmiths in Hope."

"Nope." He saw a crack in the wall of opposition. "But you have a lot of wagons passing through here, ma'am. Broken axles, worn-out brake shoes, rusted undercarriages—I fix them all. I can patch a rusted kettle so good you'll think it's new. I can shoe eight horses a day. There's not a kitchen tool I can't produce. And even though my work has been mostly on weapons, I reckon I could learn to make and repair any farm tool you hand me."

"I see. Well, that's a useful trade." Rosie looked at Caitrin again. Then she elbowed her husband. "Isn't that a useful trade, Seth?"

The man's blue eyes focused on his wife. "Rosie, what are you up to?"

"I just think—" she twisted her hands—"I think Hope could certainly use a blacksmith. There *are* a lot of wagons. And that hinge on the door of our oven's firebox has been giving me no end of trouble."

"I fix hinges," Jack inserted.

"Your best shovel split clean in two the other day, Seth."

"I fix shovels," Jack said.

"And you can be sure we'd sell every ladle, knife, pothook, and trivet we could put in the mercantile." Rosie's eyes took on a light Jack had seen that evening in the barn. Only this time her ardor worked in his favor. "If we could repair the hoop on that big barrel by the barn, Seth, we could catch rainwater in it. Just yesterday I noticed that the bucket in the well has sprung a leak. And you were wishing for a new set of tools to build our house not three days ago. Seth, there *would* be value in a blacksmith. I think every one of us would profit, don't you?"

"Rosie." Seth shook his head and hooked his thumbs in his pockets. "Rosie, it's not any old blacksmith we're talking about here. It's *him*."

"I'll stand up with your wife, Seth," Caitrin said, walking to Rosie's side. "Mr. Cornwall has given his word he'll not trouble you again."

"He's troubling me right now," Seth said.

"Aye, but 'tis all in how you look at the matter. You cannot deny it took great courage for Mr. Cornwall to walk unarmed into our midst today and beg a boon of you. Something has driven him to it, Seth."

"I wouldn't doubt 'twas the devil himself!" Jimmy cried. "He's up to no good, Seth. Send the villain packing. And, Caitrin Murphy, you'll sit yourself down before your sister flies into a fit of apoplexy."

"How can you be sure 'tis not God who has driven Mr. Cornwall to you, Seth?" Caitrin said. "Sure, he's asked you for peace and forgiveness—"

"He's asked for your land!" Sheena shouted. "Don't give him a fleck of dust, Seth. He's Cornish, so he is, and they're all a pack of liars and cheaters—"

"Give him a chance, Seth," Caitrin cut in. "Clearly the man has shown a change of heart."

"Trickery! All trickery!" Sheena hollered.

"Seth, you could let the man work at the back of the mercantile after you've built the new barn," Rosie said. "He could have my bed in the loft."

"Run him off!" someone shouted.

"Can you fix a plow, Cornwall?" another called out.

"Send him packing!" Jimmy cried.

"I think now maybe this is goot man, Seth," the blond giant said. He held out his arms like a pair of tree limbs, and the crowd quieted. "Man is fighting you before. But now is vit no gun coming. Is ask vorking for you. Rolf Rustemeyer say yes. Is goot man now. Seth, you give vork this man."

"Hope does need a blacksmith," Casimir Laski added.

"A livery would bring in lots of customers," Rosie said.

"Don't do it, Seth." Jimmy shook his fist at Jack. "He'll ruin you. He'll destroy our town."

"He's asked for godly love," Caitrin reminded Seth softly. "How can we deny this man?"

Seth folded his arms across his chest and stared into Jack's eyes. "Can I trust you, Cornwall?"

"Yes."

"Prove it."

"That'll take time. Will you give me time, Hunter?"

"You're asking for more than time. You're asking for a place to live, a place to work, a chunk of my land, and a lot of my good-will. Why don't you go on back to Missouri, Cornwall? Why work here?"

Jack's focus flicked to Caitrin for an instant. At the sight of her flushed cheeks and sparkling emerald eyes, he felt his resolve grow. "I need a fresh start," he told Seth. "Kansas is wide open and raw. Out here, a man can let go of the troubles in his past and make a new life for himself. You did that, Hunter. I'm asking for the same chance."

"For all I know, your troubles will follow you here." Seth studied his boots for a moment; then he shook his head ruefully. "Well, I reckon I'm a pretty big fool, but I'm going to give you permission to set up shop on my land. You can sleep in the barn loft. Rosie's made it a nice enough place. I'm not in the business of handing out loans, but if you can scrape together the cash, you can build yourself a smithy here by the main road and take in whatever work comes your way."

As the realization of victory coursed down his spine, Jack's spirits soared. "Thanks, Seth. You won't regret it."

"Yeah, well, we don't have any official peacekeepers around here, so we'll have to trust you to keep your nose clean. One slip, and we'll run you out of town so fast you won't know which way is up. Got that?"

"You won't have to worry about me for a while, anyway. I'm going back to Missouri to check on my family and take care of some unfinished business."

Seth nodded. "See you later, then."

"Later." Jack tipped his hat at Rosie and gave her the warmest smile he could muster. The young woman had risen to his defense . . . and her words had made all the difference. He felt sure he knew why she'd had a change of heart.

Caitrin Murphy was standing to one side as Jack mounted his horse. It was all he could do not to take her in his arms and thank her, tell her how deeply her words and actions had affected him, kiss her sweet lips in promise of the day he would return. But he could feel the hostility still emanating from the crowd, and he knew any sign he made toward Caitrin would cause her trouble in the town.

"I'll be back," he said. He gave her a last glance before he tugged Scratch's reins and headed for Topeka.

$\sim$

"I told you he wouldn't come back." Sheena leaned over a wooden chest in the mercantile and set the stack of paper valentines back into their box. "You stood up for him at the Hunter wedding. Rosie stood up for him. Rolf stood up for him. Even dear Seth stepped out and offered the scoundrel a place to work and a clean bed to sleep in. But he rode away without a backward look.

"Now what's it been? Three months? More? Not a soul has glimpsed a single sight of Cornwall's hairy hide. You thought he would return at Christmas, Caitrin. You mentioned he might appear for the New Year's Eve fancy dress ball. Then you speculated he'd show up for the Valentine dinner. Now you speak of Easter. As far as I'm concerned, Jack Cornwall is long gone and good riddance. I don't know why you even think of the rascal."

Caitrin wound lengths of red satin ribbon back onto their spools. She didn't know why she thought of him either. Jack Cornwall had stepped into her life for a few brief days. He had spoken sweet words and touched her heart with his bold request of Seth. And then he had vanished.

In the passing weeks Caitrin had invented all sorts of reasons why the man hadn't returned as he had promised. Something had gone wrong with his plans for his dear sister. Perhaps Jack hadn't been able to manage poor Lucy after all. Maybe she had fallen physically ill. On the other hand, the weather might have prevented Jack's return. It certainly had been a frigid winter, with so much snow that everyone had stayed cooped up for days at a time. Huge drifts had covered the roads, making travel difficult and communication all but impossible. Perhaps Jack had run into trouble with Bill Hermann, the man in Missouri who was trying to hunt him down and involve him in some sort of trouble. Or maybe his wound had taken a turn for the worse. Or he couldn't find the money to buy his equipment for the smithy. Or . . .

"He's no different from the rest of his kind," Sheena said as she packed a stack of lace-edged tablecloths into the chest. "Our father warned us never to trust a Cornishman, Caitie. Sure, you and I saw the devils time and again in the fish markets. We knew firsthand the havoc they caused with their sneaking boats and their low prices. Our own papa denounced them, and if you can't trust Papa's word, who can you trust? The Cornish are liars, cheaters, and tricksters. Troublemakers. Jack Cornwall proved it with his wicked behavior toward Seth and Chipper. And the way he was casting sheep's eyes at you during the wedding feast! He's a scoundrel—can you deny it?"

Caitrin handed her sister the spools of ribbon. "He seemed sincere enough to me."

"Aye, and you'd believe a turnip was a gold nugget if someone looked into your green eyes and told you it was. That's the trouble with you, Caitie, my love. You see things for what they could be . . . and not for what they are."

"Is that so wrong? Rosie believed this barn could become a profitable mercantile. She worked hard to bring the vision to life. And when she became a married woman and busy in her new house, she passed that dream along to me. Now look at the place."

Sheena lowered the lid of the chest, sat down on it, and studied the room. Caitrin couldn't deny the pleasure she felt as she stood on the brand-new plank floor and surveyed glass cases filled with merchandise, walls lined to the ceiling with shelves, and long plate windows gleaming in the afternoon sunlight. She had long nourished the idea of adding a small restaurant area to the mercantile, and she hoped she could talk one of the men into building a room or two at the back to rent out to passing travelers. Though her dreams of a husband and family had come to nothing, Caitrin felt sure God had given her a new goal, and she took satisfaction in her achievements.

"Rosie had a good idea," Sheena said. "And you helped her transform this smelly barn into an honest-to-goodness mercantile. But, Caitie, you can't change everything you set your mind on. You certainly can't change people. Take Rosie herself for a perfect example. Each time the community gathers for a party, you dress Rosie up in your Irish finery, pin *shingerleens* into her hair, and push her feet into pointed-toe slippers. And halfway through every celebration, she races back to her house and changes into one of her ginghams so she can dance better with Seth. She pulls all the glitter out of her hair, puts on her worn boots, and turns back into our dear Rosie."

"I don't mind."

"Of course not, because that's who she is. She's *Rosie*. She'll never be a fine lady in silks and taffetas. She doesn't want to. And Rolf Rustemeyer will never be a gentleman speaking the King's English. He's a German farmer, so he is. He works all summer long in the dirt and heat. He's built half the church by himself this winter. He'd rather climb a ladder and nail shingles all day than try to learn the proper way of holding a fork and knife. Caitie, people are what they are. You can transform a barn into a mercantile, but you'll never turn a lying Cornishman into an upstanding citizen. You must permit Rosie to dress herself for the next party, and you must allow Rolf to eat everything on his plate with a spoon if he wants. And you must stop believing that Jack Cornwall will be true to his word and turn up in Hope again. He won't. He's not coming back."

Caitrin traced Sheena's flaming red hair and bright green eyes. How could two sisters brought up in the very same country, the same house, the same family arrive at such different beliefs? But they had, and they loved each other deeply in spite of it.

"Oh, Caitie," Sheena said, standing and taking her sister's

hand. "It's not that I want you to feel bad about all you've done. Sure, I wish only for your happiness. I rarely see you truly happy these days, and I think it stems from all your wishing and dreaming. Look at Jimmy and me. He's as skinny as a fence post, so he is . . . and I'm so wide around the middle these days I can hardly tie on my apron."

"Are you going to have another baby, Sheena?" Caitrin asked with alarm.

"Oh, who can tell, and what of it? If I'm not nursing one child, I'm bearing another. That's what I'm trying to tell you. I'm me, that's all. And I'm happy. 'Tis because I accept my skinny Jimmy, and my vast brood, and my widening girth that I can find joy in each day that the Lord brings. I'm not always trying to change everything." She let out a deep breath. "Maybe if you'd stop looking on Rolf as a project in need of fixing, you might see he's a very good man in search of a wife."

Caitrin swallowed. "I don't want to marry Rolf."

"Why not? You expect him to be perfect like Sean O'Casey? Ooh, he was a fine one, prancing down the street with his black curls and his tailcoat. But he went off and married the mine owner's daughter, Caitie, and that makes him a poor match for someone as good-hearted as you. But Rolf—now Rolf would make a loyal husband, hardworking and true. If only you could accept him. If only you could change your attitude—"

"Now you're wanting *me* to change, Sheena!" Laughing, Caitrin flapped her apron at her sister. "Shoo with you! Back to your skinny husband and your brood of *brablins*. If I must stop having visions for what people can make of themselves, then I must stop being me. I must change, and I'm no more inclined to do that than any of these others."

"Aye, and you'll live a single, lonely life all your days." Sheena grabbed her basket of leftover heart-shaped cookies from the counter. "Stop waving that apron at me! I'm going, I'm going."

"Come and visit me tomorrow in the soddy," Caitrin called. "I think I've thought of a way to hang wallpaper."

"Wallpaper in a soddy!"

Her hearty laughter broke off as Rosie rushed into the mercantile. Face as pale as the snow that crusted the windowsills outside the store, she clutched her stomach and leaned against the wall, breathing hard. A long tendril of brown hair had come down from its pins. She brushed it aside and stared hollow-eyed at the two women.

"Something terrible has happened," she whispered.

"Rosie?" Caitrin hurried to the younger woman. "What's the matter? Is it Jack Cornwall?"

"Oh, Caitie!" Sheena squawked. "Must you bring up that scoundrel again?"

"This is worse than Cornwall," Rosie murmured. "Much worse."

"Sit down." Caitrin shoved a chair into the back of her friend's knees. Rosie collapsed and buried her face in her hands. "Is it Seth? Is it Chipper? Please, Rosie, you must tell us!"

Lifting her head, Rosie dabbed at the tears on her cheeks with the corner of her apron. "I have just realized the most awful thing," she said. She swallowed hard. "I'm dying."

"Dying!" Caitrin sank to her knees and took Rosie's hands. "Are you ill? Do you need a doctor?"

"It's been coming on very slowly," Rosie explained through trembling lips. "A slow, creeping sickness. It might be consumption . . . only without the cough."

"Consumption without the cough?" Sheena snorted. "I've never heard of such a thing."

Rosie shook her head. "I'm wasting away. I've watched my skirts' waists growing wider and my ribs starting to stick out."

"Are you eating?"

"Hardly. Everything I put into my stomach comes right back out. I can't tolerate the smell of Seth's coffee in the morning, and the fish poor Chipper caught the other day nearly knocked me flat. I've never been so sick. I've always worked like a twister—that's what Seth calls me, his little twister—but now I can hardly drag myself out of bed."

"Your cheeks are still rosy," Caitrin offered.

"Seth is going to be a widower again," Rosie wailed, "and Chipper will lose his second mother. Oh, I'm so upset, I can hardly think. How am I going to break the news to Seth? What will he say? We've just moved into our new house, and he's preparing for the spring planting. I don't want to die! It's not that I'm unhappy at the thought of heaven. Far from it. But you know I'd love to watch Chipper get bigger, and I want to have lots of babies and be a granny someday. I want to grow old with Seth!"

"Oh, Rosie!" Caitrin threw her arms around her friend. How could this terrible fate befall someone so precious? If anyone deserved a long life, it was dear Rosie. Now this!

"The truth hit me just a few minutes ago," Rosie said, dabbing under her eyes with the corner of her apron. "You see, I was in the kitchen counting the loaves of bread in storage. It seems like I'm having to make more and more loaves every baking day, just to keep up with the appetites of those two. Anyway, I got to figuring how many times I've baked bread this month. And then I counted up last month's baking days, and the month before . . . and . . . and . . . I suddenly realized that this is the third time that . . . that . . ."

"That what?" Caitrin implored, wondering what baking had to do with Rosie's impending demise. "This is the third time that *what?*"

"That she's missed her monthly!" Sheena exclaimed. "Of course Rosie can't eat, and she's losing her breakfast, and she's missed her monthly three times in a row. She's gone with child!"

"What?" Rosie and Caitrin said together.

"You're going to have a baby, Rosie, my sweet. Didn't anyone tell you the signs? Well, I suppose your caretakers at the orphanage forgot to pass along the important things mothers tell their daughters. Aye, I can see it as plain as the shoes on my feet. You're pregnant."

Rosie sat in stunned silence, her brown eyes fastened on Caitrin's face. Caitrin soaked in the news and squeezed her friend's hands. "A baby, Rosie," she whispered. "Sheena ought to know!"

Rising slowly, Rosie clutched the shawl at her throat. "Sheena, are you sure I'm not dying?"

"I'd lay my life on it. You should move past the morning sickness part of it any time now, and then you'll start eating so much Seth will go into shock. You'll have to let out all your skirts. You'll grow twice the hair you had before. And when you walk, you'll waddle like a duck."

"A baby!" Rosie shouted, twirling on the tips of her toes. "I'm not dying! I'm going to have a baby. Oh, miracle of miracles! Oh, joy and gladness!"

Caitrin laughed as Rosie danced around the chair onto which she had so recently collapsed. "Thank God!"

"Yes, thank you, Father!" Rosie whirled toward the mercantile door. "I've got to tell Seth! He'll be so surprised! He won't know how it happened!"

"I suspect he will," Sheena put in with a chuckle.

Rosie threw out her arms and spun out into the open, stumbling momentarily into the silhouetted shape of someone approaching the mercantile. Standing on tiptoe, she gave the man a kiss on the cheek.

"I'm going to have a baby! Glory hallelujah!" She popped her head around the doorframe. "Oh, Caitie, isn't this the most amazing day? I'm going to have a baby. And Jack Cornwall has come back!"

CHAPTER 7

"OUT!" A plump redhead shrieked as she gave Jack a shove on the chest. "Out with you, devil!"

He took off his hat, looked over the shoulder of the woman attempting to eject him from the mercantile, and let his gaze settle on Caitrin Murphy. So, he hadn't dreamed her up. There she was, as real as life. Curly auburn hair piled high on her head. Bright green eyes and pink cheeks. Long, white neck. He was afraid he might keel over.

"Jack," she whispered, her lips barely moving.

"Get out of here, you wicked man!" The other woman bopped him on the arm with her basket. Heart-shaped cookies went flying. "We won't have the likes of you in our town. We don't want your kind. Wait a minute—where do you think you're going? You can't come inside here—"

"Miss Murphy," Jack said, stepping past the woman who seemed determined to beat her basket to shreds on his arm. "How have you been?"

"Finely and poorly," she said softly. "And you, Mr. Cornwall?"

"About the same." He thought his heart was going to jump straight out of his chest. "Mercantile looks good. You've been working hard."

"Aye."

As he came closer, she bit her lower lip and fumbled with a wisp of hair that had fallen onto her forehead. "I've come back," he said.

"No, you haven't!" The other woman whacked him again. "You shut your gob and listen to me, Mr. Cornishman. You'll not be casting sheep's eyes at my sister. You'll get onto your wicked black horse and ride back into the hole you crawled out of, so you will!"

Jack glanced at the stout woman and tried to make her resemble Caitrin in any way. Except for the hair and the eyes, they couldn't look more different. All the same, he realized this must be Jimmy O'Toole's wife, Sheena, in whose barn he had spent a good bit of time.

"Mrs. O'Toole," he said, nodding deferentially. "Pleased to make your acquaintance."

"Blarney!" she declared. "You'll not win me over with your sweet words. Sure, I know the likes of you. You shot at our Seth, so you did. You tried to kidnap poor little Chipper. You fought with—"

"I know what I did, ma'am. I was there at the time." Jack turned his hat brim in his hands. "Point is, Seth Hunter gave me permission to build a smithy on his land. I'm aiming to do just that."

"Never! We won't have any Cornish people in our town. We won't allow Cornish—"

"And what's wrong with the Cornish, may I ask?" a high-pitched voice cut in.

Jack groaned as his mother strode into the Hope Mercantile. "Mama," he said, "maybe you ought to wait out in the wagon."

"Stuff and nonsense! I should like to make acquaintance with the inhabitants of my new hometown. And if I'm to do most of my shopping in this mercantile, I want to become familiar with the place." Her gray eyes sparked like flint as she studied Sheena O'Toole. "Jack, you didn't tell me the town was infested with Irish."

"Infested!" Sheena exploded.

"Mrs. O'Toole, Miss Murphy," Jack addressed the women over the hullabaloo. "I'd like you ladies to meet my mother, Mrs. Felicity Cornwall. Mama, this is Mrs. Sheena O'Toole and Miss Caitrin Murphy."

If calling on her sense of social decorum wouldn't calm his mother, nothing would. Nostrils white rimmed with distaste, Felicity gave the women a brief half curtsy. "Charmed, I'm sure," she said, patting her brown hair that lately had grown threaded with silver.

"Miss Murphy is one of the women who manages the mercantile here in Hope." Jack allowed himself a glance at Caitrin. Her cheeks were drained of color, and she had wadded up the end of a red ribbon she was holding. Though wishing he could speak to her alone for a moment, he knew he had no choice but to smooth out the trouble between the other women.

"Miss Murphy can show you around the store," he said to his mother. "Isn't that right, ma'am?"

"I should be happy to help you, Mrs. Cornwall."

"Is this the maid who hid you in the barn, Jack?" his mother asked. "Is she the one who took care of your wound after that brutal man shot you in the shoulder and then turned around and tried to beat you to death?"

Sheena gasped. Caitrin moaned. Jack rolled his eyes. This was not going well. He took his mother's elbow. "Weren't you asking about fresh eggs this morning, Mama? I believe I see a basket of brown eggs on the counter right over there. Maybe Miss Murphy—"

"You hid Jack Cornwall in *our* barn, Caitie?" Sheena demanded of her sister. "You hid from us the very devil himself?"

"My son is far from a devil, Mrs. O'Toole!" Felicity snapped. "I'll have you know he won a medal for bravery during the war, and I keep it right here in my bag. Show it to her, Jack!"

"Mama, please."

"Your son is a Confederate, so I'm told," Sheena said. "A soldier in the army that fought to keep the black man in chains. The army that burned cities. The army that looted the farms of good, honest people."

"It was Yankees who destroyed *our* farm! We had a beautiful place. My husband built our home with his own two hands the very first year we came to America."

"From Cornwall?"

"Yes, indeed." Felicity tilted her chin in the way Jack knew meant trouble. "We hail from the lovely seaside town of St. Ives. Perhaps you have heard of it."

"Me? Ooh, certainly not. And I have naught but pity for those who would choose to live on such barren, windswept cliffs. The Murphys, from whom my sister and I proudly descend, come from the parish of Eyeries in the township of Castletownbere in County Cork."

"Miners," Felicity said through pinched lips.

"And fishermen." Sheena's cheeks glowed.

"Amazing there's not a mackerel or a bit of tin ore in the whole state of Kansas," Caitrin said. "God has blessed us indeed to bring our families to such a bountiful new land. Mrs. Cornwall, you must be exhausted from your journey. Would you care for a cup of hot tea?"

"Just a half dozen of those eggs, Miss Murphy," Jack said before his mother could continue her argument with Sheena. "We've got to set up camp for the night."

"Camp?" Caitrin asked. "But Seth offered you the loft."

"We won't stay in an Irishman's store," Felicity said firmly.

"Seth Hunter isn't Irish. He's American—as are we all. Mrs. Cornwall, you're more than welcome to take lodging in the loft. There's a good bed, a chair, and even a table. I'll fetch a lamp."

"No!" She held up her hand. "We've caused a confloption just by our appearance here this afternoon. I had understood my son to say we'd be welcome. But I can see that the Irish community keeps to its accustomed clannish manners even in Kansas."

"And why should we welcome troublemakers—"

"Sheena!" Caitrin cried.

"Jack Cornwall tried to steal Chipper, so he did."

"My son was honor-bound to return my grandson to me!" Felicity huffed. "I raised Chipper from the day he was born."

"And kept the news of him from his rightful father," Sheena accused.

"Stuff and nonsense!"

"Stop your ballyragging!"

"Jack . . . oh, Jack." Caitrin's trembling voice silenced the argument. "Jack, someone's coming into the mercantile. Who is that?"

Expecting to see Seth Hunter armed to the teeth or Jimmy O'Toole with weapons drawn, Jack swung around to find a shrouded figure weighted with chains stumbling into the building.

He glanced at Caitrin and Sheena. "Ladies," he said, "this is . . . ah . . . this is my sister, Lucy Cornwall."

⟩~

Caitrin stared in horror at the ragged creature whose hollow gray eyes gazed back at her in a lifeless trance. Heavy wrought-iron chains weighted down her thin wrists and clamped her bare feet together. Long brown hair hung in tangles that covered her cheeks and fell in uneven, limp wisps to her waist. Drooping shoulders barely supported the thin fabric of a dress with a torn neck. A ragged shawl trailed from the woman's elbow to the floor. A dark stain on her neck and a smudge across her forehead attested to the fact that she had not bathed in a long time.

"*This* is Lucy?" Caitrin asked.

"My daughter is not well," Mrs. Cornwall said tersely. "Jack, take her back to the wagon at once."

"No, Jack!" Lucy held out her manacled wrists. Her fingers, their nails bitten to the nubs, stretched toward her brother. "Jack, don't leave me out there."

"It's okay, Lucy." He shoved his hands down into his pockets and walked to her side. "We'll all go outside together. Come on, Mama."

"I'm scared, Jack," his sister whispered.

"Nobody's going to hurt you here, Lucy. This is a good place. Remember I told you about the mercantile and Miss Murphy who runs it? This is Miss Murphy, right here. She's a good woman."

The empty eyes focused on Caitrin. "Does she . . . does she know about . . . about the soldiers? . . ."

"Keep quiet, Lucy!" Felicity cut in. "You know you're not to talk of family matters in public."

"She doesn't know anything, Lucy," Jack said. "You don't have to be afraid."

"I'm happy to meet you, Miss Cornwall," Caitrin said. When she extended her hand, Lucy shrank back as if in fear she'd be struck. Caitrin lowered her hand and smoothed out her apron. "Sure, you must be worn from all your travels, Miss Cornwall. Once I open my restaurant in Hope, I'll treat you all to a good meal. As it is, I can only offer a few chairs and that small table. But I'll be happy to lay out an afternoon tea for everyone. I've fresh rolls baked this morning, and perhaps I can even find a few sweets left from the Valentine party."

Sheena gaped at her sister, but Caitrin didn't care. If Jesus had treated all people with respect and honor, why should she be any different? Maybe Jack Cornwall was a wicked fellow, his sister troubled, and his mother ill tempered. Jesus had washed the dirty feet of his disciples, dined with prostitutes, and healed the slave of a rich man. Her Lord had been a servant, and she would do no less. Marching across the room, she began clearing the table of the receipts she'd been entering into her ledger.

"Sheena, will you please set the kettle on the stove?" she called. "Mrs. Cornwall, do you like sugar and milk with your tea?"

"Caitie, be reasonable!" Sheena hissed.

"Thank you for your offer of tea, Miss Murphy, but we must be going." Felicity Cornwall began moving her family toward the door. "We shall set up our camp near the Bluestem Creek, and Jack will begin building his smithy in the morning. Good day."

Caitrin set the ledger and receipts back onto the table as the visitors exited the mercantile. If the good citizens of Hope had thought of Jack Cornwall as a troublemaker before, she could hardly imagine what they were going to say now. What sort of man must he be to keep his sister in chains? Vile! And the mother— how could she allow her poor daughter to go unwashed and uncombed? It was disgraceful.

"Miss Murphy?" Jack Cornwall poked his head back into the mercantile. "Suppose I could talk to you a minute?"

"I should think not!" Sheena exclaimed.

"Oh, please, Sheena, do take your basket and go home to Jimmy. I must close the shop in a moment anyway."

"My husband will not be pleased when he hears the news that Jack Cornwall has returned," Sheena said, leaving the store with her nose in the air. "And neither will Seth."

Caitrin crossed her arms around her waist as Jack approached her in the empty building. Suddenly she wished she hadn't sent her sister away. The man was taller than she remembered, broader across the shoulders, and more deeply tanned. She had forgotten how he filled a room, as though the everyday things inside it had shrunk into themselves. But she hadn't forgotten his gray eyes.

"I owe you my thanks, Miss Murphy," he said, his hat in his hands. "That's three times you've come to my defense."

"I hadn't much choice in the barn when you lay injured. And at the wedding . . . well, I thought it bold of you to come unarmed and place your request before Seth. But I doubt my support will count for much in the days ahead, Mr. Cornwall."

"I know I'll have to earn the town's trust. I can do it, too . . . if they'll give me time."

Caitrin ran her hand along the edge of a counter. She tried to think of polite words to fill in the silence between them, but she and Jack had never spoken lightly. Their conversations of the past had always been urgent and often heated. Perhaps it was best that way.

"Why do you keep your sister in chains?" she spoke up. "You're a blacksmith. Surely you could remove them."

"I'm the one who made them."

"You made those dreadful manacles?" Caitrin stared at him. "But you're treating Lucy as badly as the most pitiful of slaves are treated! She must shuffle along instead of walking. She can barely even lift her hands."

"I know." He rolled his hat brim. "Look, Miss Murphy—Caitrin— you're the only human being I've run into lately with a lick of kindness. Don't judge my family until you know the truth."

"I'll not judge you even after I know the truth. But it's hard to stand by and watch a woman be treated in such an abhorrent manner."

Jack let out a deep breath and looked away. "We *have* to keep Lucy in chains."

"Why?"

"She tries to hurt herself," he said in a low voice. "There have been times when she . . . when she tried to take her life."

"Oh, Jack."

"The chains aren't to punish Lucy. They're for my own peace of mind. I have to protect her from herself. Not too long ago, she got loose from Mama, climbed up onto the roof of the house, and tried to jump off. I barely got up there in time to stop her. We don't have a choice in this, Caitrin. My sister may be chained, but at least she's alive."

Caitrin tried to absorb the terrible significance of what Jack had told her. "What kind of a life can she ever hope to lead?"

"Lucy has no hope . . . and she doesn't want to live."

"But God offers everyone hope for an abundant life. If only she knew her heavenly Father—"

"There's no easy answer to this, Caitrin," Jack cut in. "I told you before, nobody can fix Lucy."

Caitrin shook her head. "I cannot believe that. Perhaps if you bathed her, she would start to feel a little better. At the very least you could brush her hair and dress her in a pretty skirt."

"My sister won't let anyone touch her. If you get too close, she screams. When I walk near Lucy, I keep my hands in my pockets so she'll know I'm not going to lay a finger on her. She can't stand anybody washing her or combing her hair. We can't even get her out of that dress," He eyed Caitrin. "That's the way it is. But Lucy's my sister, and I'm going to stand by her no matter what."

"That's a good thing . . . but the chains are not. People here will think badly of you for keeping her in shackles."

"So, help them understand."

Caitrin swallowed. That was a grand wish. She couldn't even get her sister to be civil to the Cornish in their midst. Hope certainly had its share of different nationalities in the community— Rolf Rustemeyer, the German farmer; the Laskis from Poland; the LeBlancs from France; and the Rippetos from Italy. Thus far, the families had lived in harmony. She had a terrible feeling that was about to change.

"I shall try to make your family welcome," Caitrin said. "I'll do as the good Lord commands, but—"

"But how do *you* feel about it?" He touched her sleeve. "Caitrin, I told you I would come back, and I have. I'm not the man I was when I left Hope the first time. I've changed, and I want you to understand that."

"What has happened, Jack?"

"One night last fall, after I left the O'Tooles' barn .... well, it was the lowest night of my life—and I've had some pretty bad times. Right out on the road, I got down on my knees, Caitrin, and I prayed so hard I thought I'd bust. It sure seemed like God was talking to me that night, forgiving me for my wrongs and welcoming me into a new life. I knew right then I had to come back here and get Seth to let me build the smithy. And I knew I needed to see you again. Every day I was gone, I thought about you. Thought about the words you said to me in the barn that first night. Did you think of me, Caitrin?"

Heat crept up the back of her neck. "I . . . I suppose I did, aye."

"Did you miss me, Caitrin?"

"I hardly knew you well enough."

"You knew me. Blazin' Jack and Fiery Caitrin, remember? You understood me better than anyone ever has." He searched her face. "And I understood you."

"Aye."

Though her heart had softened toward this man, she could not forget how the people in Hope would view him—as a hot-tempered avenger, a difficult and demanding presence, a man who would not be pushed around. Such a person would find it difficult to fit into a warm, loving community and become part of the team working to build the town of Hope. Though Jack professed a newfound commitment to the Lord, only time would allow him to live out his faith. And Caitrin could not be sure people would give him that time. She felt all too certain that the Cornwalls would not stay long, and her heart could not afford the pain of another loss.

"The people of this town will find it hard to accept you," she told him. "Sure, you might as well realize that. Not only have you brought your own less-than-shining reputation, but you've brought other difficulties."

"Lucy."

"She's very troubled."

"My sister hasn't always been this bad off, Caitrin. Things got a lot worse when she found out Papa was about to die."

"Your father died? You didn't tell me! When did it happen?"

"Not long ago. That's why I couldn't get back here sooner. Papa took sick, and he lingered through the winter. We buried him one day and set out for Kansas the next. I reckon I don't need to tell you that Mama wanted to stay in Missouri. The only thing that calmed her was knowing she'd get to see Chipper again. Lucy loves the boy, too."

"Oh, Chipper! But that makes things even worse! I doubt if Seth will want the Cornwalls spending time with his son. He's very protective of the child. And now Rosie is . . . well . . . Seth will probably draw his family close around him. He loves them so much, and you caused such trouble before. Now things are going to be so . . . so difficult."

"Tell me a time when things aren't difficult." Jack gave a humorless laugh. "You're right in saying I brought more than my reputation along. I brought a group of decent people—the folks I care about most. Lucy has her problems, but I don't know a family that's perfect. Do you?"

Was he daring her to bring up the O'Tooles as the shining example of a family? Caitrin knew that must include her sharp-tongued sister. Aye, Sheena had her flaws. All of them did. No one in the close-knit Irish family could be called perfect, but at least they blended. Sheena had accused her sister of believing she could change everyone to fit an ideal image. But Caitrin obviously could do nothing to make Jack Cornwall blend into the peaceable community of Hope. Or the prickly Felicity. Or Lucy.

"No one is perfect," Caitrin said, untying her apron. "As the Good Book says, 'For all have sinned, and come short of the glory of God.'" With a sigh, she picked up her workbasket. "I won't lie to you, Mr. Cornwall. I was hoping you'd come back to Hope. You brought a bit of a spark into my life, so you did. And when you turned up at Rosie's wedding, you lit a little fire under the people here. You set them to thinking. You challenged them to move beyond their fears. You forced them to take a step toward forgiveness. But now that I see you again, I'm afraid."

"I never intended to scare you, Caitrin." His voice was low.

"Aye, but you have. Your Cornish mother and your troubled sister are naught but kindling to the fire you started last autumn. I'm afraid that fire will grow and spread until it changes into a roaring inferno that could destroy the town of Hope."

"No!" Jack hammered his fist on the counter and set the glass to shivering. "The only inferno I intend to light is the one inside my forge. I came here to work and take care of my family. I came for a fresh start."

"Only God gives fresh starts."

"I know that!" He took a step closer to her. "Caitrin, my past has been one rung after another on the ladder that proves a single man can't change the world. First, I thought I could bring Missouri a fresh start, so I fought in a bloody war that came to nothing. Next, I thought I could join up with a gang of vigilantes and keep the cause alive even when it was doomed. Not only did I fail to set Missouri free, but now one of my former friends is trying to track me down and haul me before the law. Then I got the notion to save Chipper. I lost that one, too. After that, I believed I could protect and help my sister. I stay right beside her every minute, but it's all I can do to keep her alive."

Jack lifted his hand to a tress that had tumbled from Caitrin's bun, and he sifted the strands of auburn hair between his thumb and forefinger. "When you told me you loved me—and God loved me—it was the first time in my life I realized there was hope outside myself. After I left you and Rosie that night in the barn, I got to thinking about all I'd tried to do and how it had come to nothing. I wondered if maybe I *didn't* have to change the world myself.

That was when I realized there was only one way to get a fresh start. Only one Person who could turn things around for me."

"The Lord," Caitrin whispered, amazed at his repeated avowals of conversion to a living faith in Christ.

"I figured you were the person who could best help me to understand the nature of Jesus. And when I saw how everybody in Hope stuck together and helped each other out, I realized they were living the way God says folks should. So I thought I'd better come back here and join in. And then maybe things would get better."

"Oh, Jack, you mustn't look to *me* if you want to know who *God* is." Caitrin took both his hands in hers. "You mustn't set your eyes on the people of—"

"Cornwall?" Seth Hunter stood silhouetted in the open door of the mercantile. Behind him, Jimmy O'Toole stared, shifting a rifle he carried over his shoulder. Rolf Rustemeyer, an axe in one hand, made the third in the party.

"Yeah, I'm back." Jack moved away from Caitrin and took a step toward the men. "I reckon you remember agreeing I could build a smithy on your land."

"I haven't forgotten. I figured maybe you had."

"Mr. Cornwall was nursing his ill father," Caitrin said, joining Jack. "He recently passed away. The family has come to Hope for a new beginning. I'm sure we'll be happy to have them here."

The three men stared at Jack.

"My wife tells me you're a Confederate," Jimmy spoke up. "Kansas is an abolitionist state, so it is."

"And the war is over," Jack replied.

"You'd better not set your eyes on any of our women."

"Jimmy!" Caitrin cried. "What a thing to say. We shall include Mr. Cornwall as one of us, just as Christ welcomed all men into his presence."

"Sheena is say you haf crazy woman here bringen." Now Rolf

addressed Jack. "Vit chains. Maybe she is hurting children. Maybe killing."

"Lucy is my sister," Jack said. He squared his shoulders. "She will not hurt the children. She loves children. She . . . she trusts them."

Jimmy gave a snort. "Perhaps, but she's Cornish—as are her mother and brother. I lived my early life in Ireland, and I've run into your kind many a time. We're growin' into a good little village, so we are, with a church and even talk of a school. There'll be no Cornish tricks goin' on about the town of Hope, let me tell you that. Sure, the first time you cheat somebody or tell a lie or make any trouble—"

"Do you expect the man to be perfect, then, Jimmy O'Toole?" Caitrin asked. "The last time I read the Holy Scriptures, I saw there was only one man perfect in all history. And the likes of us managed to kill him on a cross. Nay, Mr. Cornwall won't be perfect every minute, nor will you. All he's asked for is a chance. Will you not give him that much?"

"If his crazy sister comes anywhere near my *brablins*—"

"If you so much as lay a finger on Chipper, Cornwall—"

"If you haf plan to hurt anybody here—"

"Oh, it's the Welcoming Committee!" Rosie cried, dancing into the midst of the three men and slipping her arm around Seth's elbow. "We used to have a Welcoming Committee in Kansas City. When I lived at the Christian Home for Orphans and Foundlings, I'd see the committee sometimes after I'd climbed up into the big oak tree to pray. Come to think of it, that old tree is where I met Seth, isn't it, honey? And Mr. Cornwall, too, as a matter of fact. Anyway, sometimes when I was up in the tree, I'd see the Welcoming Committee marching down the street to visit the newest family in town. Five or six women in their Sunday best would take along baskets of fresh bread and candy treats for the children. All the businesses would donate gifts in order to introduce themselves to the newcomers. Well, now that's a grand idea!

Mr. Cornwall, would you take your family a little something . . .
a little . . ." She looked around the store.

"Eggs," Caitrin said, sweeping the basket off the counter. "Take
these eggs to your mother as a welcoming gift."

"Thank you, Miss Murphy." Eyeing the men who stood gaping
in the doorway, Jack accepted the basket.

"And you must present your sister with this brush and mirror,"
Caitrin added, laying the gifts on the eggs. "Tell the family they
must come to tea tomorrow here at the mercantile. Isn't that right,
Welcoming Committee?"

Seth cleared his throat. Jimmy shifted from one foot to the
other. Rolf stuck his hand in his pocket.

"My mother enjoys a good afternoon tea," Jack said to Caitrin.
"But I might ask Lucy to stay at the camp. Sometimes she's a little
uncomfortable around strangers."

"That would be fine," Caitrin said. "Wouldn't it, Rosie?"

Rosie smiled. "Yes, that would be fine. Wouldn't it, Seth?"

When he didn't answer, she jabbed her elbow into his side.
"Uh, yeah, I reckon," he said. "Welcome to Hope."

CHAPTER 8

CAITRIN sat beside the stove in the half-empty soddy and tried to think about wallpaper. Stripes. Flowers. Ivy. She would need a bucket, thick white paste, a brush. Scissors, too. She would start papering beside the front door and . . .

"Oh, this is hopeless!" She slapped her hands on her knees and stood. "I'll never make paper stick to these sod walls. Brown, ugly sod walls with grass roots growing right into my sitting room!"

Night had fallen, but the dim light cast by the oil lamp on the table revealed all but the darkest corners of Seth Hunter's old soddy—Caitrin Murphy's new home. Choking down tears, she stormed to the front door.

"Leather hinges," she said. "Dear God, why have you given me leather hinges? And no windowpanes! Couldn't I at least have glass windowpanes instead of this—this ridiculous half-rotted gauze?"

She hung her head. Was it wrong to shout at God? Was it wrong to moan and complain when she was blessed with her own warm home, loving relatives, and honest work to do each day? Shouldn't she be singing praises on this moonlit night?

"Spiders!" she cried, stomping the small black insect that scurried in front of her foot. "I hate spiders! Dear Father, why have you given me spiders and blacksnakes and prairie dogs? I wanted heather, bracken, sandy shores, and fishing boats. I wanted Ireland.

I wanted Sean O'Casey! And now I must live out my life as a spinster shopkeeper on this freezing, blistering, grasshopper-infested plain with hardly a stick of furniture but this broken chair!"

She picked up the rickety chair and shoved it under a table Seth Hunter had built long ago. The end of one table leg had been chewed to splinters by Stubby, the Hunters' enormous mongrel dog. As the table wobbled back and forth, the lamplight flickered.

"Yes, I know they're only worldly goods," she said into the hollow room. "But, God, you created me, and you know the kind of woman I am. I adore lovely things! I dream of castles and ivy-covered walls. I want silk pillows and Persian carpets. At the very least, I should like a set of dishes that match!"

Picking up a chipped white plate with a central rose bouquet that had been half-scoured away, she searched for her reflection. She could make out nothing but the thousand scratches where knives had cut into meat or bread through the porcelain's glaze. She turned the plate over, hoping to find the insignia of a pottery in some exotic city. Perhaps it had been painted and kiln-fired in Staffordshire, Paris, or Japan.

"Ohio." She ran her finger over the raised, knobby letters on the back. Then she peered closer to discover that someone had misspelled the marking to read, *Mad in Ohio*.

"Oh, I just hate this!" Caitrin cried. "Shabby!"

She hurled the plate at the sod wall. The puff of dust, the burst of breaking porcelain, and the tinkle of falling shards were followed by a soft knock on the door. *Oh no!* Caitrin clapped her hands over her cheeks and realized they were damp.

"Caitrin?" It was Rosie's voice.

"One moment." Caitrin dabbed her eyes with the corner of her apron. She toed the bits of shattered plate into a pile and set a basket on top of them. Then she tucked a strand of hair back into her bun.

"Rose Hunter, what are you doing out and about after dark?"

114

Caitrin asked as she opened the door. "And in your condition! Do come inside at once. Does Seth know you're here?"

"He and some of the other men are meeting over at the mercantile." Hand in hand, Rosie and Chipper walked into the soddy. Stubby followed, his great tail thumping into Rosie's long, blue-gingham skirt.

"Looks different around here," Chipper said, surveying the soddy. "You don't gots very much furniture, do ya, Miss Murphy?"

"Not a great deal." Caitrin chewed on her lower lip as she followed the boy's gaze around her new home. Just as she feared, his eyes went straight to the basket perched atilt on the pile of plate shards. He and Stubby set off to investigate.

"It's broken glass," she warned.

"Oh no, it's that beautiful plate I left here for you!" Rosie hurried to Chipper's side and knelt beside the fragments. "This was my favorite of all the plates we had. Did you notice there were three roses in the center, Caitie? The one on the left was a bud, and the one on the right had just begun to unfold. But the rose in the middle—bright, glorious pink! Petals like velvet! Every time I washed this plate, I was sure I could smell that precious rose."

Caitrin sank onto her chair and rested an elbow on the rickety table. "I'm sorry," she mumbled.

"It's not your fault. Heaven knows I've let plates slip through my fingers before." Rosie pulled a stool to the table. "One time back at the home in Kansas City I was washing a teacup. It was the only cup I had . . . and almost the only possession I had, other than my bonnet that blew away last year in a storm. I had discovered the teacup lying in the neighbors' trash with just a little chip out of the rim. You know how people are so careless about what they throw away? There was no saucer, but oh, that cup was beautiful! It had been painted a pale, pale green with purple violets on the side. Anyway, wouldn't you know? I had covered the cup with soap, and it slid right out of my hand—*crash*—into the basin. The handle broke off. There were just two little nubs sticking out, so you couldn't hold it anymore without burning your fingers, but—"

"I threw the plate," Caitrin whispered.

"Threw it?" Rosie repeated loudly.

Chipper turned around, his blue eyes wide. "How come you threw Mama's good plate?"

"I was . . . I was angry." She wished she could crawl under the table. "I'm very sorry. It was the wrong thing to do. I'm afraid I got carried away shouting at God about my terrible lot in life. Such a dreadful thing to do after all the blessings he's given me."

"Nobody should shout at God," Chipper said.

"I'm not sure of that," Rosie said. "God is our Father. Every moment of every day, he knows exactly how we feel inside, what we're thinking, what we want, and what we need. It won't do any good pretending you're not mad if you're really seething. You'll never fool God. You might as well go ahead and tell him exactly what you think."

"But yellin' and throwin' plates?" Chipper asked. "That ain't good."

"The Bible tells us the Spirit prays for us in groanings that can't be expressed in words. _Groanings_ . . . that's the very thing it says. And we know that Jesus prayed with such agony in the garden that he sweated great drops of blood. So if groaning and sweating blood are perfectly acceptable ways to talk to God, I don't see what's wrong with a little shouting and plate throwing."

Chipper laughed, and Caitrin couldn't hold back her grin. "Maybe all my ranting at the good Lord caused him to send you two along tonight," she said, laying her hand on her friend's arm. "I'm glad of your company."

Rosie's face broke into a smile. "I've been so excited about the baby, I just can't stop chattering. What do you think of Lavinia?"

Caitrin blinked. "Who's that?"

"It's the name of our new baby," Chipper said, crawling into his mother's lap. "Let's see, we gots lotsa names already. Lavinia and Priscilla and Vanilla—"

"Valerie!" Rosie said with a chuckle. She kissed Chipper on the cheek. "There's something so beautiful about the name Lavinia, don't you think, Caitie? It just rolls right off the tongue."

"I want a brother," the little boy announced, "an' I don't want him to be named Lavinia."

"Lavinia is a girl's name, silly. Oh, Caitrin, I'm just praying every moment for this baby. I so want her to be healthy. And why are you throwing plates?"

The change in subject caught Caitrin by surprise. "Because Jack Cornwall came back," she blurted, which wasn't at all why she believed she'd thrown the plate. "No, that's not it. It's really the wallpaper. And the table is wobbly, and the chair is rickety, and I don't know how Jack is ever going to fit in. Poor Lucy in chains. You should have heard Sheena! I could have stuffed a sock into her mouth. She was shouting *Cornish this* and *Cornish that*, hitting Jack on the arm with her basket. Then, in came Mrs. Cornwall talking about Irish infestations. Jack said that some former colleague is still trying to take him to court, and I gave poor Lucy a comb and brush, but it's not going to help at all!"

"Is she bald-headed?" Chipper asked.

"No!" Caitrin exploded, pushing back her chair and standing. "Of course she isn't bald-headed."

"Hide the plates!" Chipper shouted. "She's gonna start throwin' 'em again."

"Caitrin?" Rosie tugged on her friend's hand. "Do you remember what you told me to pray for last fall? You said, 'If you wish to pray about Jack, Rosie, pray for his soul.' You asked me to pray that the Spirit of God would fill Jack's heart. You wanted me to pray for his family and his safety. And last of all, you asked me to pray that

Jack would find a good woman who has the courage to love him as he deserves. Do you remember that?"

Caitrin slumped into the chair again. "Aye. I've prayed for him myself. But what hope does a man like that have to make a fresh start of his life?"

"Hope is the very name of our town, Caitie! If Jack Cornwall can't find hope here, where can he find it?"

"But how can he have hope if he must keep his sister in chains, Rosie?"

"Paul and Silas were put in chains. That didn't stop God's love from touching them."

"Perhaps, but can Jack ever hope the people here will love him? You know the trouble he's caused."

"Folks will just have to forgive Jack's past and open their hearts to his family."

"But there's not a chance Jimmy and Sheena will accept the Cornwalls. Their Irish pride is so strong, and Jack's mother is thoroughly Cornish."

"And I'm a foundling from a livery stable." Rosie smiled, an inner triumph lighting her huge brown eyes. "I used to hate admitting that, but now I know it doesn't matter where we come from, Caitie. In time, people learn to look beyond such things. Folks around here have learned to love me, and they'll love the Cornwalls, too."

"Even if Jack can overcome all those things, a man is trying to find him and take him back to Missouri. He's being tracked."

"Uncle Jack tracked *me*," Chipper put in. "An' he found me. Now he's gonna live here with us. And Gram is, too. So maybe trackin' ain't all bad. I can't wait to see Gram tomorrow. Mama said she'd take me down to their camp first thing."

"It's going to be all right, Caitie." Rosie gave her friend's fingers a squeeze. "If God could create the miracle of life inside me, what can't he do?"

"You hear that, Laviliva?" Chipper said, his mouth against the soft apron around Rosie's waist. "Mama says you're a miracle."

"*Lavinia.* Oh, that name's never going to work." Rosie pursed her lips for a moment. "Why don't we throw a welcoming party for the Cornwalls? It could be a spring festival with fresh flowers and punch. We could hang a big banner over the mercantile's door: To the Cornwall Family—Welcome to Hope."

Caitrin smiled. "It's a lovely idea, but—"

Before she could finish, the soddy door swung open and Seth Hunter strolled in. "We made a decision," he began, stopping when he saw the women's surprised faces. "Uh, 'scuse me, Miss Murphy. I forgot I don't live here anymore."

"No, please. You're welcome any time." Caitrin stood as Jimmy O'Toole and Rolf Rustemeyer followed Seth into the small room. "Shall I put on a pot of tea?"

"*Ja,*" Rolf said, grinning broadly. "Fery goot maken tea. I like."

"It's late, Rustemeyer." Seth clamped a hand on the big German farmer's shoulder. "We'd better leave Miss Murphy in peace tonight. We just wanted you ladies to know we've decided to let the Cornwalls stay in Hope—for one month."

"One month?" Caitrin cried. "But Mr. Cornwall will hardly have time to build his smithy. And you know the bridge travel won't get busy until late spring."

"A month's grace," Jimmy explained, "to see how they get along here. Round St. Patrick's Day, we three men will have another meetin' and judge if we'll allow the family to stay on. If Jack Cornwall causes one stime of trouble, he'll be out on his ear. His mother's to keep her Cornish gob shut tight, especially where my Sheena is concerned. They're to stay to themselves. And if we see the mad girl anywhere about, the whole family will be asked to leave."

"So you'll permit the Cornwalls to stay in Hope," Caitrin said, "as long as they keep themselves hidden, say nothing, do nothing, and contribute in no way except to bring business to the community. The rest of us, meanwhile, are to keep a sharp lookout so as to catch their slightest misstep. We're to turn our heads the other way when they walk past, and we're to pretend they're invisible at all times. Yet we'll be nosing about their business to find any flaws. Sure, in a month, we'll have caught them at *something*, so we will, gentlemen. Then we can be rid of them like so much dust shaken from our boots."

Caitrin crossed her arms and leveled a stare at the three men. Never had she witnessed a more prideful act or heard a more unchristian decision than this one. Seth gave his wife an uncomfortable glance. Rolf rubbed the back of his neck and stared at the floor. Jimmy stuck his thumbs under his suspenders and regarded his sister-in-law.

"Shall we hold everyone in Hope to such exacting standards then?" Caitrin asked the men. "If so, we must run Rolf away immediately for his unforgivable misuse of the English language. And Seth, I'm afraid you'll have to go as well. Only yesterday you were helping Rolf frame up the church, and you must have hit your thumb with a hammer, for I heard a most unholy word escape your lips."

"Seth!" Rosie gasped.

"Well . . ." Seth shifted his weight from one foot to the other. "Well, it hurt. I'm sorry, Miss Murphy. It won't happen again."

"Too late for that, I'm afraid. Under the rules you gentlemen have laid out, one infraction is cause enough to be run out of town. We may be known as the town of Hope, but we certainly offer not a measure of grace. Jimmy will have to go as well, I'm sorry to say. Sure, he's been known to walk outside of an early morning and put on a most unacceptable display of stretching, hawking, spitting, blowing his nose, scratching his—"

"That'll be quite enough from you, Caitrin Murphy!" Jimmy said. "You'll not be makin' light of our decision, young lady. Your own behavior toward Jack Cornwall has not gone unnoticed. Sheena told me you harbored that *sherral* in *my* barn last winter, so you did. You kept his presence a secret, fed him our grub, hid our own enemy from us. If you were not my wife's sister, I'd put you out on your grug for such wickedness. Sheena tells me she saw Cornwall throwin' sheep's eyes at you today, and you back at him. She said she left the two of you in the mercantile havin' a great cuggermugger, all cozy and sweetlike. What have you to say for yourself, lass?"

"I've nothing to say for myself. I'm not the person on trial here. It seems that Mr. Jack Cornwall has already been sentenced to a stoning by the likes of you Pharisees, so I'll speak for him—"

"You've spoken for that devil enough already," Jimmy snapped. "I never thought I'd see the day when one of my own family would turn against me. I gave you a home, food, and my good care, Caitrin. Is this the thanks I get? That you keep deadly secrets from us, that you speak out in defense of our enemy, that you accuse *us* of injustice?"

His green eyes were sharp as they stared into Caitrin's face. She felt her cheeks flush with heat. Half of her wanted to scream at the three pious men. But she couldn't deny that Jimmy had been correct in his accusations.

"I apologize to you," she told her brother-in-law. "I had no right to hide Mr. Cornwall from you last autumn. I put a stranger's well-being above loyalty to my own family."

"Aye, you did. I thank you for your repentance, and I'll welcome a change in your behavior. Never forget that you're Irish, lass. You're a Murphy from County Cork. Don't be swept away by that wicked stranger when you've better men here at home. And don't trade your allegiance to your Irish heritage for a few sweet words from a proven liar, a fighter, and a thief. Stay close to your own kind, Caitie. We love you, so we do. We'll see you're looked after."

"Thank you, Jimmy." Caitrin swallowed at the gritty lump in her throat.

"I am goot man here at home," Rolf said, thumping his massive chest. "Maybe you marry vit me, *ja?* Haf many childrens."

"Oh, dear Rolf," Rosie cut in, laying her hand on the German's brawny arm. "I think it's time for us to move past basic English and into learning good manners."

"Goot manners?" He grinned and shot a victory glance to the other men. "*Ja*, we are all goot manners, Seth, Jimmy, *und* me. I am goot man. Fery goot man. Tank you, *Frau* Hunter, for saying."

Rosie laughed. "You *are* a good man, and you will learn good manners in time. Maybe you can start by escorting Miss Murphy to the welcoming party for the Cornwalls."

"What?" Jimmy cried.

"We have to give the family a party, of course. Oh, don't worry yourselves, Welcoming Committee. Caitie and I will plan everything." Rosie gave Chipper a playful pat on the back. "Come on, sweetie. Grab that big ol' dog of yours, and let's head for home. I'm so tired! It's a good thing I'm having a baby, or I'd be sure this was another sign I was on the road to my own funeral."

Waving a cheery good-bye, Rosie hurried her family out the door. Jimmy settled his hat on his head and followed. Rolf gave Caitrin an awkward bow.

"You come to velcomen party vit me," he said. "I am fery goot manners."

"And *you* are Irish, Caitrin Murphy!" Jimmy called over his shoulder. "Don't forget it."

As the door slammed shut behind the men, Caitrin let out a breath. "I may have been born in County Cork," she said into the empty room. "But I live in Hope, Kansas. I'm not Irish; I'm American . . . and I won't be bound by petty prejudice."

All the same, she knew Jimmy had been within his rights to chasten her. Her loyalty should lie with her sister and the O'Toole family. And no sweet words from a gray-eyed man could change that.

Jack set a block of sod on the slowly rising wall of his smithy, then stood back to survey his new domain. Though he had worked all day and his muscles ached, it would be another week before he could put a roof on the building. Cutting, hauling, and laying the heavy sod was tedious labor, but the natural material would keep his workplace cool in summer and warm in winter. More important, it wouldn't burn as easily as would the dry timber of a frame building. He sure didn't cotton to the idea of lighting his forge the first time and burning down the whole place.

Good thing Seth Hunter had allowed him to build near the mercantile, Jack thought as he trimmed the grass from another sod brick. Any wagon coming from east or west was bound to see the sign he would hang outside his door. In fact, he'd already had his first customers. Though he hadn't even built his forge, he'd managed to shoe five horses and patch a hole in a passing farmer's water bucket. The jingle of coins in his pocket sure felt good.

Whistling, Jack heaved the brick onto the wall and edged it into place. He'd seen Caitrin Murphy coming and going from the mercantile, but she had made herself scarce around his work site. He could hardly blame her.

After Jimmy O'Toole's unpleasant visit to his camp the night of the Cornwalls' arrival, Jack wasn't exactly on speaking terms with the family. Like some kind of self-appointed policeman, O'Toole had marched over and laid out a bunch of rules and regulations the Cornwalls were to follow. Then he'd announced they would have one month to demonstrate their good behavior, or they'd be expelled from the town. Jack's mother had responded with a flurry of loud verbal assaults about Irish slothfulness and stupidity . . . and that had ended the conversation.

"Hey, Uncle Jack," Chipper said behind him.

Jack swung around. At the sight of the little boy, he felt like the sun had just risen. An unexpected truth filtered into his heart. In spite of losing the child to Seth last autumn, Jack had been granted Chipper's presence—his snaggletoothed grin, his deep chuckle, his cheery conversation were a part of Jack's daily life again. God had given him the boy after all.

"Hey, Chipper," Jack greeted him, kneeling to give his nephew a hug. "I haven't seen you all day. What have you been up to? Trouble, I reckon."

"Naw!" Chipper giggled. "Me an' Will O'Toole was fishin' at the creek almost all day. Didn't catch nothin', though. I gotta go pick buffalo and cow chips for Mama now. But first, lookit what I brung you!"

He pulled half a cookie from the pocket of his overall bib. "Oops, I guess it busted when you gave me that squeeze. It's a sugar cookie. Mama made it."

Jack accepted the crumbly gift and took a bite. "Mm-mm. Now, that's one good cookie. You tell your mama I appreciate her thinking of me."

"Oh, Mama didn't send it to you. She baked a big batch of cookies to sell in the mercantile. Caitrin Murphy gave this one to me when I was in there fetchin' a coupla hooks for me an' Will this mornin'. It was warm, an' it smelled so good. I had all I could do not to eat it. But I saved it just for you!"

"Miss Murphy told you to give this to me?" Jack felt a ripple of satisfaction run up his spine. "What exactly did she say to you?"

"She said, 'Give this cookie to your uncle Jack.'"

"And that's all?"

"She said in her funny way of talkin', 'It takes time an' hard work to build castles, so it does.' An' I reminded her that you was buildin' a smithy, not a castle. Then she told me the smithy is your

124

castle, an' you're gonna build all your dreams right inside it. Is that true, Uncle Jack?"

"I reckon it is." Jack smiled and rumpled the boy's dark hair.

"But I thought you was gonna build stuff outta iron inside your smithy. Like wagon wheels and plows."

"I am. And with the money I earn, I'm planning to make my dreams come true."

Chipper tilted his head to one side. "Know what, Uncle Jack? I think Jimmy O'Toole was dead wrong the other night at Miss Murphy's house when he called you a liar an' a fighter an' a thief."

Fighting the fury that rose inside him at the child's repetition of O'Toole's slanderous words, Jack studied Chipper's bright eyes. "I have done some wrong things in my life, little fellow," he said. "Same as everybody. But you know what Miss Murphy told me once? She said God thinks I'm precious. He loves me. This winter I did a lot of praying and reading in the Good Book, and I found out she was right. The God who made this very sod we're standing on loved me enough to come down here and die for me. Now if he cares that much about an ol' scalawag like me, I figure he can help me leave behind whatever wrong I did and walk along a new road. And if Will's papa would look at who I am instead of who I was, maybe he could see that."

Chipper pulled the other half of the cookie from his pocket and handed it to his uncle. "I bet you're right, Uncle Jack. Well, I gotta go pick up cow chips for Mama. Guess what? We're havin' stew and corn bread tonight!"

"Yum! Come by and visit me tomorrow," Jack called as Chipper ran off to do his mother's bidding. "And tell Miss Murphy thanks for the cookie!"

The boy's laughter was ringing in the air as the mercantile door opened and Caitrin Murphy herself stepped outside. Jack caught his breath at the sight of the woman. In the past few days, he had reminded himself a hundred times to stand back and give her room. If he inserted himself between her and her family again, it would only cause trouble.

Besides, she wasn't all that special, he had told himself again and again. Just a red-haired gal, a little too skinny, and a lot too mouthy. Just a common working woman. A spinster at that. She was past the age when most women married—her midtwenties at least. And she had all those obnoxious relatives. . . .

As she turned, Caitrin's green eyes flashed in Jack's direction. Behind her, the setting sun lit her hair like a roaring inferno. Her brown dress shimmered and glowed like molten bronze as it flowed down to her toes in cascades and swirls of fabric. She bent to insert a brass key in the mercantile door, and a lock of loose, curly hair slid over her shoulder. Jack had never seen a volcano, but that tress had to be like lava the way it burned and tumbled slowly forward.

He dropped the sod brick he was holding and started toward her. These past months he'd been praying so often that words seemed to form in his heart without his planning them. He knew God heard him, even though he couldn't always feel his Master's presence and couldn't always hear an answer to his constant request. *Father, I've tried to stay back,* his soul lifted up. *But there's something about her. Something I need. You brought me back here in spite of everything. Help me now. Help me to bridge gaps. . . .*

"Mr. Cornwall," she said, clutching her workbasket in front of her. "Good evening to you."

"And to you, ma'am." Belatedly, he remembered to take off his hat. "I . . . ah . . . I thank you for the cookie. Chipper gave it to me."

"Rose Hunter baked it."

"Tasted good."

She brushed the lava hair back over her shoulder and looked in the direction of her soddy. "Well, 'tis late. I must be getting home."

"I'll walk you."

126

"No!" The green eyes darted up at him. "Thank you, Mr. Cornwall, but I know my way."

He didn't care how much his presence unnerved Caitrin. He had seen the look she flashed him from the mercantile door, and he fully intended to spend a few minutes with her.

"I'll walk you anyhow," he said. "It's getting dark."

She let out a breath and picked up her skirt. "The sun is still on the horizon."

"Perfect time for the wild things to come out and feed."

Her focus darted his way as they started along the narrow path toward the soddy. "I'm not afraid of wild things."

"Really?" he said, matching her stride for stride. "Danger lurks in the most unlikely places."

"Does it now?"

"In empty barns on autumn nights."

"I'm not afraid of barns."

"On isolated paths across windswept prairies."

"I'm not afraid of paths."

He followed her to the door of her soddy. "In lonely hearts at sunset."

"I'm not afraid—" she paused and looked full in his face—"I'm not afraid of a lonely heart at sunset."

"You should be," he said.

CHAPTER 9

CAITRIN held her workbasket at waist level, hoping in vain that Jack might keep his distance. Instead, he rested one hand against the soddy, leaning on his arm and trapping her beside the open door. If she ducked inside, he might follow . . . and she could never allow that. Her back to the rough wall, she lifted her chin and met his eyes.

"Mr. Cornwall, you must not—"

"Jack," he cut in.

"As I was saying, Mr. Cornwall—"

"Jack."

She moistened her lips. "You must not come to my house, *Jack*. The men have allowed you only one month to prove yourself. If Jimmy sees you talking with me, he'll want to run you off."

"I don't care what Jimmy O'Toole sees. And I don't care what he thinks, either. The only opinion I care about is yours. What do *you* want, Caitrin? If you don't want to talk to me, tell me right now. I'll back off."

Caitrin could hardly believe how the man's very presence stirred her. This was nothing like the giddy, girlish sentiment she'd felt for Sean O'Casey . . . where pride in his position and his good looks had impelled her love. The force of Jack's determination cut into her, hewing down everything in its path. Jimmy had called him a liar. Yet she felt certain that this man, like none other she had ever known, was completely honest. He spoke his inner-most thoughts aloud. He acted on his sincere convictions. And for the sake of peace, *she* must be the one to hide the truth.

"I think," she began, "I think you must not speak with me, Jack."

"I didn't ask what you thought. I asked what you wanted."

What did she want? Countless things! She wanted this man to take her in his arms and hold her day and night for the rest of her life. She wanted him to be her champion . . . to fight off every adversary that came between them. She wanted his deep voice ringing in her heart. She wanted his touch, his breath on her skin, his tender kisses. She wanted a world of passion and dreams come true!

"I want you to stay away from me, Jack," she choked out. "Because I don't want you to leave."

"What do you mean by that?"

She shook her head. "You cannot be seen with me, or the men will send your family away. I heard the words they spoke of you, so I did. Sure, Jimmy looks upon you as the devil himself, Jack. Seth doesn't trust you. Rolf is confused by you and probably a little jealous. Do you want to leave this town?"

"Do you want me to go?"

"No, and that's why you must not come near me."

"What's the point of staying if I can't talk to you, Caitrin?"

"Sure, you didn't come to Hope just for me! You wanted to make a fresh start. You wanted to build your smithy. You wanted to find a place of solitude and protection for Lucy. You wanted to earn a living for your family."

"I wanted to be with you." He took a step closer, all but engulf-ing her in his presence. "When I met you, I was sure God had abandoned me a long time before. One bad thing after another had happened in my life, and I blamed him. But then you walked into Jimmy's barn that night, and everything turned around. You're the only good I've known in many years, and I'm sure God put you in my life. I'm not about to back off unless you tell me to."

"Jack, God is not like a capricious fairy, showering us with bad luck or good according to his whims." Fearful of being seen, Caitrin tried to look over Jack's shoulder at the path to the mercantile. But the solid slab of muscle blocked her view. Praying for wisdom, she spoke quickly. "Life unfolds before us, good and bad. Often the bad is the consequence of our own personal sin. But sometimes . . . as with Lucy . . . dreadful things just happen. 'Tis the same with the good in life. Usually, we reap what we sow, and if we plant good seed, then good things happen in return. But sometimes the Lord permits good, even if his people don't deserve it."

"You're the good God brought into my life."

"But you mustn't look to *me* if you want to know *God*. I'm a human, and I make many mistakes. I'm willful and mouthy. I shout and weep, and I . . . I throw plates."

"Plates?"

"You must keep your focus on the Father, Jack. Talk to him and grow in him. Please . . . please don't view my presence in your life as a sign that God loves you. He has loved you always, through good times *and* bad. You must have a strong enough faith that when things take a turn for the worse, you won't believe God has deserted you. That's when you will need him the most. And if the men here chase you away—"

"No one's going to run me off, Caitrin. I'm a stubborn man." He fingered the tumble of curly hair that lay on her shoulder. "My convictions run deep, and I don't give up easily. You saw the way I went after Chipper. Last autumn I was sure God had robbed me of the boy, and I held the Almighty responsible for yet another loss in my life. But it hit me this evening when Chipper brought along that cookie . . . I didn't lose the boy after all. God gave him to me anyhow, just not in the way I'd planned. I'm beginning to think

God has good plans for me, and he can turn the worst problems into blessings."

Caitrin studied his gray eyes, reading the earnestness in them. How she loved to hear him speak! Though he was a common laborer, Jack might have been a scholar for the profound analysis he gave to his life and the world around him.

"When you look at it that way," he said, "you could say I've blamed God for a lot of losses that turned out to be gifts. I fought in the war for the cause of freedom from tyranny. The South lost the war, but God gave me freedom anyhow. Look at me out here, carving a life from this prairie. That's freedom, Caitrin. That's hope."

"I don't want them to take it from you," she whispered, her eyes misting. "Oh, Jack, please go away. Don't let the men see us together. They'll rob you of that freedom. They'll steal your hope . . . and mine."

"What hope do we have if we can't even speak to each other, Caitrin?" He drew her into his arms. "I want to hear your passionate words and see the flash of fire in your eyes. I want to get close enough to smell that scent you wear."

"Lily of the valley," she murmured, dropping her workbasket and slipping her hands up the broad expanse of his chest. "Jack, hold me tight. Sure, my head is running in circles, and my heart . . . my heart . . ."

His lips pressed against hers in a tender kiss. She melted into him, reveling in the utter power of his embrace. For this moment she did not have to hold herself up. She could surrender . . . drift at peace in his strength . . . rest in the security of this man's presence. His hands slid into her hair as his lips found her cheek, her ear, her neck. Struggling for control, he drew her close and nestled her head in the curve of his shoulder.

"I don't care what they say, Caitrin," he mouthed, his breath warming her hair. "I don't care what they try to do to me. Unless you tell me to go, I won't abandon you. I'll never leave you. It's a promise."

With a last crushing embrace, he set her apart. Turning his back, he walked away into the dusk. Caitrin gripped the edge of the door behind her. In the distance she could just make out the glimmering light of oil lamps shining in the O'Tooles' soddy across the creek . . . and in the Cornwalls' small camp along the sandy bank.

"Lord, oh, Lord," she whispered in prayer. "Bring us light. May it be the light of your love and forgiveness, and not—" she stifled a sob—"not the spark of a fire that will destroy us all."

$\nearrow$

"*Three* pickles?" Caitrin eyed Mr. Bridger, the man who carried mail to and from Topeka. "Are you quite sure? You'll be thirsty enough to drink up the whole of Bluestem Creek before you're halfway home."

The man laughed. "They're not all for me. I've been raving about these pickles so long, my wife ordered me to bring her one. And then little Johnny piped up wanting a pickle of his own. If word gets out—and with my wife around, it will—you may have to shut down the mercantile just to make enough pickles to supply Topeka."

"That will be my sister's task, so it will. Sheena's the pickle maker of the town. I'll be sure to tell her of your abiding admiration."

"My admiration for her *pickles*," he clarified. "That Jimmy O'Toole may be skinny as a telegraph post, but I sure don't want to tangle with him over a misunderstanding about his wife."

Caitrin handed Mr. Bridger the wrapped dill pickles, their pungent green marinade already seeping through the brown paper. She needed to tend the customers who had ridden in on the mail coach, but she knew her first loyalty belonged to the mail carrier. It was he, after all, who brought the others.

"I'm sure Jimmy knows you're not the first to appreciate Sheena's skills," she said. "He's a good man, so he is."

"You're right about that, but I've heard stories about the hulla-baloo he put up over the building of the Hope bridge. And I know he wouldn't allow the church to be raised on his land. O'Toole's a tough old buzzard, if you ask me. You make sure he knows it's the pickles that interest me, and not the wife."

"I'll do it," Caitrin said with a chuckle. "But you mustn't think too harshly of Jimmy—"

"Excuse me, ma'am." A short, bullnecked man leaned across the counter. "I don't mean to interrupt you, but when does the coach to Manhattan get in?"

Caitrin glanced up at the store clock. "It should be here already. It usually gets here the same time as the mail coach, and I can hardly catch my breath for the traffic. Are you bound for Man-hattan, sir?"

"Yep." He squared his shoulders inside the ragged gray Confed-erate army coat he wore. "Headin' west. I'll cover the whole state of Kansas before I'm through, if need be. Fact is, I'm on the look-out for an old friend of mine. Name's Jack Cornwall. Ever hear of him?"

Caitrin's heart dropped to her knees. "Cornwall," she mumbled. "Is that a . . . a Cornish name?"

"Don't know and don't care." He rubbed the stubble of dark whiskers on his chin. "Near the end of the war, Jack Cornwall ran with my bunch over in Missouri."

"Your bunch?"

"Group of men, soldiers mostly. We kept the cause alive, pro-tected the poor farmers gettin' eat up by Yankee aggressors, that sort of thing—not to mention a fair amount of drinkin', cuttin' up, and carryin' on with women." He gave a laugh. "Hoo, that Cornwall was a wild one, you know. Big tall feller, kind of a rough face, gray eyes. He worked as a blacksmith durin' the war—shoulders from here to here, arms like blocks of steel. Drove the ladies crazy. You'd remember him if you saw him."

Her back to the visitor, Caitrin busied herself tucking letters into the mail slots. "I'm sorry I can't help you," she said.

"If you run into my man, tell him Bill Hermann's lookin' for him."

"I'll do that." Through the window beside the mailboxes, Caitrin spotted Jack Cornwall dusting off his hands and starting for the mercantile.

"See, back around the end of the war, our bunch ran into a little unfortunate trouble," Hermann continued. "Messy business."

"What sort of trouble?" Caitrin asked, praying that Jack would change his mind and turn around.

"There was a lynchin'. Easton was the feller's name. After that, the bunch split up for a while. Cornwall went back to his family, and we ain't seen hide nor hair of him since."

"Does . . . does the bunch want him back?" Caitrin's heart slammed against her chest. Jack stopped to pat Stubby on the head as Chipper scampered up. *Go with Chipper*, she pleaded silently. *Go with your nephew*.

Jack knelt to talk to the boy. Chipper pulled something out of his pocket and the two bent to examine it.

"Yeah, the bunch wants his help," Hermann said. "See, most of 'em wound up in jail after the Easton troubles, but if Cornwall would testify that he was at the cabin that night and that none of the bunch was involved in the lynchin', the fellers might get off scot-free. 'Course Cornwall doesn't want to swear he was there for fear of gettin' his own hide strung up on the hangin' tree, and he's been runnin' ever since the trouble. Folks told me the Cornwall family had moved south, around Cape Girardeau. All I found out down there was that he'd gone to Kansas chasin' some kid. I rode across the state line lookin' for him, and folks said he'd come right here. To this town."

Caitrin could hardly breathe. "Is that right? I'm a newcomer myself. Not long of County Cork, in Ireland."

"You musta missed him. I hear he caused quite a ruckus—typical of Cornwall." He laughed again. "And then he headed back to Missouri. I spent most of the winter searchin' for him. But when I tracked him to the house where he kept his mama and his lunatic sister, the folks livin' around the place told me he'd up and took 'em off to Kansas."

Caitrin gulped as Jack stood and looked toward the mercantile door. "You're very dedicated to your purpose."

Bill Hermann stretched and twisted his bull neck, causing a series of crackling pops to echo through the mercantile. "I got motivation, ma'am," he said, giving his knuckles a similar bone-crunching flex. "Cornwall's testimony is the only thing that can get the bunch off the hook. The trial's scheduled for a couple of months from now, and I gotta get Cornwall back to Missouri in time."

He handed her a card. "This here's the place to write if you hear of Jack Cornwall. You'll let me know, won't you, ma'am?"

"'Bill Hermann,'" she read from the card.

"That's me. Well, I hear the Manhattan coach pullin' up. Gotta go."

He started for the door just as Jack turned toward the smithy, putting his back to his former comrade. With the crazy notion that she could somehow protect Jack, Caitrin followed Bill Hermann out of the mercantile. *Dear God, don't let the men see each other!* she pleaded. *Please, don't let them see each other.*

When she stepped into the frigid February air, she realized she had broken a sweat. Mr. Bridger, the mail carrier, heaved a sack of letters onto his coach as his passengers climbed aboard. The driver of the stage bound for Manhattan was just stepping down from his seat.

"I'm sorry, Miss Murphy, I won't have time to stop today," he called out to her. "I know you always want customers, but I'm runnin' late."

"That's quite all right," she said. "Bring me twice as many the next time, will you?"

She squeezed her hands together as Bill Hermann followed a couple of other passengers into the coach. The driver latched the door behind them. When the horses began to pull away again, Caitrin waved and gave the driver her brightest smile. Inwardly groaning, she brushed a tendril of damp hair from her forehead. If Hermann had seen Jack . . . remembering the man himself, she swung around toward the smithy. Chipper had just darted away with a wave of farewell.

Jack Cornwall straightened, caught sight of her, and grinned. "Well, well," he said. "This day just got a lot brighter."

Caitrin bit her lip to keep from bursting out with all the suppressed tension of the past few minutes. "Hello, Jack."

"Looks like Chipper found the first tadpole of the year."

"Bill Hermann was here," she blurted, rushing toward him. "Oh, Jack, 'twas Bill Hermann himself, the man who's been tracking you! He just rode away on the Manhattan stage. He knows you were in Hope last autumn. He'll be back, I'm sure of it. And he says you were part of . . . part of a lynching."

Jack crossed his arms over his vast chest. "Bill Hermann is lying."

"Can you prove it?"

"Do I need to?"

"Hermann says you can testify on behalf of your bunch."

"I'm not going to testify. I don't have anything to tell a judge, because I wasn't around at the time of the Easton troubles. I don't know a thing about that lynching."

"Why does Mr. Hermann believe you were there if you weren't?"

"It was night. Dark."

Caitrin looked away. "And you *were* one of his bunch?"

"Yep." He took her shoulders and forced her to face him. "But I wasn't there that night, Caitrin. I swear it."

"Sure, you don't need to swear such a thing to me. All I ask is that your words be true."

"I'm telling you the truth. I had gone to Sedalia that day. You can ask Lucy. We were together the whole time."

"Then Lucy can testify for you!"

"No." Jack shook his head. "She can't. She won't."

"But why not? Aye, the judge must listen to her words."

"I'd never ask Lucy to stand up for me." Jack raked a hand through his brown hair. "Look, let me handle this, would you, Caitrin? It's my problem. I can take care of Bill Hermann and the old bunch. I've put my past behind me, and I'm facing the future. I'm not afraid."

"You may have put your past behind you, but obviously your cronies haven't. Many of them are biding time in jail until their trial. They'll have plenty of good reasons to toss the past straight into your face . . . and Bill Hermann is their ringleader."

"Let it go, Caitrin. You'll never fix this one."

"What am I to do then?" She could hear the intensity in her voice, the edge of frustration knifing through her words. "Yesterday, you risked your position here in Hope by kissing me in full view . . . and it was all I could do to fall asleep last night for thinking of that kiss. Am I to be swept off by you, then, Mr. Cornwall? Is my heart to be placed in your hands? Is my very soul to be meshed with yours—only to have you ripped away by some demon from your past? And you ask me to stand by and do nothing! You promise you won't abandon me—yet I can almost see them coming now to drag you away. Am I to sit idly and watch?"

Jack enunciated each word slowly, "You *can't* fix this one, Caitrin. Leave it alone."

"Then you must fix it. You must help Lucy to write a letter to the authorities in Missouri."

"Never."

"Why not? She would do it for you."

The muscle in Jack's jaw flickered. "I won't ask her, Caitrin. Neither will you, and I'm counting on you to abide by my request. Do you understand?"

Caitrin lifted her chin. "Then do not expect me to allow you any further liberties with my affections, Mr. Cornwall. If you refuse to defend yourself and you will not permit me to help you, then I want nothing to do with you."

"Aw, Caitrin." Jack took her arm and pulled her close. "Get off your high horse, woman."

She trembled as his hand slid down her arm. "Jack, I cannot bear this. 'Tis bad enough that I must listen to the people here drag your family's reputation through the mud. I can't imagine you will ever win their hearts. But the thought that this man from your bunch—"

"It happened a long time ago, Caitrin. Almost a year. I've changed."

"Have you?" She rested her cheek against his chest. "I fear I'm a terrible weakling, Jack, unable to bear the pain of another loss. If you are genuinely innocent, prove it. Rid yourself of this millstone around your neck."

"When the time comes, Cait, I'll do that." He kissed her forehead. "But I have to walk this new life step-by-step. I can't alter the past. I can't fix up the whole world. And neither can you. I know I'm precious to God, remember? If I put this in his hands—"

"Caitrin Murphy!" Sheena squawked, racing toward the couple. "By all the goats in Kerry, Sister, what are you doing? Get away from her, Cornish devil!"

"Oh no, it's the deadly basket again," Jack cried out, raising his arms in mock defense against Sheena's swinging workbasket.

"Get away from my sister!" The puffing woman clobbered him across the chest. "See to the children, Caitie!"

Caitrin gaped as Erinn and Colleen came to a stop just behind

Sheena. At the sight of their mother whapping the brawny man, Colleen popped her thumb into her mouth, and Erinn blinked in shock. Crouching beside the girls, Caitrin threw her arms around them.

"Is that Mr. Cornwall?" Erinn asked.

"Aye, and you mustn't be afraid of him. He's a very nice man, so he is. A good man."

"Then why is Mama hitting him?"

"Because he's . . . he's Cornish."

At that moment another stage rolled across the bridge and came to a stop in front of the mercantile. A fresh load of customers clambered out of their tight quarters. Caitrin sucked down a breath and turned to greet them. "Good afternoon, everyone," she called over the hubbub of her sister's drubbing. "Welcome to Hope. Won't you go inside and have a look around the mercantile?"

Dumbfounded at the sight before them, the visitors clustered together, wives clutching their husbands' arms. Caitrin turned to Sheena and attempted to grab the flailing basket. "Please, Sheena!" she hissed. "Please stop!"

"He's a villain, a very demon!" Sheena stood back, panting for breath. "A kidnapper!"

The crowd in front of the store broke into murmurs of surprise.

"This man is an attempted murderer!" Sheena cried in triumph, presenting her enemy to the gasping bystanders. "And now I have caught him in the very act of seducing my sister!"

"Listen here, feller!" The stagecoach driver pulled a pistol from the holster at his waist. "I don't know what you done to upset Miss Murphy's sister, but you better put your hands in the air and walk over here nice and slow."

"This is ridiculous," Caitrin said, stepping in front of the gun. "Mr. Cornwall is an upstanding citizen of Hope."

"I'll defend myself, Miss Murphy." Jack edged her to the side, his hands held well away from his body. "Ladies and gentlemen, I'm

140

the town blacksmith. Mrs. O'Toole and her people have a little running feud with my kinfolk back in the old country, but you have no need to be alarmed. If you'll just step into the mercantile, I'll head over to the smithy and get back to my work."

The stagecoach driver glanced at Caitrin, then at Sheena. "Shall I let him go?"

"No," Sheena said.

"Aye," Caitrin overruled. "Of course, you must let him go. Good day, Mr. Cornwall."

"He was here to woo you, wasn't he, Caitie?" Sheena queried as Jack stood his ground. "Ooh, to think that my own sister . . . my beloved little Caitrin would—"

"I've done *nothing* wrong, Sheena." Caitrin didn't know whether to rush to her sister's comfort, try to ease her customers' trepidations, or run away with Jack Cornwall and never look back. "Sheena, please—ladies and gentlemen, do go inside and look around. We've plenty of freshly baked bread, and I received a parcel of bright new fabrics just yesterday."

"I hear Mrs. O'Toole's pickles are the pride and joy of Hope," Jack said, addressing the nearest woman. "Fact is, folks come from miles around just to taste them."

"Indeed," Caitrin said, encouraged by the flush of pink in her sister's cheeks. "Only moments ago, the Topeka mail-coach driver bought three whole pickles. Two for his family and one to eat on the way home. He's predicting a rush of orders from the city."

"Pickles?" A thin man took off his hat and stepped forward. "Dill pickles?" The stagecoach driver lowered his pistol. At that moment Felicity Cornwall raced up from the camp beside the Bluestem. Waving her arms over her head, she gave a wild shriek and headed for Jack. Women gasped. Men grabbed for their children. The driver accidentally discharged a shot into the ground.

"Jack, come quickly!" Felicity cried. "It's Lucy. She's drowning in the creek!"

CHAPTER 10

"L ET'S GET out of this town," a customer called as Jack pushed through the crowd and sprinted toward the creek with Felicity following right behind. "These folks is crazy!"

"No, wait!" Caitrin held out her arms, but it was too late. Even the driver fled toward the stagecoach without a backward look. Swinging around, she grabbed Sheena's arm. "I must go with them to Lucy!"

"Caitie, this is not your business," Sheena insisted, clutching at her sister's hands. "Stay here and mind the mercantile. Let the Cornwalls tend to their own."

"How can you say such a thing?" Caitrin pulled back in disbelief. "Would you have the poor woman drown?"

"I would have you know your place, Sister!" Sheena's green eyes crackled. "Sure, you must choose between them and us, Caitie. You know we'll never permit that Cornish devil to become one of us. If you keep on championing him, letting yourself be duped by his charms, stumbling into his traps, we'll have no choice but to disown you. Please, Caitie, come into the mercantile with us now. Help Erinn and Colleen choose peppermint sticks and lemon drops to take to the boys."

Caitrin glanced at the little girls whose bright eyes stared in confusion. "Erinn, Colleen," she said softly, "Jesus commanded us to serve those less fortunate, did he not? Poor Miss Lucy, who cannot seem to find any joy in life, is certainly less fortunate than we. And that is why I must go to the creek and try to be of some service to her." She caught both her sister's hands. "You must understand, Sheena. Please, understand."

Without waiting for a response, Caitrin raced past the smithy toward Bluestem Creek. Lucy was nowhere in sight.

Felicity Cornwall darted back and forth along the sandy bank, shrieking in despair. Up to his chest in the creek, Jack was wading deeper as he called out the young woman's name.

"Jack!" Caitrin shouted, hurtling down the bank. "Where is Lucy? Where has she gone?"

"Drowned, drowned!" Mrs. Cornwall wailed.

Caitrin dashed into the frigid water just as Lucy's dark head bobbed up in midstream. The young woman drifted in the swiftest part of the current, her back to the shore. Gasping in shock at the icy chill that gripped her ankles, Caitrin waded to Jack's side.

"She's not done for yet," he panted. "She's got her feet on the bottom, but she keeps letting herself float off under the water."

"She's wearing those heavy chains. Sure, they'll drag her down."

"Lucy!" Jack called out, reaching toward his sister. "Lucy, it's Jack. Can you hear me? Don't go under again, Sis."

"Lucy, Lucy!" Mrs. Cornwall shrieked. "Get out of that water at once! Do you hear me, young lady? Come here immediately!"

Lucy's head sank beneath the surface. Caitrin watched in horror as Jack lunged toward the spot, disappearing himself. Toes numb, she squeezed her hands together. Should she go ashore and calm Felicity? Her keening was only making things worse. No, there was no choice in this matter.

"Can you swim, Miss Murphy?" Felicity cried as Caitrin set out into the middle of the stream.

"Not much." She cast a backward glance. "If you're a praying woman, Mrs. Cornwall, now's the time."

Hardly able to catch her breath in the numbing water, Caitrin plunged ahead. When Lucy bobbed to the surface again, she was many yards downstream from the place Jack had been searching. Caitrin made for her at once. *Give me words, Father,* she pleaded. *And give her hope!*

"Hello, Lucy," Caitrin called in the most casual and unagitated voice she could manage. "It's a bit cold out here, don't you think?"

Lucy stiffened at the sound of the unexpected voice. Her hair streaming, she slowly turned to observe the woman approaching. Caitrin was horrified to see that Lucy's face had turned an ugly shade of gray, her lips a pale blue.

"Miss Murphy," Lucy whispered.

"Did you get the brush and mirror I sent with Jack?" Caitrin asked, working her way toward midstream. "They were meant as gifts for you."

Hollow-eyed, Lucy gazed in silence.

"It was a small tortoiseshell brush. I've a comb to match it in the mercantile." Teeth chattering, Caitrin kept walking closer until she was up to her chin in the bracing water. "I'd noticed that caring for your hair might be a bit difficult, and I thought perhaps you'd enjoy something pretty."

Lucy stared.

"I'm so glad you've come to Hope," Caitrin continued, chatting as though they were seated in a parlor somewhere. "Sure, all the women who live close round here are married and busy with families. But I live alone, and the company of someone for tea now and again would be lovely. Perhaps you could come for tea this afternoon? I've Earl Grey, but please don't tell. It's wicked of me, but I don't want to share such a treasure with just anyone."

She stopped a pace from the young woman, hardly breathing in fear that Lucy would drift away again or that she herself might collapse from the cold. Ashore, Mrs. Cornwall had stopped shrieking, and Jack stood unmoving at the corner of her vision. Forcing her stiffened lips into a smile, she looked into Lucy's eyes.

"I'm a bit cold; are you?" Caitrin searched for recognition. "Can you feel the cold, Lucy?"

"I . . . I'm sorry . . . ," she mumbled.

"I think in the summer the water must be rather nice. The children enjoy paddling about in it, so they do. But it's awfully chilly right now."

"I don't . . . don't feel anything."

Caitrin cocked her head to one side. She could feel *everything*—the swift current tugging at her legs, the sucking mud beneath her feet, and the bone-aching cold creeping ever inward through her body. But Lucy's words had been filled with a kind of resigned peace.

"I suppose," Caitrin said softly, "I suppose you like it when you can't feel anything, Lucy. Sometimes . . . sometimes I can hardly bear the weight of my own thoughts. Do you know what I did the other day? I got so angry I threw a plate. Smashed it right against the wall."

Lucy gaped, blank-faced.

"And just now, right outside the mercantile, I shouted at my sister," Caitrin went on. "Chipper says we shouldn't shout and throw things, but I think it's far more important that we be honest. God knows everything about us, and he's not going to punish us for sharing our true emotions with him. It's quite all right to feel what's inside your own heart, you know."

"No," Lucy mouthed. "I don't . . . I can't . . ."

"Grab her!" someone shouted from the shore.

"Get her now!"

Lucy's eyes darted away from Caitrin's face. A look of terror suffused her ashen skin. "No . . . no . . ."

"I'm not going to grab you, Lucy," Caitrin promised quickly. "Jack told me you don't like to be touched, and I certainly understand that. Sometimes I just want to hide, I feel so—" A movement caught her eye. "Oh, have a look at that blue jay on the other bank! Can you see it? Spring is almost here, Lucy. I can hardly wait. Did you know Rose Hunter and I are planning a welcoming party for your family? What's your favorite color?"

Lucy's focus shifted again from the shore to Caitrin's face. "I don't . . . I can't think. . . ."

"Well, that's probably because it's so cruel cold out here." Aware that her legs had gone numb and the current was clutching at her with icy claws, Caitrin knew she had only moments before she would be forced to leave the water. "I've an idea, Lucy. Would you like to come to my house right now for a spot of tea? This very moment?"

"They'll . . . they'll . . ."

"No, they won't. I won't let them touch us. Jack will protect us, won't he? He loves you so much, Lucy. Sure, I'll tell him to take off those ridiculous chains so you can lift your teacup. How's that? Will you come for tea? Do say yes."

Lucy turned toward the shore. Caitrin could see that a crowd had gathered—the Manhattan coach passengers who had let their curiosity get the better of them, Seth and Rosie, a horde of children. Even Sheena and the girls had traipsed down from the mercantile.

"Oh, good heavens," Caitrin said. "You'd think they'd never seen anyone taking a dip in the creek. Come along, we'll walk right past them, so we will."

Lucy shook her head and started for the center of the creek, the deepest part where the current surely would carry her off. Caitrin gulped down a cry and reached out to her. When she laid her hand on the young woman's shoulder, Lucy stiffened.

"'Tis the other way," Caitrin said, sudden tears clouding her eyes. "Please, Lucy, you must turn and go the other way."

There was a moment of utter silence, and then Lucy drifted toward Caitrin. Frail arms brushed against her. Huge liquid eyes blinked up at her. "I like Earl Grey," Lucy whispered.

"It's the bergamot flavoring." Caitrin let out a breath of relief and slipped her arm around the young woman's bony shoulders. "I think bergamot is a sort of herb, but then again it might be a fruit. The taste is rather citrusy, don't you think?"

"Yes," Lucy murmured.

"Because of that," Caitrin continued, beginning a slow walk toward the shore, "I should think one would want to drink it with a slice of lemon and a dollop of honey. But shall I tell you the truth? I love my Earl Grey with milk and sugar. Lots of sugar!"

Casting a pleading glance at Jack, Caitrin tried to think how to prolong the conversation. If only the people would go away and stop gawking like stupid cows. If only Caitrin's toes would come back to life so she could tell where the bottom of the creek was. If only she could touch . . . but she *was* touching Lucy, holding her close, speaking as one friend to another.

"I'll stoke up the fire in my oven," she said. "We'll be as warm as toast in a few minutes, and while we thaw, the tea water will have time to boil. You never did tell me your favorite color, Lucy. Mine is emerald green. I think I'm rather vain about green, but it really does go so well with my eyes."

"Blue," Lucy whispered as she and Caitrin straggled onto the shore. "I'm . . . I'm . . ."

"Teal blue?" Caitrin drew her closer, silently daring the gaping crowd to make a move as she led Lucy through them. "That's the color of a duck's back, you know. Sure, I like that shade. But I'm rather partial to a soft cornflower hue."

"Baby blue." Lucy's chains clanked as she tried to keep up with Caitrin. "Baby."

"Jack, do come and take these off!" Caitrin called in frustration. At this rate, it would be an hour before they arrived at the soddy. Already she felt certain her skirt had frozen to her legs and her toes were going to chip off inside her wet boots.

Breathing hard, Jack knelt, dripping, at his sister's feet. As he inserted a key in the heavy padlock, his gray eyes searched Caitrin's face. She understood the terrible fear that consumed him.

"Lucy and I are going to take tea at my house," she told him, praying her words would reassure the man. "I'm sorry to say, but we can't invite you, Jack. This is a ladies' tea, and it's only for the unmarried women of Hope. That's Lucy and me, so there you have it. Now, please open the lock on her wrists."

Jack stared into Caitrin's eyes. "You take care of Lucy, hear?"

"I know you love your sister, Jack. Don't you?" She nodded. "Don't you love her?"

"I sure do. I . . ." His voice faltered as he bent to unlock the chain that bound his sister's wrists. "I love you, Lucy."

Jack knocked on the door of Caitrin's soddy, and then he gave his mother a solemn nod. Mrs. Cornwall stood to one side, as bug-eyed as a frog. They had waited more than an hour at their camp, talking over the terrible mistake they'd made in allowing Lucy to walk about unguarded. She'd headed straight for the creek, and Felicity had noticed her barely in time. If Caitrin hadn't come along . . .

"Well?" Felicity demanded. "Can't the woman be bothered to answer her own door?"

Jack gave his mother a warning look. "Miss Murphy won't like it that we're here in the first place. She wanted to be alone with Lucy."

"They've been alone long enough. That Irish maid doesn't have a single notion how to manage my daughter. She'll turn her back the first time, and Lucy will grab a pair of scissors—"

"Jack?" Caitrin opened the door to a narrow slit and peeped through. "What are you doing here? Mrs. Cornwall, I told you I would be taking tea with Lucy."

"Where is my daughter?" Felicity demanded. "She's sure to catch her death after all that swimming about in frigid water."

"Lucy is asleep," Caitrin said. "While she was warming up by the stove, she drifted off and hasn't awakened since."

"Typical!" Felicity said. "Lucy would sleep all day and all night, too, if we'd let her. She's the laziest maid you ever clapped eyes on. We must wake her at once and get her back to the camp."

"I should like your permission to keep her here tonight, Mrs. Cornwall." Caitrin turned her focus to Jack. "Please let Lucy stay with me."

"Never." Felicity's eyes hardened. "My daughter belongs in her own bed. And without the chains, one can't be sure—"

"You can't fix Lucy's troubles, Caitrin," Jack said over his mother's harangue. "Look, can I come inside and talk to you for a minute?"

Green eyes bright, Caitrin glanced from Jack to his mother and then back again. "Only you, please, Mr. Cornwall. I shouldn't want anyone to wake Lucy."

Jack let out a breath as he stepped into the soddy. That comment would set his mother off all over again—abandoned outside on a chilly February evening, as though she didn't have the sense to know what was best for her own daughter. Of course, Felicity probably *would* try to stir Lucy, and then Caitrin might fly off the handle. What a mess.

Standing just inside the door, Jack discerned his sister asleep on the rough-hewn wooden bed near the stove. Damp hair spread across the pillow in a dark tangle, she was covered with layers of thick quilts. Her long, angular frame lay perfectly still. His heart contracted at a sudden thought. How many nights had his sister been forced to sleep with her ankles and wrists bound by the chains he had forged? She looked so comfortable there on Caitrin's bed. So much at peace.

"Please speak to your mother about that constant carping, Jack,"

Caitrin whispered. "She must learn she will never shout poor Lucy into wholeness."

"And you'll never coddle her into it, either." Jack took her arms in his hands. "Caitrin, everyone in my family has done their level best for Lucy. We're all exhausted from constantly watching over her, trying to protect her, trying not to upset her. We've concocted every scheme imaginable to bring her out of these doldrums, but the doctors have told us Lucy's condition is incurable. Sometimes she'll seem a little better, but she goes right back into it. I don't want you to be fooled because you were able to bring her out of the creek today. Lucy does make forward strides. But in a few days or even a few hours, she always slides back into her black pit. Please listen to me, Caitrin—you *can't* change this."

"All I've asked is that Lucy be permitted to stay the night with me." She slipped her hands over his. "Jack, I'm not a fool. I know I haven't the training to manage Lucy. I certainly don't understand what caused this madness in her. But I do care about her. I want her to have one night of undisturbed rest. Please, Jack, allow her to stay."

His heart thudded as he looked into this woman's earnest face. Caitrin was so *good*. So perfect. And yet, one mistake with Lucy, and she'd be changed forever. If Lucy figured out a way to harm herself while she was in Caitrin's care . . .

"I'll stay here, too," Jack said.

"You can't do that!" Caitrin laughed in disbelief. "Sure, I won't have a lone man in my home. What would people think?"

Jack fought the grin that tugged at his mouth. Caitrin Murphy didn't give a hoot what anyone thought about her relationship with Lucy or Mrs. Cornwall. But heaven forbid they should get any ideas about her and Jack Cornwall.

"I'll sleep just outside the door," he said. "That way you can holler if you need me."

"I won't need you, and I won't have you putting up a camp in my front yard." She set her hands on her hips. "Go along with you now. Your mother, too. You said yourself that everyone's exhausted from the constant care of Lucy. Relax then, and leave her to me this one night."

"Caitrin, if something happened—"

"Jack?" Lucy sat up in the bed, her eyes blinking in confusion. "Jack, I'm . . . I'm . . ."

"You're here at my house, Lucy," Caitrin said, going to her. "We were just about to have tea when you dropped off to sleep. Earl Grey, remember? Here's a dressing gown you can wear. Let me help you."

Jack shifted from one foot to the other, feeling awkward and useless in Caitrin's house. Though he was a little surprised at how sparsely furnished the place was, he could tell it was her private domain. She was completely capable of managing her life here, and she didn't need any interference.

"Good-bye, Jack," she called. "You can come over tomorrow morning and have breakfast with us if you like. Bring your mother with you. We'll have hot biscuits and gravy. It's an American dish, rather heavy if you ask me, but everyone seems to like it."

Jack watched as Caitrin helped his sister into a bright pink dressing gown, tied a big silky bow at her waist, and then began combing that tangle of brown hair. Combing! Caitrin was combing Lucy's hair! Jack stared at the two women in amazement.

Is it possible, Lord? he prayed. *Have you sent Caitrin to help Lucy? Oh, God, let Lucy get better. Please make her well again.*

"Ta ta, Jack," Caitrin called, giving him a wave of dismissal. "See you in the morning."

Jack stepped outside the soddy and pulled the door shut behind him. His mother stared at him in dismay, her face pinched. "You left Lucy in there?" she demanded. "You're going to let her stay the night with Miss Murphy?"

"That's right."

"Oh, Jack, you are besotted with that young Irishwoman!" she cried, frustration raising her voice to a falsetto. "How could you risk your sister's life? She'll be dead by morning."

"She'd be dead right now if Caitrin hadn't saved her," Jack said, brushing past her and starting for the camp. "Lucy's sitting in there wearing a pink gown and a bow. And Caitrin is brushing her hair."

"What?" his mother exclaimed behind him.

"Caitrin is brushing Lucy's hair."

"Really, Jack? Really?"

Jack paused and wrapped an arm around his mother's shoulders. "Really, Mama."

⤳

Caitrin woke in the night and felt the warmth of her new friend beside her in the bed. Odd how comfortable it was to share her little home with Lucy Cornwall. The place didn't seem quite so empty, so cold, so forlorn.

They'd had a good evening, sipping tea and munching sandwiches. If she hadn't seen Lucy drifting in the river hours before, Caitrin would hardly have believed anything was wrong with the young woman. They were almost the same age, and they kept up a comfortable conversation until the fire died down . . . planning the welcome party, discussing favorite foods and hairstyles. Lucy's speech was halting but lucid.

In fact, Caitrin realized as she lay in the darkness staring up at the ceiling, Lucy actually might have talked more freely if her hostess hadn't interrupted her every ten seconds. Chagrined, Caitrin mulled over the number of times Lucy had started to talk and then had fallen into her pattern of saying, "I'm . . . I can't . . . I don't know . . ." And Caitrin—with all good intent—had covered the awkwardness with cheerful chatter, changing the subject from one topic to another.

Rolling onto her side, Caitrin frowned into the blackness. Why hadn't she just listened to Lucy? Maybe her friend would have been able to share her deepest thoughts. Maybe she could have opened her heart to Caitrin if she hadn't been so rudely interrupted time and again.

Jesus, do you heal people like Lucy? Caitrin wondered. *The man you met in the cemetery had been as destructive to himself as Lucy—cutting his flesh with stones and screaming out in his anguish. But your touch brought him back to his right mind. Does Lucy have a demon inside her? Has she sinned in some terrible way to be tormented like this? Is it a dreadful sickness that one day will kill her? Oh, Father, I don't understand what's wrong with Lucy, but please touch my friend! Please make her well.*

"Caitrin?" Lucy had risen on one elbow and was gazing at the other woman. "You're tossing."

"Forgive me, Lucy. I didn't mean to wake you."

"No, I thought . . . I thought I might have . . ."

"You didn't disturb me at all. I've been thinking about . . ." Caitrin suddenly couldn't be honest. "I've been thinking about wallpaper lately. I want to paper the soddy, but I don't believe—"

Be still, a voice inside her spoke. *Be still.*

"I don't believe wallpaper will work," she finished.

"I'm not sure," Lucy said. "I can't . . . I can't think. . . ."

"It's so late, and here I am chattering away—" Caitrin squeezed her fists. *Be still.* She let out a breath and finished, "Chattering about wallpaper."

Lucy was silent. Caitrin could hear her breathing softly. Her thin fingers picked at the tufts of yarn on the quilt that covered the two women.

"I don't think wallpaper will stick," Lucy said finally. "Your walls are dirt."

"I know."

"But I can't . . . I can't . . ."

"You—" Caitrin bit her lip to keep herself from blurting out some vapid nonsense.

"I can't think very clearly about wallpaper," Lucy said. "I don't . . . don't know . . ."

She lapsed into silence again. Caitrin thought perhaps she had fallen asleep, but then she sighed. "It's hard to think, you know," Lucy said softly. "My thoughts go around and around. I don't . . . I can't stop thinking about things that bother me."

"Like—" Caitrin cut off her own sentence.

"Like Mary. When she got sick. I adored Mary." Lucy's voice was high and fragile. "My big sister was golden haired and so beautiful. She loved to dance and flirt with all the men. But then . . . then . . . I can't . . ."

Caitrin managed to hold her tongue.

"Can't remember what happened to Mary," Lucy went on. "Oh yes, it was Seth Hunter. She fell in love with him, and Papa got out his . . . his shotgun . . . and how sad Mary was. She told me she had married Seth in secret. And then the baby . . ."

"Chipper?"

"Did I say there was a baby?"

"Yes."

"I'm not permitted to talk about that. We must keep our secrets well hidden. Others will stare at us if they hear the truth. No one has to know a thing."

"Who has told you to keep secrets, Lucy?"

"Mama." She lay quietly for a long time. "Some things can be mentioned. Mary died. The Yankee soldiers came. Oh, dear . . . I'm sorry, but I can't talk about that either. Jack was fighting in the war. And then Seth stole Chipper. Papa took sick. They put me in chains. I'm insane, you know."

"Are you sure?"

"Oh yes." Lucy nodded on her pillow. Her hand slipped across the quilt and covered Caitrin's. "Please don't be afraid of me. It's because of the thoughts going around and around. I can't make them stop. I try, but I can't. . . . I can't . . ."

"You've had a great many sorrows," Caitrin whispered.

"Mary. The soldiers. The war. We lost the farm. Papa took sick." She trembled. "People die. There's such loss . . . and I can't . . ."

"I don't believe you're insane."

"No?"

"Anyone with as many griefs as you've known would find it difficult."

"Difficult to go on living."

"Aye, 'tis hard sometimes." Caitrin's thoughts wandered to Sean O'Casey and the terrible agony she had felt at his loss. But now—oddly—she no longer sensed that emptiness. There was something else . . . someone else . . .

"I have many sorrows," Lucy said. "And many, many secrets."

CHAPTER 11

I T WAS Rolf Rustemeyer's turn to lead the Sunday services. Jack heard that the big German farmer had been practicing his sermon on Rosie Hunter, but rumor had it there'd be slim pickings on the spiritual smorgasbord today. All the same, families from the homesteads around Hope began to gather in the mercantile around nine o'clock. By the time Jack walked in, the room was filled with the aroma of hot cinnamon buns, fresh coffee, and apple strudel.

In the short time he'd lived in Hope, Jack had tried to learn the names of the people who passed his smithy on their way to the mercantile for supplies. Few ever spoke to him, and when they did, it was only to ask how soon he'd be able to repair a plow or mend a wagon wheel. But Caitrin Murphy always followed her customers out the mercantile door to wave good-bye. "Come again, Mr. LeBlanc," she would call. "See you next week, Mrs. Rippeto!" And Jack would memorize the names.

They had all come together to worship on this bright, late-winter Sunday, and Jack had made up his mind to walk among them as one of the community. He'd been given a month to prove his peaceful intentions, and this gathering would be the perfect opportunity to do just that.

"Mornin', Mr. Laski," he said, extending a hand to the Polish

157

fellow who owned a stagecoach station several miles down the road to Topeka. "I'm Jack Cornwall. Good to see you today."

The man's eyes narrowed. "Oh yes," he said. He gave a quick nod and turned away.

Jack shrugged. He wouldn't get angry. Couldn't afford to. Things were just now beginning to look up for the Cornwall family. Caitrin had convinced Felicity to let Lucy stay at the soddy a few days. His sister had lived with the young Irishwoman for almost a week now. And though no one had seen much of either one, Jack sensed that the community was beginning to relax about the notion of having a "madwoman" residing there. His mother—the only person from the creek episode to catch a cold—had stayed busy at the camp, either working or lamenting her drippy nose. Freed from his responsibility to help keep an eye on Lucy, Jack spent every free hour working to build the smithy. He would have the forge up and burning by Monday night.

"Mr. Rippeto," Jack said, giving the Italian homesteader his warmest smile. "Good to see you and Mrs. Rippeto here today."

"Keep your eyes off my wife," the man muttered, pointing a beefy forefinger. "Stay away from my family."

"Listen here, you—" Jack bit off his words. Swallowing his fury, he found a bench near the side of the mercantile, sat down, and opened his Bible. He'd be lucky to get through this morning without punching somebody in the nose.

"Hi, Jack," a voice whispered beside him.

He turned to find his sister slipping onto the bench. A cloud of Lily of the Valley perfume drifted around the startling array of braids and curls in Lucy's upswept brown hair. Clad in a silky dress of pale blue, she arranged her skirts to allow the tips of her kidskin shoes to peep out. Flushing a vivid pink, she patted the sagging bodice.

"It's too big," she whispered. "This is really Caitrin's dress."

Jack smiled. "Well, I reckon you look mighty pretty in it, Lucy."

His sister bit her lip and focused on her hands knotted in her lap. "I've been feeling better, Jack. You know . . . Caitrin lets me cook."

"Cook!" Jack instantly thought of the number of weapons Lucy could lay her hands on—knives, ice chisels, meat forks . . .

"I baked those cinnamon buns on the table over there," she said shyly. "Please don't tell, just in case they taste awful."

Jack took a deep breath. "Does Caitrin stay with you? Is she nearby all the time?"

Lucy nodded. "She or Mrs. Hunter. They take turns tending to me and the mercantile. Caitrin says . . . she says she's been dreaming of opening a restaurant one day, and she would like me to help with the cooking. We might build a little kitchen and have our own pots and pans. I could plan the menus."

"Is that so?" Jack hadn't seen his sister so animated in years.

"Caitrin's very good to me. I'm afraid I've worn her out, and Mrs. Hunter, too, but please don't make me come home, Jack. I really . . . I can't . . . can't . . ."

"It's okay, Luce," he said, calling her by her pet name. "I'll talk to Caitrin and see how she's doing."

The Irishwoman herself entered the mercantile in a vision of shimmering emerald green. Jack thought he might fall right off the bench. Red hair swept up in a mass of sparkling combs and doo-dads, she fairly radiated as she greeted one person after another. Little girls swarmed her, touching the emerald fabric and lifting the hem of her skirt to peep at the rows of petticoats underneath. Caitrin laughed and chatted, her focus roving the room until it came to rest on Jack.

His heart slammed against his chest as she gave him a brilliant smile and started across the room. At that moment, Felicity Cornwall marched into the mercantile, sneezed loudly, and made straight for Jack's bench. Cutting in front of Caitrin, the woman swept down beside her daughter and began to blow her nose on a violet-strewn handkerchief.

"I cannot believe this wretched cold," she announced. And then she noticed her daughter. "Lucy, how lovely you look! The dress is gorgeous—although two of you could fit inside it, of course. You didn't intend to wear that necklace, did you? Silver would look much better than gold with that blue."

Lucy dropped her focus to her lap and laid a hand over the offending necklace. Jack clenched his jaw. Two paces away, Rolf Rustemeyer tapped Caitrin on the shoulder, gave her a dramatic bow, and began to describe in detail his plan to escort her to the upcoming spring festival. Jack picked up his Bible, opened it right down the middle, and searched for an appropriate psalm to fit his dark mood.

"Let us begin with a familiar hymn," Casimir Laski announced, drawing everyone's attention. While people scurried to find places on the benches, he began to sing in Polish. As though directing a hundred-voice choir, he waved his hands to and fro, bellowing out the song at the top of his lungs.

The congregation listened in silence, bewildered by the unfamiliar tune and the foreign words. Jack fought a grin. So much for harmony in Christ. He'd located one of David's psalms pleading with God for justice upon his enemies. Jack found it particularly satisfying.

"Today morning, I talk about Gott," Rolf Rustemeyer said, taking his place at the front. Huge shoulders squeezed into an ill-fitting jacket, the German had attempted to comb his unruly blond hair into some semblance of grooming. As he held up a heavy Bible and stumbled through the Galatians chapter 5 passage about the fruit of the Spirit, his jacket sleeve worked its way up his arm almost to the elbow.

"Gott is maken beautiful day," Rolf said. "Fery goot the sunshine. Spring vill come soon, *ja?* But I haf question. Is spring inside you? In heart?"

Jack closed his Bible and tried to concentrate on Rolf's sermon.

His attention wandered over to Caitrin, seated with the O'Toole family two benches in front of him.

"*Ja*, I know I am goot man," Rolf said. "And many of you are goot manners. Excuse me, goot men. Goot vomens, too. And childrens. But in mine heart is sometimes bad things, *ja?* Maybe I am telling a story not true. How you say in English, Rosie?"

"Lying," she called out.

"Lying is bad thing. Or maybe I am want to have Jimmy O'Toole's fery nice mule, *ja?*"

"Coveting," Rosie spoke up.

"You are farmers, and in spring clear out all bad things from fields. Hoe, plow dirt, kill bugs, *ja?* Is because goot things cannot grow in bad dirt. So my question again. Is spring inside you? In your heart? Better you get all bad things out of your heart. Better you tell Gott, 'I am sorry. Forgif me.' No more hating, no more lying, no more covering—"

"Coveting," Rosie corrected.

"Let Gott bring spring into heart of *you*," Rolf continued, his eyes blazing. "Then goot things vill grow. You can be happy, kind, forgif other people, *ja?*"

He looked around. Jack felt sure the sermon of the day was over, but Rolf crossed his arms over his chest and stared out at his congregation. It occurred to Jack that the German was probably a very intelligent man, no doubt frustrated at his inability to convey his thoughts as clearly as he'd like. But he had brought a good message. One they needed to hear.

"I say to you," Rolf boomed out, "no more talk bad about each other. Get rid of veeds! *Amen.*"

"Veeds?" Lucy whispered as Rolf returned to his bench and Casimir Laski stood to lead another song.

"Weeds," Jack translated.

Lucy nodded and smiled. The transformation on her face lifted Jack's heart. He could have kissed Caitrin Murphy right here in front of everyone. Lucy was better. *Thank you, God. Thank you.*

Another Polish hymn sung solo by Casimir Laski was accompanied by many dramatic gestures intended to encourage the congregation to sing along. As they hummed some semblance of the unfamiliar melody, it occurred to Jack that he ought to join Rolf Rustemeyer as often as possible in the final construction work on the new church. This town needed a pastor. And a song leader.

"How you like my talking?" Rolf asked, striding toward Jack as the congregation rose to make their way to the tables and sample the rolls and pies. "You understand what I say?"

"Perfectly," Jack said. He gave Rolf's huge hand a hearty shake. If anyone had determined to get rid of weeds in his heart, it was the German. He seemed to have decided Jack Cornwall was a friend, and his broad smile and strong white teeth displayed his acceptance of a former enemy.

"Who is pretty lady here with you, Jack?" Rolf asked, giving Lucy a little bow.

"Mr. Rustemeyer, meet my sister, Miss Lucy Cornwall." Jack reached for the young woman, but she shrank backward, a look of horror filling her gray eyes.

"Oh no," she mouthed. "No . . . please . . . I can't . . ."

"It's okay, Lucy," Caitrin said, joining the group and slipping her arm through her friend's. "Rolf, your sermon was an inspiration."

"Inspiration?" He squinted his eyes, clearly uncertain whether he'd just received a compliment.

"'Twas very good," Caitrin clarified. "Sure, you might want to apply for the position of minister yourself. And, Mr. Cornwall, how are you today?"

"Better now," Jack said, drinking in her bold green eyes and pink lips. "A lot better."

She laughed. "I'm certain you've heard about the spring festival that Rosie and I—"

"Lucy," Felicity Cornwall interrupted, "you'd better come back to the camp with me now, dear. I'm sure Miss Murphy has had quite her fill of mollycoddling you this week. And I know for a fact the mercantile has gone untended so often that rumors are spreading amongst the customers."

"Rumors?" Caitrin asked.

"I was in for eggs just two days ago," Felicity said. "No one behind the counter, of course, and the mail coach from Topeka pulled up. The driver told me you had ignored two sets of customers, you had left the mercantile doors wide open day and night, and you'd completely run out of pickles."

"Mr. Bridger," Caitrin gasped. "He wanted more pickles?"

"I realize you intended to do a good deed by watching over my daughter," Felicity continued, "but abandoning your commitments is quite irresponsible."

"My Caitie—irresponsible?" Sheena O'Toole said, approaching with a huge cinnamon bun in one hand. "I should think not! Caitrin Murphy took on *your* responsibilities when she welcomed this poor madwoman—"

"Well," Jack said loudly as his sister cowered behind him. "I reckon it's time to head out into the sunshine. Beautiful day! Great sermon, Rustemeyer. Mrs. O'Toole and Miss Murphy, good to see both of you this fine morning."

He shepherded Lucy toward the mercantile door, praying she wouldn't collapse before he could get her outside. Caitrin followed close at his heels, and he could hear Sheena and his mother exchanging volleys of insults. He hurried his sister out the front door.

"Mr. Cornwall!" Caitrin cried. "Won't you stay for a cup of coffee?"

The man stopped and faced her. "No, Miss Murphy. I won't be joining the citizens of this town for their Sunday fellowship."

"Why not?"

"Weeds," Jack snarled, scooping his wilting sister up in his arms. "Too many confounded weeds."

⁂

Caitrin hammered the last nail on the big sign outside the mercantile. "'Welcome to the Spring Festival in Hope,'" she pronounced, reading the black letters she had painted on a white sheet. And then she muttered, "Hope, Kansas . . . home of the meanest, nosiest, grouchiest, and most intolerant people this side of the Mississippi River. Welcome one and all."

She gave the nail head a final whack and started down the ladder. The festival was doomed. People were already driving their wagons across the bridge, and she hadn't even bothered to dress for the occasion. What was the point? No doubt the event would erupt into another brouhaha just like the recent Sunday service. The guests of honor probably would be run out of town by the kindly folk of Hope. It would be a festival of welcome . . . and good riddance.

"I sound just like Lucy," Caitrin mumbled to herself as she stomped back into the mercantile. "One bad thing after another. Perhaps her disease is contagious after all, and I'm destined to spend my life in chains of my own making."

In frustration, she kicked at a marble one of the children had abandoned on the floor. The missile flew through the air, barely missing the glass counter that displayed men's white collars and ladies' lingerie, hit the wall on the other side, and bounced to the floor. Clapping a hand over her mouth in horror at the near catastrophe, Caitrin stood trembling. It was those horrid chains!

She couldn't stop thinking of poor Lucy . . . back in chains for jumping in front of the Topeka stagecoach and nearly succeeding in killing herself. The horses had panicked, the coach had careened across the bridge with screaming passengers hanging on for dear life, and Mr. Bridger, the driver, had tumbled from his seat and broken his wrist. Lucy was found huddled at the foot of the bridge, her pale blue dress covered in mud. Chains again.

Caitrin heard the mercantile door open behind her and a group of excited children pour into the room. "It's a party for Gram and Uncle Jack," Chipper told the others. "Aunt Lucy might even get to come."

"I thought she was crazy," Will O'Toole said.

"She is, but only if you look at her or touch her." Chipper tugged on Caitrin's skirt. "Are we gonna bob for apples at this festibal?"

"Not this one, Chipper," she said. "We'll have to wait until autumn for apples, so we will."

"Auntie Caitrin, where are all the fancy *shingerleens* you usually put into your hair?" Erinn inquired. "Sure, I thought you were going to wear the purple dress again, but you've got on this old brown thing."

Caitrin tried to smile. "The color is bronze," she said. "Can't you see the fabric is all shot through with metallic threads? In the proper light, I shall fairly glow."

"Ooh!" Erinn closed her eyes, clearly imagining the moment. "Will I be as lovely as you one day, Auntie Caitrin?"

"Lovelier."

Caitrin bent to give her niece a kiss on the cheek as the Laski and LeBlanc families filtered into the mercantile. She was a little surprised they had come to the festival. After all, none of them had had a civil word for the Cornwalls. Of course, a quilt auction was planned for the late evening. Proceeds would be used to purchase the wood for pews in the new church. The women would want to see whose winter handiwork would bring in the most money. Certainly it wasn't the prospect of welcoming the Cornwall family that drew them.

In moments the mercantile began to fill. A self-designated band gathered near the canned goods and tuned their instruments.

Lines of children and their parents formed in front of the little booths erected around the room.

As the festival officially got under way, Rolf Rustemeyer's harmonica provided a collection of tunes for a cakewalk. Carlotta Rippeto manned a make-believe fishing pond from which children could draw little candies, reed whistles, or corn-husk dolls. A group of young people gathered in a corner to play "graces," using crossed sticks to toss a hoop from one member of the party to another. Many of the unmarried farmers assembled near the food table and sampled the slices of pie and plates full of cookies.

"Hello, Caitrin!" Rosie fairly skipped across the room to her friend. "Guess what. I didn't spit up a single time today!"

"Wonderful," Caitrin said, mustering a smile. "Perhaps you're over the hump."

"Hump is right. You should take a look at my stomach! I ate all day long. Tonight I could barely button my bodice."

"Making up for lost time."

"I guess so. I started with tinned peaches, went on to half a loaf of fresh bread, then oysters, lemonade, and salt pork. Do you have any of those wonderful pickles Sheena makes?"

Caitrin chuckled. "As a matter of fact, I restocked the pickle barrel three days ago. It's right over there by Mrs. LeBlanc."

"I hope I don't make a pig of myself. Seth might stop calling me his little twister and start calling me his great big oinker!"

Rosie gave her friend a quick hug and started through the crowd. Caitrin searched the room for any sign of the Cornwalls. Not six months ago, Jack Cornwall had stirred up more than a little trouble in this very room—appearing at a party and accosting Rosie, and later fighting with Seth right outside the front door. Could the people of Hope ever put those events behind them? She had her doubts. Farmers had long memories, and Jack had branded himself a villain, as simple as that.

"Food is all gone from cakewalk," Rolf Rustemeyer said, coming up beside Caitrin. "I gif away already six pies, three cakes, and whole jar of peppermint sticks."

"Peppermint sticks?" Caitrin looked up into the German's smiling face. "But they weren't meant to be part of the cakewalk. We sell them in the store."

He shrugged. "I haf no more cakes and pies. Then I see peppermint sticks on counter, gif to children. Is okay?"

"Yes, it's okay," she said with a sigh. She hoped nobody else manning a booth would decide to give away merchandise as prizes.

"Is time for danzing now, *ja?*" Rolf slipped his heavy arm around Caitrin's shoulders. "You look fery beautiful tonight, Miss Murphy. Danz vit me?"

"Well, I—" Caitrin looked up to see Jack Cornwall and his mother stepping into the room. "Oh, the guests of honor are here! Excuse me, Rolf. I must ask Seth to introduce them. I wonder what they've done with Lucy."

Catching Jack's eye, she hurried away from Rolf. Poor Rolf! He was such a fine man, and so earnest. But Caitrin could hardly imagine an evening clomping around the dance floor with him, let alone a lifetime. He was desperate to marry, and Rosie had been his first choice. When she had elected to wed Seth Hunter instead, he turned his attentions to Caitrin. She was *not* desperate, however, and she certainly had no desire to marry in haste.

"Marriages are all happy," she muttered, quoting her mother's favorite Irish proverb. "It's having breakfast together that causes all the trouble."

She caught up with Seth beside the dessert table and asked him to announce the newcomers. Though everyone in the room already knew the Cornwalls by reputation, it would help their standing in the community if Seth would give them a public welcome. After avowing he wasn't much for speech giving, he motioned the band into silence and climbed up on a chair.

"I want to thank everybody for coming tonight," he said. "Are you folks having a good time?"

The question was answered with a cacophony of whoops and hollers. Caitrin made her way across the room to Jack. Dressed in a clean white shirt and the gray trousers of his army uniform, he had clearly done his best to spiffy up for the occasion. Caitrin began to wish she'd taken time to arrange her hair and change into a fancy dress.

"Where's Lucy?" she whispered, as Seth welcomed by name the various families in the community.

Jack shook his head. "Mama didn't want to bring her along. The chains, you know."

"Did Lucy want to come?"

"Hard telling. She didn't say much—although she spent the whole day yesterday washing that blue dress. This morning she ironed it stiff as a sheet of tin."

"She *wants* to be with us, Jack. Please go and fetch her."

"Better not. We've got her locked up safe. She'll be all right, and I'll go check on her now and again."

Caitrin twisted her hands together. "Oh, please bring Lucy, Jack. How will she ever be accepted if she's locked away as though she has some shameful disease?"

"She does . . . in a manner of speaking."

"I'm not ashamed of her. Are you?"

"No." He rubbed the back of his neck. "All the same, if there's any trouble—"

"I'll take the blame, so I will," Caitrin said. "Gladly."

Jack let out a breath of resignation and started for the door. Seth's words stopped him. "We wanted to get together tonight," his former brother-in-law said, "to welcome the newest folks in Hope. I know a lot of you have been watching the smithy going up across the road. Well, that's Jack Cornwall's new place of business, and we're glad to have him here. If you need a new branding iron or a pair of tongs, Jack's the man to see. And I have it straight from the horse's mouth—or maybe I should say the mule's mouth—that he can nail on a shoe quicker than anybody around. Rumor has it he's never been bit or kicked either. Now how many of you can say that?"

Amid the chuckles, Seth continued. "Jack is a good man, an honest worker, and my son's favorite uncle. I'm proud to call him a friend. Folks, would you give a nice welcome to Jack Cornwall?"

Caitrin held her breath as the smattering of claps gradually grew into a swell of applause. She noted that the crowd had looked uneasy at Seth's warm welcome of his former enemy. She really couldn't blame them for their misgivings after the things Jack had done in the past. Though Hope might appreciate having a smithy, Jack Cornwall himself was still on probation.

As Jack acknowledged the welcome and then slipped out to fetch Lucy, Seth began to introduce Felicity Cornwall. Caitrin belatedly remembered that years ago her husband had run off Seth with a shotgun and that the Cornwalls had treated their daughter's husband as if he didn't exist. But Seth had managed to grow beyond his own memories of past hurts. He reminded everyone that Mrs. Cornwall was a recent widow, and he quoted Scripture admonishing Christians to take care of orphans and widows. *Rosie must have put him up to that*, Caitrin thought.

"Welcome to Hope, Mrs. Cornwall," Seth said. "We trust you'll be happy here."

Patting her silver-streaked hair, the woman nodded. "Thank you, Mr. Hunter. I always do my best to find a measure of joy in whatever circumstance God has placed me—no matter how bleak."

A rumble of mutterings at her comment crossed the room. Mrs. Cornwall simply stood there looking as though she'd just eaten one of Sheena's dill pickles. Caitrin studied the woman in disbelief. Did she *enjoy* causing dissent? Could she possibly think God wanted his holy name included in the context of an insult?

"Now we're going to dance awhile," Seth said, holding out his hands to quell the tide of dissent. "And then we'll have us a quilt auction!"

The roar of enthusiasm drowned out any bad feelings in the crowd, and the band struck up a lively square-dance tune that drew everyone from toddlers to grandparents to the middle of the floor. Rolf strode across the room and grabbed Caitrin before she could protest. As he charged around in circles, occasionally stomping her hem with one of his big work boots, she saw Jack and Lucy slip into the shadows in one corner of the room.

"Ouch, you great galoot!" Caitrin cried when Rolf's attempt at a two-step landed his foot directly on her big toe. "Oh, Mr. Rustemeyer, you really must take some lessons."

"I take many lessons. Talk English fery goot now, *ja?*"

"You need dancing lessons." She looked into his eyes and saw that he wasn't having much more fun at this than she. *Dear God, please send someone for Rolf,* she lifted up. *And don't let it be me!*

"Ven you marry vit me, is okay the mercantile," Rolf said. "I don't get angry. You can vork all days until baby comes."

"When I marry you?" Caitrin repeated numbly, her feet slowing. "Sure, I never agreed to marry you, Mr. Rustemeyer."

"*Ach!*" He stopped dancing and gave his forehead a sound slap. "In German, *wenn* means *if*. I say this one wrong. I mean, *if* you marry me, is okay the mercantile."

"But I'm not going to marry you, Rolf," Caitrin whispered. "I . . . I love someone else."

"*Ja,* Sheena tells me about *der Irländer* you lof. But he is far away gone. Better you not to be alone. Better you to marry, *ja?*"

"Perhaps," Caitrin said, meeting Jack Cornwall's gray eyes. "Perhaps."

CHAPTER 12

AS SOON as she could disengage herself, Caitrin hurried over to the corner where Jack Cornwall stood beside his sister. Though Lucy looked haggard and pale, she had dressed in the silky blue gown Caitrin had given her, and she had made an attempt to put up her hair. A flicker of life leapt into her gray eyes as her friend approached.

"Lucy, you came!" Caitrin said, extending her hands.

"Oh . . ." Lucy drew back for a moment. Then she let out a breath and clasped the outstretched fingers. "Caitrin."

"That dress is positively stunning on you."

"Well, I . . ."

Lucy fell silent, and Caitrin waited.

"I got it dirty the other day," she whispered. "I'm sorry. I just . . . I can't . . ."

"It looks lovely tonight." Caitrin took a tentative step forward and folded the trembling young woman in her arms. "I'm so happy to see you, Lucy. I was sorry to hear you weren't feeling well. Sure, you've no idea how I've missed your cinnamon buns for breakfast."

When Caitrin drew back, Lucy was smiling. "I just . . . I . . . I like to bake."

"And when we build our restaurant, the food will be famous thanks to you."

"Would you make some cinnamon buns for me, Luce?" Jack asked. "I've never tasted your cooking."

Lucy pursed her lips for a moment. "Usually I wear those . . . those chains."

She pointed to the iron handcuffs hanging from Jack's back trouser pocket, and Caitrin frowned. "I'm quite certain those aren't necessary tonight," she said. "Why did you bring them, Jack?"

"Just in case." He shifted from one foot to the other. "You know, Lucy's not real comfortable around crowds of people."

"Who is? I'd far rather be sitting in the soddy eating cinnamon buns and drinking tea with Lucy than allowing Rolf Rustemeyer to make minced meat of my toes. But here we are, and we'll make the best of it. Lucy, would you like something to drink?"

The wide gray eyes turned to her. "Punch," Lucy whispered. "And a slice of pie, please."

Caitrin gave Jack a victory smile. "I'll fetch us all something to eat."

When she returned, they still were seated side by side in the half-dark corner of the mercantile. Lucy was tapping her toe in time to the music, and Jack had managed to slip his hand around his sister's. Caitrin could have wept. *Father, please*, she pleaded in silent prayer. And when she couldn't think of words adequate to express her feelings, she turned the matter over to the Holy Spirit. *Groanings*, she thought. *Oh, God, my soul groans for Lucy.*

"This is one of my favorite tunes," Lucy shared as Caitrin joined her on the narrow bench. "Mary used to dance to this tune. But now . . . now Mary's . . ."

"Would you like to dance with me, Luce?" Jack asked his sister.

"No," she whispered. "You and Caitrin. Please, dance together."

Jack glanced at Caitrin, and she read the uncertainty in his eyes. Leave Lucy alone, and who knew what might happen? He would not likely abandon his sister.

"Where is your mother?" Caitrin asked. "She could sit with Lucy."

Jack grunted. "Mama's over there by the table. I don't want to bother her."

"Sure, I can't see why not. She's only arranging the food—setting pies and cakes this way or that. Fetch her at once, Jack. She'll accompany Lucy while you and I dance."

Jack raked a hand through his thick brown hair. "Mama's had an ornery look on her face ever since I brought Lucy in here. She won't cotton to—"

"Mama doesn't like me to go out in public," Lucy said. "She's afraid I'll . . . I'll say something or do something shameful."

"Oh, Lucy, I'm sure that isn't so."

"I can stay here," she whispered to her brother. "I'll watch you dance. I would like it."

"Well, I don't know." Jack studied his sister. "You might get to thinking about things."

"I'll try not to. I promise."

Caitrin understood the man's concern, but she couldn't help feeling that this overprotectiveness was bad for Lucy. The young woman seemed fine at the moment, drumming her fingertips on her knees and chewing a bite of apple pie. *What is it that eats away inside Lucy, Father? What are these terrible secrets that gnaw at her soul and tangle her reason?*

"I don't think dancing is such a great idea," Jack said finally. "We'd better stay close."

Caitrin glanced at Lucy and absorbed the longing in her eyes. "Please escort me to the floor, Jack. After the dance, Lucy and I shall watch the quilt auction together. It's to start right after this song."

"Go on, Jack," Lucy said.

"Come along, Mr. Cornwall." Caitrin stood and looped her arm around his elbow. "If you don't take me out onto the floor at once, my feet will simply start dancing of their own accord."

"I'll be right back, Lucy," he said as he drew Caitrin into the midst of the crowd. The moment he stepped away from the darkened corner, a familiar teasing light filtered into his eyes. "Feet dancing on their own? Now that would be a sight. Allow me to ease your distress, madam."

"With pleasure, sir."

As Jack Cornwall whirled Caitrin through the crowd, she thought he was the most thrilling partner she had ever had. Though he wouldn't know the intricate steps of the Irish dances Sean O'Casey had performed, she began to understand that her young love's action had been just that—a performance. Sean had displayed his theatrical style with all the flair of a strutting rooster. Caitrin had been a flattering arm piece, a perfect foil to direct everyone's attention to the man himself.

But Jack Cornwall's focus was riveted to his partner. His whispered compliments sent her head spinning. His strong arms kept her close. He escorted her down a promenade, circled left and right, and fairly lifted her from the ground as they stayed in step with the music. By the time the music slowed, she was breathless.

"That was a delight!" she exclaimed. "I can't think when I've had such fun."

Jack gave her an extra twirl that lifted her skirts from her ankles. Laughing, she clapped her hands together as he caught her against his chest, dipped her low, and touched her lips in a warm kiss. "Caitrin Murphy," he said, "I could get lost in those green Irish eyes."

But when he lifted his head and looked across the room at his sister, his face sobered. Caitrin followed the direction of his gaze to find Lucy huddled into herself and staring blankly down at her lap.

"She's thinking about her troubles again," he said in a disheartened voice.

"I've missed your sister greatly," Caitrin whispered. "How is she, Jack? Please tell me the truth."

"Sometimes—like tonight—I start to think she's perking up. I tell myself I don't see any trouble, even when it starts to crop up again. I try to convince myself it's all right that Lucy sleeps day and night, and she won't get out of bed even to eat. Maybe she's just tired, I think. And when she sits staring at her lap for hours on end, I try to believe she's working out some kind of a tricky problem or something. But after a while, it's no use pretending."

"She told me her thoughts go around and around. She can't make them stop." Caitrin was aware that the crowd had moved toward the tables heaped with food. This rare moment with Jack must not be wasted. "What is Lucy dwelling on, Jack? What are these thoughts that plague her?"

"Memories, Caitrin." His face was solemn. "She's got a lot of worries and a lot of bad memories. Lucy always has been more sensitive than most folks to things that happen around her. Even as a little girl, she used to cry a lot. But she always laughed louder, hugged tighter, and loved deeper than everyone else, too."

"Maybe the trouble is something within the very essence of her spirit. Perhaps 'tis something she was born with."

"I reckon you might be right. And, too, she's had some pretty big hurts."

"Mary's death, your absence during the war, the loss of the family farm and your father." Caitrin recited the list. "Is there anything else, Jack? Did something else happen to Lucy?"

He looked away. "She just couldn't hold up under the pile of troubles."

"She said she has many secrets."

"I reckon so," he said. "In the Cornwall family, you keep certain things under wraps—no matter what. Lucy's always been the peacemaker of the bunch. She's so sweet, so trustworthy, that she's had a lot of confidences shared with her."

"Such as?"

He was silent a moment. "Seth Hunter, for one. Not until

everything had blown sky-high did I learn that Mary had been seeing him on the sly. Seth was just one of our farmhands, you know. He didn't have a hope in the world of earning Mary a good living, and he was a Yankee sympathizer to boot. Mary confided to Lucy about Seth, but Lucy kept the information to herself. Then Seth and Mary got married in a hush-hush ceremony, and before long there was a baby on the way—and not a soul knew about any of that except Lucy."

"Oh my. What other troubles has Lucy borne?"

"When Papa took sick, he kept his illness a secret. The only way anybody found out was that Lucy used to empty his chamber pot every morning. She saw the blood, and that's how she knew. Papa made her swear she wouldn't tell Mama, but then when—"

"It sounds as if Lucy is the only Cornwall keeping secrets," Caitrin said. "'Tis as though she's been the hiding place for the entire family's sin and pain. What guilty knowledge have *you* laid on her fragile conscience?"

"Me? None." His eyes went hard. "Don't try to blame *me* for what's happened to Lucy. When she's feeling bad, she's like a sledder on top of a big snowy hill—going down fast and nothing can stop her. Once she's over the crest, you might as well give up. But I'll tell you one thing. It's never been me who gave her a push at the top. I've always stood by my sister and protected her."

"By clamping her in chains?"

"It's that or an asylum."

"For heaven's sake, Jack, why must you—"

A shrill shriek cut off her words. Caitrin swung around in time to see Lucy scramble from the bench, fall to her knees, and crawl into the corner. Rolf Rustemeyer leapt over the bench toward her, and Casimir Laski grabbed the German man by his suspenders.

"Stay away from that woman!" Laski shouted at Rolf. "She's crazy! A madwoman!"

176

"What I haf done?" Rolf said, turning toward the crowd in dismay. "I bringen her chocolate cake, no more."

"Get the Cornish strumpet out of here!" Jimmy O'Toole cried, pointing toward Lucy, who began to sob. "We won't have a lunatic—"

To Caitrin's horror, a string of foul language and denigrating epithets spewed from Jimmy's mouth. Lucy held her hands over her head as though she were being physically beaten as she screamed like a wounded coyote. Jack left Caitrin's side and shoved his way through the throng.

"Shut your mouth, O'Toole!" Jack shouted at the Irishman. "And you, Rustemeyer, get away from my sister. Leave her alone."

"*Aber* I only bringen *torte!*" Rolf returned, stumbling into his native language. He held up a plate bearing a slice of chocolate cake. "*Ich bin sehr* . . . I am fery goot man, *ja!* Not hurt nobodies."

"And you, O'Toole," Jack snarled, "if I ever catch you talking like that to my sister again—"

"You're as insane as she is!" Jimmy hurled back. "Your whole family is a pack of filthy Cornish—"

"Lemme tell you something, buster." Jack shoved his finger in the man's chest. "You stay away from my family or I'll—"

"Jack, Jack!" Felicity Cornwall grabbed her son's arm. "Get Lucy. You must get Lucy!"

Caitrin stood nailed to the floor, staring in disbelief while Felicity raced for the door as though ravenous wolves were after her. Jack scooped up his weeping sister and followed his mother out into the night. As the door banged shut, a hush fell over the room.

Finally Jimmy O'Toole cleared his throat. "'Tis a good thing they're gone. That family has no business in our mercantile. God created the different races to be separate and apart. The Cornish and the Irish. The black and the white. The Indian and the Spaniard. There is to be no mixin' of people."

An assenting murmur ran through the gathering. Caitrin glared at the self-righteous group—Poles, Italians, Germans, French—all a medley of racial backgrounds. Jimmy nodded importantly.

"Mr. O'Toole," Caitrin spoke up. "Could you please remind me where that particular verse is located in the Bible? Sure, I'd like to read for myself the Scripture where God tells us he wants the different races to remain separate and apart."

The Irish immigrant folded his arms across his bony chest. "Tower of Babel," he said. "Genesis, I believe."

"At the Tower of Babel, God confounded the *language* of the people," Rosie Hunter spoke up. "Because of their conspiracy to reach God through human effort, the people were given many different languages. But the Scriptures in Genesis say nothing at all about the color of folks' skin or the place of their birth, Mr. O'Toole. Isn't that right, Seth?" She looked at her husband for confirmation.

"Well . . ."

She lifted her chin. "You said, 'Rosie, let's start at the beginning of the Bible and read all the way through.' And just last week we read that passage about the Tower of Babel. The story is not about the races; it's about languages. I remember the passage very well."

"Me, too," Chipper chimed in.

"My father told me that everythin' is in the Bible," Jimmy insisted. "Everythin' right and true. And he said 'tis true that the Cornish folk are wicked, and they cannot turn to good. For myself, I can hardly believe that a Cornishman has a soul. They're not completely human, but more like the devil himself, and so it cannot be right for us to have aught to do with the Cornish."

"No soul?" Salvatore Rippeto interrupted. "Then you are saying the Cornishman is like an animal, O'Toole? Maybe you think it's okay to *own* Cornishmen? Maybe you think slavery was a good thing, too. Is this what you say, O'Toole? You wanted Kansas to go to slavery?"

"Why do you think the girl is crazy, Rippeto?" Casimir Laski stepped into the argument. "God has given this illness to her because of some unconfessed sin! Sin drives the Cornwall woman mad. Sin from her past torments her day and night."

"I am an abolitionist!" Mr. LeBlanc roared. The miller leapt onto a bench. "I believe that all men have souls, Jimmy O'Toole! Cornishmen, black men, all men! I say it is wrong to own slaves."

"But if we'd had slaves," Laski shouted, "we could have gotten through that grasshopper plague a lot better last year! We could have replanted twice as fast!"

"Settle down, everybody," Seth Hunter hollered. "This is supposed to be a party, and we've just run off the guests of honor. Now everybody better get calm, while I go try to—"

"Down with slavery!" someone cried.

"And down with the Cornish!" Sheena O'Toole bellowed. "Down with soulless Cornishmen!"

"Defeat to the Confederacy!"

"All hail the Union!"

"Calm down everybody!"

"Secede! Secede!"

"Yankee!"

"Reb!"

Caitrin clapped her hands over her ears. As Salvatore Rippeto's fist smashed into Casimir Laski's nose, she ran toward the door. With the crack of a bench breaking and the wail of a child crying behind her, she let the blackness of night gather her into its arms.

Jack could hear the sounds of the quilt auction inside the mercantile as he strode toward it from the creek bank. The good citizens of Hope must have settled down after their hysterics, namecallings, fist swingings, and general conniptions. Cruel people. Sinners one and all. If he didn't have to go back inside and fetch

Lucy's handcuffs from where they'd fallen out of his pocket, he wouldn't come near the place.

Ever again.

It was time to leave. He should have known better than to return to Kansas—flat, dried-up old plain anyhow. Bunch of prairie dogs scratching out a living. He'd heard their cruel accusations against poor Lucy. Lucy had never done anybody a bad turn in her life.

"Sunshine and Shadows!" Seth Hunter called out from the mercantile. "This quilt was made by Mrs. Violet Hudson. Why don't you tell us about it, ma'am?"

Jack stepped into the crowded store as a woman stood holding a small baby. Five or six little children clung to her skirt. "It's the dark and light colors that make up this Log Cabin pattern we call Sunshine and Shadows," she said. "I used scraps from the dresses I made when my husband was alive. And then . . . well . . . I sewed myself some widow's weeds, so I had the dark scraps, too. So that's it, Sunshine and Shadows."

Thankful the crowd was facing away from him, Jack walked to the corner of the room where he had sat with Lucy. The whole mess was Caitrin Murphy's fault, he thought. She was so determined to do her good deeds and make her pious proclamations that she'd run everything straight into the ground. *Go and get Lucy, Jack. Please fetch your sister, Jack.* If he hadn't been swayed by her constant belief that all would be well . . .

As he picked up the chain, the clink of iron drew the attention of the crowd. Straightening, Jack stared at the onlookers, daring them to speak a word. Seth Hunter tossed the quilt onto a bench and took a step forward.

"Jack," he said. "I . . . ah . . . I was planning to come talk to you later. I hope everything's all right. Your sister, I mean."

"Same as ever." Jack squeezed his fist around the chain. Words of venom and bile filled his mouth and soured his tongue. He gritted his teeth.

"I am fery sorry for trouble I make you," Rolf said, standing. "I do not mean bad to your sister."

"That's right, Jack," Seth added. "I'd like to apologize to you and your family for the ruckus tonight. I guess things got heated up around here and . . . ah . . . well, some of us got a little carried away."

"Yep," Jack said. "I reckon you did."

The chain dangling from his hand, he walked toward the door. *Thanks for the welcome party,* he wanted to say. *Thanks for your show of neighborhood unity. Thanks for your godly example of Christian love and brotherhood.* But he swallowed the words and stepped outside.

So much for Hope.

Caitrin nearly cried aloud in fear when she saw the huge, shadowy figure moving toward her. But then she heard the clink of an iron chain and recognized the outline of the man's shoulders.

"Jack." She stood from the bench outside her soddy. "How is Lucy?"

"Needs her chains. And don't sass me about it, either. There's nobody to keep an eye on her while we pack up."

"Pack?" Caitrin took a step toward him, aching to touch and soothe but aware she had already caused so much trouble. "Are you leaving us, then?"

"It's for the best."

"Please don't go." The words slipped out before she had weighed them. "Oh, Jack, I know some of the men were unkind, but—"

"They spoke badly of Lucy. She's my sister, and I'll stand up to anyone who sullies her name. Fact is, before her troubles, Lucy was one of the sweetest little gals anybody ever knew—a good, upstanding Christian who showed her religion by her actions better than anybody around here. Jimmy O'Toole had no right to cuss her like that. I've been trying my best to pray, read the Bible, and walk the straight and narrow. But if I ever get my hands on that skinny little Irishman, I can't promise he'll live to see another day."

"Sure, Jimmy is my own sister's husband," Caitrin said, recoiling at the harshness in his voice. "In spite of his ill behavior tonight, he's a fine, hardworking man and a good father to his five children. You mustn't threaten his life, Jack. And the people of this town are not so wicked, either. Please try to remember they probably haven't met anyone like Lucy before, and they don't know what to make of her. Few of them have had such troubles in their own families. They haven't had time to get to know Lucy as a human being."

"Which they don't consider her to be. You heard what O'Toole said about us—Cornishmen have no souls. Aren't we worthy of God's love? Don't we deserve a measure of friendship from the townsfolk?"

"Of course you do."

"I reckon not. Ever since I started building the smithy, not a person in Hope has said more than two words to me beyond asking me to mend a shovel or patch a bucket. How's my family ever going to show our true nature if people judge us as demons?"

Caitrin lifted her eyes to the moon. She'd been sitting for almost an hour in prayer, begging God to show her answers to these very questions. Instead of a peace that passes understanding, she felt turmoil and anger. Fury raced through her veins at the cruel words that had been spoken and the wicked things that had been done. And now Jack Cornwall was forcing her to defend the very people who had disappointed her so deeply.

She let out a breath that misted white in the chilly night air. "I don't know how you can prove yourselves," she said softly. "But you certainly won't do it if you leave town."

Jack leaned his back against the wall of the soddy and dangled the chain against the toe of his boot. For a long time he said nothing. Then he hooked a thumb in his pocket. "All we wanted was a chance," he said.

"The question is not what *you* wanted, Jack. What does *God* want of you?" Caitrin rubbed her hands up and down her arms, trying to warm them. "Do you think I would have chosen a sod house on a barren prairie as my lot in life? Certainly not. But I felt the Lord leading me here to Sheena and Jimmy. I didn't understand why at the time, and perhaps I still don't. At first I felt I was to help my sister with her children, perhaps to start a small school and teach them their letters. Then I began working at the mercantile, and it seemed God brought my skills into use there. And then you came along. . . ."

She studied his face, the hard line written across his mouth, the rumple of his brown hair, the anger in his gray eyes. *Oh, Jack Cornwall. Why do you stir my heart and cause my very bones to ache? What is it in you that touches me so deeply?*

"'Tis not what we want," she whispered. "If we've given our hearts to the Lord, we must do his will no matter the cost."

"How's anybody supposed to know what God wants?" he asked. When Caitrin didn't answer, he mused for a moment. "If I were to put myself in God's shoes, I'd ask just one thing from folks—and it wouldn't have a thing to do with running smithies or mercantiles. I'd want love."

Caitrin tried to force down the lump in her throat. "Yes," she managed. *Thou shalt love the Lord thy God with all thy heart. . . .*

"I'd want people to love me so much that they had to tell everybody they met," Jack said. "And they'd show their love for me so clearly in everything they did that other folks would ask why . . . and then start begging to get to know me for themselves. If I were God, that's what I'd want."

Love, Caitrin thought. It was what Jack himself wanted and what she'd begged God to give him. How amazing that this often unloved and unlovable man understood so clearly the heart of his Lord.

He studied the moon. "I thought if I built a smithy here I could take care of my family," Jack went on. "I've got plans, you know. Dreams. And I sure thought God had led me back here to Kansas to make them come true. But after tonight . . . well, I'm not certain there's room for me in this town."

Caitrin gulped down a sob. How could she ever express the torment she felt over his words? She couldn't even make herself speak for fear she'd burst into tears. And what could she tell him? *Give these people time, Jack. Be patient, Jack. Let them learn to care for you . . . as I do.*

"If God didn't send me to Kansas to build that smithy," he said, still staring at the moon as though it were his companion on this night and not Caitrin Murphy, "if God didn't send me here to build that smithy, then why did I feel so sure I was supposed to come back? It was almost like I heard him talking to me that evening last winter after I left the O'Tooles' barn."

"You heard the voice of God?"

"In a way." He reflected a moment. "I told you about that night on the road when I got down on my knees and prayed for God's forgiveness. It was almost like God *told* me to come back to Hope. Why? Why did he want me here?"

Caitrin blotted her cheek with the corner of her handkerchief. *Why, Lord? Why anything? Why was Lucy so troubled? Why did Sheena scorn Felicity? Why didn't she have the answers for Jack? Why, why, why?*

"Because I'm supposed to love God here, and that's all," Jack said, his voice filled with an unexpected calm. "No big dreams. No big plans. Just love. *That's* why he wanted me to come back to Kansas. God wanted me to love him so much—right here in this podunk town with its mean-mouthed citizens—that people could look at me and see for themselves that God changes men's hearts."

Caitrin dabbed her eyelids and tried to dam the drippy faucet that her nose had become. Why did she have to cry *now*? Why this uncontrollable weeping when there was so much she needed to say? She wanted to affirm Jack, to encourage him, to beg him not to give up. She ached to reach out to him with words of acceptance and love. Instead, she gave a shuddering sob and buried her face in her hands.

"I doubt if the folks here will change, though," Jack said to the moon. "Their hate is dug in deep. Real deep."

Her handkerchief soaked, Caitrin blotted her cheeks with the cuff of her sleeve. Yes, it was true, she wanted to tell him. Hate and intolerance could spring out of the nicest people at the most unlikely times. And only God could change them. But her lip was quivering so much she couldn't form a single word.

"So I guess that's that," Jack said. He wound the chain around his hand. "If I leave, they won't have seen God in me. Not enough to touch their hearts anyhow. I reckon the Cornwalls will just have to be like that fellow Stephen in the Bible—keeping our mouths shut while folks throw their stones. It's not exactly in my nature to turn the other cheek, but I expect I better give it a try. What do you think?" He turned and looked at Caitrin.

"Oh, darlin'," he said. In a single stride he had caught her up in his arms and was kissing her hair, her damp cheeks, her wet eyelashes, her trembling lips. His warmth enfolded her.

"The first time we met, you told me you loved me," Jack said in a low voice. "I didn't know what that word meant. *Love.* Didn't really understand it. But I think I'm beginning to catch on. It's about opening your heart to what somebody else needs. And it's *you* I'm seeing that love in, Caitrin. I'm seeing God in you the way I want folks to see him in me."

He held her tightly, all but crushing the breath from her chest. "Thanks for talking to me about all this, Caitrin," he said, his lips moving against the skin of her forehead. "You're a wise woman."

With one last embrace, he stepped away from her, looked her up and down once, and then turned on his heel and walked away. She was quite sure *she* hadn't been the one talking to Jack Cornwall. And she hurried into the soddy for a dry handkerchief.

CHAPTER 13

"S OMETIMES I feel discouraged, and think my work's in vain,"
Jack sang as he pumped the bellows on his forge. "But then
the Holy Spirit revives my soul again."

Jack thrust the red-hot nail header into his quenching bucket
and heard the satisfying hiss of steam. "There is a balm in Gilead
to make the wounded whole," he belted out the chorus. "There is
a balm in Gilead to heal the sin-sick soul."

He gave the header a tap and a brand-new nail slid out into
the pile on the table. With the church going up and folks repairing their barns and wagons, Jack could hardly keep up with the
demand for nails. He was grateful for the work.

It had taken him two days to persuade his mother to stay on in
Hope and less than two weeks to convince the townsfolk they'd
be hard-pressed without him. Swallowing their pride, people had
begun trickling into the smithy from the time he had his forge up
and burning. Now a steady stream of customers dropped by wanting repairs or asking for the plows, shovels, wheels, and tools he
crafted each day.

After talking with Caitrin the night of the welcome festival,
Jack had made up his mind to keep a safe distance from her and
the incredible lure of her sweet spirit and compelling beauty. If
he was ever to have a chance of courting the woman in an open
and proper fashion, he knew he'd have to win the respect of the

O'Tooles . . . and that wasn't going to be an easy job. All the same, he had found a way to stay in touch with Caitrin. She had agreed to let him sell his tools through the mercantile. The arrangement gave her a little profit, and it allowed him to talk with her every day, if only for a few minutes.

"If you can't preach like Peter," he sang, enjoying the rich round notes of his mellow baritone filling the smithy, "if you can't pray like Paul, just tell the love of Jesus, and say he died for all."

By the time he had sung the last word, Jack had made three more nails. Every fifteen seconds he could turn one out, he thought with some measure of pride. He had learned nail making at his father's side on the farm, and even as a child he had enjoyed the creativity and challenge that went with working iron. But it wasn't until the war that he'd come into his own. Assigned to a Confederate unit as the blacksmith, he had followed the troops and worked from sunup to sundown fixing broken weapons, repairing cannon, crafting tools. Hard work, but he'd loved it.

"Excuse me, sir, but where is Gilead?" a lilting voice asked.

Jack gave the bellows a push that blew fresh air onto the glowing pocket of coke in the forge and looked up. Caitrin Murphy stood in the doorway, a smile on her face and a bent poker in her hand.

"Caitrin," he said, his breath nearly robbed from his chest by the sight of her. "You look beautiful."

"No more beautiful than the sound of your voice drifting across the road to the mercantile." Then she gave him a little wink. "Tell me, sir, what is the exact meaning of the word *balm?*"

Jack laughed. "You know, I've been singing about the balm of Gilead ever since I learned that song at a church service last Christmas, and come to think of it, I don't know the answer to either question."

"Perhaps you'd better move on to 'Jacob's Ladder,'" she said, stepping into the room. "I recall the story behind that one, so I do.

Jacob dreamed about a ladder with angels going up and down it from earth to heaven."

"He was using a rock for his pillow," Jack said. "No telling what you'll dream if you do something knuckleheaded like that."

She chuckled. "That was when God gave Jacob all the land around the place where he was sleeping and promised him a long line of children, too. 'Tis a good verse for us here in Hope, Kansas. 'And, behold, I am with thee, and will keep thee in all places whither thou goest, and will bring thee again into this land; for I will not leave thee, until I have done that which I have spoken to thee of.'"

"Great ghosts, Miss Murphy," Jack said. "Where'd you learn all that?"

"Straight out of the Scriptures, sir." She laid the poker on a table. "And now down to business. I've a poor bent poker here that I took in trade for a bridge toll. Can you make it new again?"

"That's what I do best." Jack tapped another nail out of the header and onto the pile. Encouraged by his admirer's praise, he started in on "Jacob's Ladder" as he began the next nail. "Sinner, do you love my Jesus?" he sang, all but raising the rafters on the smithy roof. "Sinner, do you love my Jesus? Sinner, do you love my Jesus? Soldiers of the cross."

As he tapered the point of the nail, Caitrin joined in. "If you love him, why not serve him? If you love him, why not serve him—"

"Tush, Jack, you'll wake the dead with all that bellowing," Felicity Cornwall said, entering the forge with a lunch basket over her arm. "Oh. Miss Murphy. I didn't know you were here."

"I brought a bent poker for Jack to mend. Your son does fine work, Mrs. Cornwall."

Felicity sniffed. "I can hear you bellowing all the way down at the creek, Jack. You'd think it was a Sunday."

"Every day's the Lord's day, Mama." Jack glanced at the basket on her arm. "What did you bring me for lunch? I could eat two horses."

"Rabbit stew," his mother said, setting the basket on the table beside the new nails. "And if you don't get your hide out onto the prairie and hunt us a deer, we're going to be obliged to eat that horse of yours pretty soon. Of course, I suppose I could make a nice pot roast out of Scratch's flank, but—"

"All right, all right. It's just that I've got so much to do around here." He slung an arm around his mother's shoulders. "Guess what Salvatore Rippeto suggested this morning?"

"That Italian?" She wrinkled her nose as she set out a bowl and spoon. "No telling."

"He thinks I should set up a livery stable."

"You don't have the money, and I wouldn't like to see you fall into debt in a place like this. We could get ourselves mired here for good."

"As far as I'm concerned, we're already stuck, Mama," Jack said. Then he looked at Caitrin, eager to gauge her reaction to his news. "I'm going to ask Seth Hunter if I can put up a soddy."

"Oh, Jack!" Caitrin exclaimed, her face lighting up.

"Stuff and nonsense," Felicity barked, clanging the lid of the soup tureen. "Not in this town, you won't! I'll not live in Hope past the summer, Jack. I've told you once, and I'll tell you again. Earn the money to get us back home. That's all I ask."

"No disrespect intended, Mama," Jack said, "but where would we live in Missouri? Too many cities. Too many people. Folks here in Hope may not be comfortable around us, but they don't stick their noses into our business much. If we go back into one of those crowded Missouri towns, they'll have the law after us to put Lucy into an asylum."

"Exactly where she belongs," Felicity said, seating herself on a stool beside the door. "And don't argue with me, Jack. You should just see your sister today. She can hardly open her eyes. She's curled into a ball of misery on her bed with the quilt drawn over her head. The girl is completely useless to anyone."

"I should be happy to drop by and visit Lucy," Caitrin put in. "Perhaps she'd enjoy having a bit of company."

Felicity gave a snort. "Don't think you're some kind of a miracle healer, Miss Murphy. My daughter has her good spells and her bad. You just happened to catch her in one of her better humors last time. You won't talk her out of this with all your chatter about tea and cinnamon buns."

Jack tugged his leather apron over his head and hung it on a hook in the door. He wished his mother could find something to talk about besides Lucy and her woes. They'd had the same conversation over and over. He could almost say her part from memory.

"Lucy has such troubling thoughts," Caitrin said.

"She doesn't think about anyone but herself." Felicity picked up the poker Caitrin had brought in and examined it as she spoke. "Lucy's selfish, that's all. She pays no heed to the trouble she causes by demanding so much of our attention. She's wrapped up in herself and all her mournful little worries, and she never stops to consider how *we* feel. I must say, I am vastly weary of it all. It makes me angry."

Jack picked up his spoon and took a bite of stew meat. "Mama thinks Lucy just ought to come out of it," he said, stating what he knew would be his mother's next comment. Felicity always delivered her assessment of her daughter's condition in three parts. First, Lucy was selfish. Second, Lucy should just come out of it using sheer willpower. And third, if Lucy were a better Christian and prayed about her problems more diligently, God would deliver her from them.

"Yes, she could just come right out of it if she had the will-power," Felicity said. "And if she'd turn her worries over to the Lord, she would see everything in a new light."

"You think she could just pray herself right out of that bed and into her right mind?" Jack asked.

"I certainly do."

He gave the stew a stir. "What do you think about all this, Miss Murphy?"

"About Lucy?" Caitrin's eyes flashed in wariness. "Though I love her dearly, 'tis not my business to assess her troubles."

"You spent a lot of time looking after my sister. Why do you think she's the way she is?"

"Sure, I don't know," Caitrin said. "But God does. I suppose the best we can do is ask him to help her."

"That's exactly what I said." Felicity nodded in self-assurance. "Lucy just needs to pray harder."

"Caitrin said *we* ought to pray, Mama," Jack corrected her. "I'm not sure Lucy can think clearly enough to pray. As a matter of fact, I don't believe she can think straight about anything. She sure isn't thinking about herself, how selfish she can be, and how much she can inconvenience the rest of us. The times she's tried to do herself in, she was just wanting everything to be over. She wanted to stop hurting."

"Hurting!" Felicity stood. "That child has everything a body could want. She's not in any pain. Stuff and nonsense, Jack. You're like putty in Lucy's hands. All she has to do is gaze at you with those big eyes, and you do anything she asks."

Jack looked up as a shadow fell across the door. Much to his surprise, Sheena O'Toole's bright red hair, green eyes, and rosy cheeks appeared in a patch of sunlight.

"Sheena?" Caitrin said. "What are you doing here?"

The woman moved one step into the smithy and stopped, as stiff as a statue. "Good afternoon," she said, her mouth tight and her focus on the rusty roasting spit in her hands. "Mr. Cornwall, I've come to seek your services, so I have."

"My services?" he asked. "You mean you want me to do some work for you?"

"Aye. That I do."

A flood of victory raced through Jack's veins. Now was his moment! He could skewer the little biddy on her own spit. He could send the Irishwoman and her sharp tongue right back outside with a message he wanted the whole town to hear: Nobody messes with Jack Cornwall. If you need me, you'd better treat me right.

He stood to his full height, towering over her. He could see the white skin around her knuckles as she clutched the rusty iron spit, and he recognized the incredible tension radiating from her. He recognized it. He had felt it himself when he went to Seth Hunter to ask permission to build the smithy.

A river of remorse washed right over the flood of victorious revenge in which he'd been about to drown Sheena O'Toole. At first he thought he couldn't even form the words that demanded to be spoken. But he'd prayed so hard that God's love would be revealed in his own life, the message just came flowing out.

"I'm glad to see you today, Mrs. O'Toole," he said, his voice more gentle than he'd ever heard it. "Looks like you've got a rusty spit bar there. That's a big problem with all those children of yours. I'll bet they want to eat day and night. If you were to put a big ol' roast on that bar, it would probably bust clean in two."

Sheena lifted her head just enough that the green of her eyes could be seen from under her dark lashes. "Aye," she said. "I was afraid of that myself."

"I can clean and mend your spit bar right here and now. But you'd do better with a new one. It would be stronger. Cleaner, too. I could have it ready for you by sunset."

"How much?"

Jack pondered a moment, and then it came to him. This was the perfect opportunity to begin building bridges between himself and Caitrin's family. The solution seemed heaven-sent.

"Tell you what, Mrs. O'Toole," he said. "You invite me to your house for a sandwich of whatever's left from the first roast on your new spit—and one of your famous pickles—and we'll call it even. I won't charge you one red cent. How's that?"

Sheena sucked down a deep breath.

"She'll never do it!" Felicity crowed. "She'll never get her Irish mitts on that new spit unless she eats humble pie, and she's too proud for that. You've caught her now, Jack. Well done!"

"Wicked man!" Sheena spat at Jack. "I came here humbly offering you an honest bit of work, so I did, and you pulled one of your Cornish tricks on me! Wait until Jimmy hears about this—"

"Hold on a minute, there, Mrs. O'Toole." Jack caught her elbow as she made for the door. "I never meant a thing by what I said. I'll be happy to fix your spit. I'll make you a new one, if that's what you want. All I intended was to—"

"To worm your way inside my house!" she hissed. "You've already taken liberties with our Caitrin, drawn her heart away from her own family. Look at her here, chatting with you as bold as a strumpet! You've already used my Jimmy's barn for a camp. And now what would you have of us? Our very privacy? As if we'd let a man like you into our house! Demon!"

"Sheena!" Caitrin cried. "Please don't be so cruel."

"You were strutting about all cock-a-hoop before, Mrs. O'Toole," Felicity said, "flinging your Irish pride in our faces. But now you've found you can't do without my son, eh? Well, you'll never see his fine work in your miserable little soddy—"

"Now hold on a minute here, Mama," Jack cut in. "I just told Mrs. O'Toole that I'd make her the spit bar. I didn't mean to—"

"Oh no, you don't!" Sheena cried. "Don't try to turn your trickery around with one of your Cornish lies, Mr. Cornwall."

"Lies? Why, you witch!" Felicity raised the bent poker and shook it in Sheena's face. "Out of here, you little red-haired leprechaun!"

"Oooh!" Sheena leapt at the older woman, rusty spit thrust

forward like a sword. "Call me that, will you? Blast your soul, you're a cheeky thing! A strap is what you are! A bold, forward, Cornish strap!"

Felicity swung the heavy poker upward to parry the thrust, and the clash of metal knocked Sheena off-balance. Recovering, the Irishwoman lunged at her opponent, and again spit clanged against poker.

"Stop this now!" Jack leapt at his mother, barely evading a jab from Sheena's spit. "Mama, put down that poker before you hurt Mrs. O'Toole."

"Sheena, don't do this!" Caitrin cried.

"Look at her, look at her!" Felicity shouted, dancing from side to side. "She's an imp of the devil himself!"

"Liar!" Sheena swung the spit, missed her target, and went spinning around in a wobbly circle. "Liar, liar!"

"Witch!" Felicity strained toward her adversary. "I'll get you now!"

In a burst of furious swordplay, the older woman fenced Sheena right out of the smithy. Jack grabbed Caitrin's hand and dashed after the two shrieking combatants. On the pale green springtime grass near the mercantile, the two women whirled and lunged at each other, their cries echoing like the wail of banshees across the open prairie.

"Stop this right now, Mama," Jack called as he sprinted toward the women. "Caitrin, help me out here."

"Sheena!" Caitrin headed for her sister, who was tottering off balance down the gentle slope toward the creek. "Jack, go after Sheena!"

"Witch, witch!" Felicity charged past Caitrin and chased after her foe, poker swinging.

"Shut your gob before I give you a sound larruping!" Sheena bellowed.

Caitrin grabbed Mrs. Cornwall around the waist, and at that

195

moment, the older woman hurled the poker at Sheena. The iron rod tumbled through the air. Jack reached for the teetering Irishwoman. Just as he put a hand on her arm, the poker slammed into her head. A bright splotch of crimson instantly appeared on her face as she slumped onto the grass. Arms covering her head, she wailed aloud in pain.

His blood racing, Jack dropped down beside the fallen woman. Caitrin turned Mrs. Cornwall loose, ran down the hill, and sank to her knees beside her sister. "Sheena!" she cried, throwing her arms around the bundle of moaning misery. "Oh, Sheena! Are you injured? Let me see your head!"

"What have I done? Oh, what have I done!" Felicity arrived at the creek bed as Sheena clutched her stomach in agony.

"My baby," the Irishwoman groaned. "I'm losing my baby! Caitie, where's Jimmy? Oh, heavens, the baby!"

"Sheena?" Caitrin exclaimed. "Sheena, you never said anything about a baby. Jack, sure, you must run to the mercantile and fetch Rosie. Bring towels!"

God in heaven, help us all, Jack prayed as he raced up the slope toward the mercantile. "Mrs. Hunter!" he shouted. "Mrs. Hunter, come out here!"

The young woman appeared in the mercantile doorway, her cheeks flushed. "What's wrong, Jack?"

"It's Mrs. O'Toole. She's hurt bad. We need towels."

"Oh, Jack!" Rosie grabbed her skirts and dashed back into the mercantile. She reemerged in a moment, arms filled with white cotton tea towels. "What happened to Sheena, Jack?"

"Trouble. Go fetch Seth!"

He headed back down the slope. Sheena hadn't budged, her body doubled up and blood trickling down her temple. Felicity hovered over her, brushing back her tangle of red hair and trying to loosen the apron at her waist. Caitrin crouched in mute horror.

Jack dropped and slid the last two yards on his knees. "Mrs.

O'Toole, can you hear me?" He dipped a tea towel into the creek and pressed it onto the gash on her head. "Mrs. O'Toole, talk to me."

"The baby!" Sheena wept. "Don't let me lose my baby!"

"We'll do all we can. Caitrin, hold this cloth on your sister's head." He settled the young woman's trembling hand on the wadded tea towel. "Push down as hard as you can. And don't let her go to sleep. How far along are you, Mrs. O'Toole?"

"Four months, the same as Rosie. I didn't want to tell it round and cut in on her joy. I've had my other babies, and this is her first, and—oh, Mr. Cornwall, where's my Jimmy?" She clutched at his arms, her pretty face wreathed in pain. "I need my Jimmy!"

"I'll get him in a minute," Jack assured her. "Calm yourself, now, Mrs. O'Toole. Take a deep breath."

"I'm going for blankets," Felicity said. She leapt to her feet and ran toward the camp.

Jack took out his pocketknife and slit the ribbon that held on her apron. "Are you cramping up, Mrs. O'Toole?"

"Aye, I am." She was crying now, tears running down her rosy cheeks. "Oh, I'm a bad, wicked woman!"

"No, you're not. Things just got a little out of hand." He lifted her head into his lap and used one of the tea towels to blot her forehead.

"But I am, I am. I was miffed at my dear Jimmy—and at God, too—when I realized I was to have another baby. I've five *brablins* already, you know, and the soddy is terrible crowded, so it is. I said—" she grimaced in pain—"I told Jimmy I didn't want the baby. I prayed . . . prayed . . ."

"Now then, Mrs. O'Toole, try to calm yourself."

"I prayed I would lose the baby!"

"Oh, Sheena!" Caitrin whispered. "You didn't."

"A terrible thing to do," Sheena went on. "Wicked and sinful of me. I was so angry about it all. But now . . . oh, now . . . I want this child! I want my baby!"

197

"Of course you do." Jack could feel his heart slamming against his chest. Caitrin sat paralyzed with shock, her face as white as her apron. Jack had had plenty of experience tending wounds on a bloody battlefield, but he didn't have a clue how to take care of a woman in Sheena's condition. And he sure didn't know anything about hearing someone's confessions.

"Oh, it hurts!" she cried out, squeezing his hand. "Help me!"

"Turn her to the side," Felicity ordered, arriving back at the site of the catastrophe. "And for heaven's sake, take Mrs. O'Toole's head off your lap, Jack. She must have her feet up, not her head. Here, put this blanket under her legs."

Glad to obey orders, he wadded up the quilt and stuffed it under Sheena's feet.

"Drink this cup of cool water," the older woman commanded. "Sometimes the cramps can come on from a thirst. Now, I'm going to check the baby, all right?"

"Aye," Sheena sobbed. "Help me, Mrs. Cornwall, please help me! Save my baby."

"I'll do what I can. Try to rest now. Pray for the welfare of your unborn child."

While his mother worked, Jack traded the blood-soaked tea towel for a fresh one and examined the gash on Sheena's forehead. Her skin had been slashed, but a few strong stitches would probably hold it together until it had time to heal. As Jack dabbed the wound with water, Seth Hunter came barreling down the slope toward the creek. Rosie, skirts flying, was right behind him. She cried out in dismay as she absorbed the scene on the creek bank.

"Seth," she shouted, "run back to the house for my medicine bag, honey."

"Medicine bag," her panting husband repeated. Then he turned right around and started up the hill again.

"I'll go after Jimmy," Jack told Caitrin, touching her hand long

198

enough to draw her attention. She nodded as she and Rosie took over the work on Sheena's forehead.

Jack ran across the bridge and covered the short distance to the O'Toole homestead. The children were playing in the yard, and the older ones directed Jack to where Jimmy was working in the field. Realizing something must have happened, they grabbed up the toddlers and started for the bridge.

"Jimmy!" Jack called, hailing the silhouetted figure whose mop of bright red hair easily identified him. "Come quick. It's Sheena!"

Jimmy dropped his plow and ran. "Where's my girl? What's happened to her?"

"On the bank. It's the baby."

"No!"

Paling, Jimmy took off like a shot. Winded from his run, Jack leaned against the O'Tooles' barn for a moment to catch his breath. At that moment, Caitrin came flying into the yard.

"Jack? Where are you?"

"Here, Cait!" He stepped out from the barn, caught her in his arms, and held her tightly. "I'm right here."

CHAPTER 14

W HAT'S happening with Sheena?" Jack asked.

"I don't know yet," Caitrin whispered. "Sure, your mother's the only one with experience in these matters. I've come to fetch Sheena's sewing basket so I can stitch the wound." She clung to him, her cheek pressed against his shoulder. "Oh, Jack, how could this terrible thing have happened? Whatever shall we do?"

He swallowed, aware suddenly that this interlude with Caitrin might be the last. The trouble between his mother and Sheena O'Toole could seal the Cornwalls' fate in the community. There would be no courtship of Caitrin.

"We'd better pray," he said. "Pray for Sheena. Pray my mother can help her hang on to that baby." He took both her hands in his. "Father, please fix this mess. Look after Sheena, and show Mama how to take care of that baby. Amen."

"Amen," Caitrin murmured. "Oh, Jack, I'd no idea Sheena was expecting a baby. Which of them started the trouble? Sure, 'tis all a blur to me now."

"They just went after each other."

"Aye, and they raced outside before I knew it. Then you and I tried to separate them. I took hold of your mother. You went for Sheena, and Mrs. Cornwall threw the poker—oh, Jack!" She buried her head in the hollow of his neck.

"I've got you, Caitrin. I'm here." As he held her close, a warmth flooded through Jack's chest and filled him with determination. At all cost, he would protect this woman from pain. He would shelter her, shield her, from the fire that raged around them.

"'Tis the end of it then," Caitrin said softly. "You'll have to leave Kansas, Jack. They gave you a month of grace, and 'tis been less than that. Your mother struck Sheena with the poker. If she loses the baby—"

"The trouble wasn't my doing. It happened between the women."

"It doesn't matter. You'll bear the brunt of it, so you will. Sure, Jimmy will latch onto any reason to drive out your family. He and Sheena have no use for Cornish."

Jack tightened his arms around Caitrin, looking into her green eyes, praying he could memorize her in case he never saw her again.

"Jimmy doesn't trust you," she said, echoing his own fears. "If he learns you were near Sheena when she fell, he'll cry for blood."

"Don't worry. I can stand up to Jimmy."

"Sure, you can't save yourself and the whole world, Jack."

"No, but I'm putting my faith in someone who can. Caitrin, look at me." He took her shoulders in his hands and forced her to meet his eyes. "Tell me you want me to stay here. Tell me I mean that much to you—and not just as a child of God. Say you want me for the man I am, and I'll tear down anything that tries to come between us."

"I do want you to know how much I care about you, and I know you love God . . . but I'm . . . I'm sometimes frightened of the fierce spirit I see inside you, Jack. How can I be sure this boldness is all for good? The things you did before were so . . . I know you had your reasons, but you were a ruthless man. You were ironfisted and unyielding. You were merciless."

"Is that what you think of me *now*, Caitrin? Do you want me to carry my past around forever like an old sack of garbage?" Hands behind her neck, he stroked his thumbs across the velvet pink of her cheeks. "You once told me I was precious to God. Those were words I'd never heard. I believed you, Caitrin. I read in the Bible that if any man is in Christ, he's a new creature. Old things pass away, and all things are made new. That's why I came to Hope looking for a fresh start. I want to be different, inside and out. But I can't do that if people tie the bad stuff in my past around my neck and make me haul it around."

"Have you truly changed, Jack?" she asked softly. "Or will some spark set the flames to raging inside you again?"

Unable to resist, he kissed her lips, pressing her tightly to him. "I don't think the flames inside me have ever stopped raging or ever will. I'll always be ironfisted. I'll always be stubborn and rough. But I've come to believe that God can take the man he created and use me for his good purposes. He used Peter, didn't he? That fellow was no angel. He was always mouthing off and doing things before he thought them through. But Christ said he'd build his church on Peter."

"Aye, but—"

"So why can't he use me, Caitrin?" He crushed her against him. "Tell me the answer to that!"

"Christ *has* put his Spirit inside you, and he can use for his good the fire that burns in your heart. But, Jack, I don't know that the people here in Hope have the wisdom and tolerance to see that far."

"I don't give a hot potato what the people here see in me," he said. "Who I am and what I do is up to God. You're the only person who matters to me, Caitrin. *You.*"

She clutched his shirtsleeves, knotting the fabric in her fingers. "Oh, Jack Cornwall, whatever is to become of us? More than ever now I see the matching zeal in our hearts. 'Tis true what I said so long ago—we *are* that pair of candles burning brightly. But I asked you before, and I'll ask it again: What future can a candle have on a windswept prairie? What do you want of me?"

"I want your fire. I want us to be a bonfire together. One big, blazing bonfire that God can use to turn raw ore into gold, a fire that everybody can see for miles around."

"Jesus taught that we're not to hide our light under a basket; we're to shine for all to witness. But, Jack, I must think of Sheena and Jimmy. I love them! I want to honor and respect their wishes. They're the only family I have. And how can I be sure something won't go terribly awry? Sure, your mother has a sharp tongue, and Lucy bears such troubles, and—"

"And people don't come in pretty little packages with bows on top, Caitrin. God loves all of us no matter what, and I reckon we should do our best to follow his example. But this is not about Mama and Lucy. This is about you and me, Caitrin. Say the word, and I'll leave town. Right now. But if you ask me to stay, I will. I won't budge an inch, no matter what anyone says or does."

As he held her, he could see the crowd hurrying across the bridge, Sheena hoisted on a blanket among them. Some of her children were crying. Jimmy was barking orders left and right. The mongrel dog yapped like there was no tomorrow as Chipper ran along beside him. Over all the clamor, Sheena's keening filled the air.

"They're coming," Caitrin whispered, turning to look.

Before she could push away, Jack bent and kissed her lips.

God, my heart cries out for her! The prayer was torn from his very soul. *Please don't take this woman from me. Make a place for us. Give us hope, Father God. I beg you, give us hope.*

"Stay," Caitrin whispered against his cheek. "I want you to stay, Jack."

"I will." His soul soared.

"But I cannot be with you in secret. If we're to be a bonfire, we can't go on hiding in the shadows."

"May I have your permission to come courting?"

She glanced up, surprise lighting her emerald eyes. "Aye," she said, a laugh bubbling from her throat as he caught her up in his arms and swung her around. "You may court me, Mr. Cornwall. I'll ask Rosie to chaperone. Now set me down before we turn the town on its head with our shenanigans!"

Before he could respond, she pulled out of his embrace and dashed for the O'Tooles' soddy. He followed, lifting up a prayer for Sheena. But his footsteps pounded out the song in his heart. *Stay! I want you to stay, Jack! Stay, stay, stay!*

"He'll have to go," Jimmy muttered. "The whole lot of them Cornish devils will have to go."

"*Whisht*, Jimmy," Caitrin said as she stood beside her brother-in-law in the silent soddy. "There may have been trouble between them, but Mrs. Cornwall is helping Sheena now. Don't spark up the strife again."

She clamped her hands together under her chin as she watched Felicity working. The younger woman lay unmoving on the bed, her head wrapped in a white bandage where Caitrin had stitched the gash made by the poker. The scent of burning lamp oil suffused the room, and the golden light gave it a churchlike atmosphere.

Felicity regarded Jimmy solemnly. "Your wife has kept her baby," she announced.

"Glory be to God," Jimmy said, letting out a deep breath. In two strides, he was at Sheena's side, kneeling by the bed and pressing his lips against her hand. Sheena stroked her husband's damp red hair. "Are you all right, my love?"

"Aye," she croaked. "The pains are going now. Oh, Jimmy . . ."

He muffled her sobs with tender kisses. "'Tis all right, my honey-sweet. Sure, 'tis going to be fine now."

"I'm so . . . so sorry."

"Malarkey. You've no need to say that."

"But I . . . I . . ."

"If you'll leave us be now," Jimmy said, turning to the three women in the room. "My wife's a *donsie* thing. She'll be needin' her rest, so she will."

"Aye," Caitrin said softly. "Sheena, I must go and tend the wee *brablins*. Will you be wanting anything more from me?"

"Nay." Sheena sniffled.

Rosie picked up her medicine bag, wrapped her arms around it, and led the way out the door of the soddy. Felicity Cornwall followed, and Caitrin took up the rear. The O'Toole children stood barefoot on the hard-beaten earth yard and stared with great emerald eyes at the women.

"Your mama is fine now," Felicity told them. "And so is the baby. God willing, your healthy brother or sister will be born in the autumn."

Their faces broke into radiant grins as the woman turned and strode toward the bridge. Caitrin stared after her, wondering what thoughts had leapt into Felicity's mind during those terrible minutes when uncertainty gripped everyone. Would she admit her guilt in the conflict? Would she beg forgiveness of Sheena? Could Jimmy ever make peace with the Cornwalls?

"Caitrin." Rosie took her friend's hand and squeezed it tightly. "We saw you with Jack. As we were bringing Sheena across the creek, we saw the two of you by the barn. He was kissing you. Jimmy saw it, and the things he said against Jack were vile. Oh, Caitrin."

"Jack's a good man, Rosie. He's begging for a chance to show that he's changed."

"He won't get it. Not with that kind of behavior."

"He was comforting me."

"They'll drive him off, Caitie. I'm sure of it."

"No," Caitrin said, her voice low and determined. "Jack Cornwall is going to stay."

꒰

"He'll have to go," Seth said, wiping his face with a red kerchief. He looked at the two women on the front porch of his new house and shook his head. "I don't care how many horses Jack can shoe in a day, Caitrin. After Sheena nearly lost her baby the other day, Jimmy's bound and determined to run him off."

"But he's living and working on *your* land," Caitrin said. "Jimmy has no right to tell Jack anything."

Seth's blue eyes flickered. "You better figure out where your loyalties lie, ma'am. Don't get me wrong now; I understand the feelings that can grow between a man and a woman. But you deserve better than Jack Cornwall. A lot better."

"How well do you know him, Seth?" Caitrin asked, her blood heating. "Only the other day Jack asked me if he must live with his past tied around his neck. Is he to be forever labeled a wicked man, with no chance to prove himself changed?"

"It's just like those tomatoes I canned last summer, Seth," Rosie put in. "I pasted the labels onto the jars with good strong glue— TOMATOES. But then I found those awful grubs in them, and they weren't fit to eat. Just the thought of it makes me sick."

"Now, Rosie," Seth warned. "Don't tie your stomach in knots again. We've had months of that."

"Anyhow," she went on. "I threw out the tomatoes—flat got rid of those nasty things. And with the strawberries beginning to leaf out, I've been doing a lot of thinking about strawberry jam. I'd sure like to put strawberry jam in the jars—but I can't get those labels off no matter how hard I scrub!"

"Aw, Rosie, these days you're always thinking about food."

"I am talking about Jack Cornwall," she snapped, her brown eyes dancing. "Everybody in this town has pasted a great big label on him that says BAD MAN, when maybe he's trying to toss out the nasty stuff and put good things inside. He needs a chance to write himself a new label."

"Maybe so," Seth said, tucking his kerchief into his back pocket. "But it doesn't really matter what I think of the fellow, good or bad. Sheena's opinion ought to be what counts the most with Caitrin. Sheena and Jimmy are her kinfolk. Jimmy holds Felicity Cornwall accountable for the troubles the other day, and I can hardly disagree with him."

"But she helped Sheena after she'd fallen," Caitrin said. "'Twas Felicity who brought the water that calmed my sister's cramps. 'Twas Felicity who examined her for the health of the baby."

"It was Felicity who went after Sheena with a poker in the first place," Seth countered.

"Will you order them to leave then?"

"I don't know what I'll do." He settled his hat on his head. "I've got sixty acres to plow, a trip to town to buy seed, a wife who's about to eat me out of house and home, and a son who ought to learn to read and cipher if I don't want him to grow up wild and ignorant. Folks are talking about the need for a schoolmarm come fall, and they've asked if I'd consider putting a school near the church. The church is built all the way up to the steeple, and people are turning to me to find a preacher. After what happened to Sheena, everybody wants me to try to talk a doctor into moving to town. We've got more people passing through Hope than we can feed and house. And I'm supposed to help Rolf and Jimmy repair one of the pontoons on the bridge."

"All that, Seth?" Rosie asked. "Why didn't you tell me?"

"I don't want to worry you, honey. Not in your condition." He gave his wife a crooked smile. When he turned to Caitrin, the tenderness vanished. "All I ever wanted to do when I moved to Kansas was be a farmer. But I'm spending half my time as the sheriff, mayor, innkeeper, and general fix-it man. Now you're asking me to be the town judge, too, Caitrin? Frankly, I don't know whether Jack Cornwall ought to be kicked out on his backside or not. And I don't much care, either."

"Saint Patrick's Day is tomorrow," Rosie called after her husband as he stalked away. "You gave the Cornwalls until then. Are you going to run them off?"

"Don't know!" he repeated. "Don't care!"

"What a grump." Rosie shook her head. "Come on, Caitrin, let's hurry this bread over to the mercantile. Ever since Seth found out I was expecting a baby, he's been storming around like a big old rain cloud. He's worried the grasshoppers will come back. He's fretting about what to plant. He's crazy to buy another cow, but he wants to keep back some savings. You'd think the whole world dangled by a thread from Seth Hunter's fingers . . . instead of being cradled in the almighty hands of the Creator himself."

"Seth only wants to be sure his family will be cared for," Caitrin said as they walked down the path toward the mercantile. "He wasn't able to provide for Chipper and . . . and his first wife. . . ."

"Mary. You can say her name; I don't mind." Rosie adjusted her skirt over the small bulge of her belly. "I know Seth was married before, and I feel sure his worries stem from that. While Mary was pregnant, he was away at the war. Then she died, and he had done nothing for her or for Chipper either. But, for pete's sake, Seth is not the same man he was back then. And *I'm* sure not a thing like Mary Cornwall. Our family can live on wormy potatoes if we have to. I'm the best around at making do on nothing." She paused a moment. "Did that sound like bragging?"

Caitrin laughed. "Of course not, silly. But I think Seth's mood has more to do with his fears than with his worries about what you'll all eat."

"What fears?"

"Mary *died*. Seth lost his first wife, Rosie. He can't rest easy at the memory of that, and he doesn't want it to happen again. The birth of your baby will be a dangerous time for you, and after that, too. Seth's mood is a measure of his great love for you. Sure, I think the loss of you would do him in. Truly I do."

Rosie stopped outside the mercantile. "Worrying won't keep me alive, Caitie. But you know something? This town *does* need a good doctor. And a preacher, too. I might just have to pester Seth about that . . . if I çan get rid of that rain cloud he's under."

Caitrin studied the three wagons rolling slowly over the bridge and mentally tallied the tolls they would bring in. Jack Cornwall emerged from the smithy across the street and cocked a hand over his eyes to watch the travelers approach.

"More customers, and this itching is just about to drive me crazy!" Rosie exclaimed, scratching her belly. "We sure could use a doctor with some good medicines and lotions on hand. You know what might put Seth into a better mood? Another party."

Caitrin groaned inwardly. "He's not that much on parties, is he? And we're just past that disastrous welcoming festival."

"I'm thinking about spring. We could have a party in April when everything's budding out. The family who lived just beyond the limestone wall of the orphanage used to have an egg hunt every spring. I always wished I could join in. Wouldn't that be fun, Caitie? We could color eggs, and the children could search for them. Maybe if the Cornwalls are still around, Lucy would be feeling well enough to help out."

Caitrin frowned as the three wagons drew nearer. It would be wonderful to include Lucy in the preparations for a party. She could just imagine the poor girl's eyes lighting up and a smile softening her pretty lips. But after the incident between Felicity and Sheena, the Cornwall camp had become as closed off as a fort. Felicity was rarely about, and Lucy hadn't been seen at all.

"We could cut cookies into the shape of bunnies," Rosie said. "And we could sprinkle them with sugar."

"Bunnies and eggs?" Caitrin regarded her friend for a moment. "Spring is for celebrating Easter and the risen Christ."

"Well, sure it is. But I've always wanted to have an egg hunt."

Caitrin slipped her arm over her friend's shoulders. "I think a good Easter sermon and a round of hymn singing would lift your husband's gloomy spirits more than colored eggs and bunny rabbits."

Coming out of her springtime daydreams, Rosie stiffened suddenly. "Look, Caitrin, it's Jack Cornwall. He's coming this way."

"Go on inside the mercantile and open up for the day," Caitrin said. "Leave him to me."

"I don't think I should. What if people see the two of you talking alone? You never know what Jimmy might do."

"Aye, but I'll not alter my ways for a man with a closed mind," she said, giving Rosie her bread basket and walking toward Jack. "What can I do for you this fine morning, Mr. Cornwall?"

He jerked a thumb at the wagons. "Looks like you've got customers, Miss Murphy. Morning, Mrs. Hunter."

"Hello, Mr. Cornwall," Rosie said, her voice wary. "We've not yet actually opened for business today. Is there something I might bring you from the mercantile before you head back to the smithy?"

"Well now, that's a kind offer, Mrs. Hunter." Jack paused before the women and took off his hat. "As a matter of fact, I do have a request. I was wondering if you had planned to attend the prayer meeting Rolf Rustemeyer has called for Sunday night."

"Me?" Rosie gaped for a moment. "Yes, of course, I am. Why wouldn't I? Rolf thinks we all ought to take time out to ask God for some rain. It's been so dry, and Seth sure is worried about the spring planting. I wouldn't think of missing that service."

"Good." He cleared his throat. "I know I'm asking a lot here, Mrs. Hunter, but would you be willing to accompany me to the service? I'd be much obliged to you."

Two pink spots suddenly popped out on Rosie's cheeks. "Thank you for your kind offer, Mr. Cornwall, but I'll be attending with my husband. I'm a married woman, you know."

Now it was Jack's turn to flush. "I . . . ah . . . I didn't mean it that way, ma'am. The fact that you're married is the very reason I'm asking you. I was needing a chaperone for the evening."

"A chaperone?" Rosie looked at Caitrin and understanding dawned. "Oh, a *chaperone*."

"I'd like to take Miss Murphy to the service," Jack said, "but I'll need someone to accompany us for the evening."

"All evening?"

"As long as need be, Mrs. Hunter. If you wouldn't mind."

Rosie pursed her lips. "This is dangerous business, Jack Cornwall. And I don't like the notion that my dearest friend could get dragged into any more trouble than she's already in. From the night I first saw the two of you together in the O'Tooles' barn, I knew Caitrin was playing with fire."

"Blazin' Jack Cornwall, that's me. But in case you hadn't noticed, your best friend is mighty fiery herself. She stood up to everyone on my behalf, and that ought to tell you something."

"It tells me you've got her bamboozled."

"I hope she's as bamboozled as you are with Seth Hunter." His smile was warm. "You're right to be concerned, Mrs. Hunter. At one time, I was rough on you and threatening to the man you loved. I was hard and mean and bullheaded. But there's something you ought to know. The good Lord put Caitrin Murphy and me together in the barn that night, and out of that meeting I became a changed man. I turned my back on my old ways, and ever since, I've been living just to love Jesus Christ. That's all I know to do, Mrs. Hunter. Just love him."

Rosie glanced at her friend. "I didn't realize."

"I may be a new man, but I'm still stubborn," Jack continued, "too stubborn to let go of the light Caitrin has been in my life. I won't walk away from Hope just because other people can't see me for what I am. I won't run from trouble. And I won't hide my head in a hole out of shame over my family. I love my sister and my mother both. I want to make a home for them here."

"Yes, Mr. Cornwall," Rosie said softly. "I understand you. I know what it means to need a home."

"Then will you help me?"

"How can I possibly do anything that would help your reputation in this town?"

"Folks admire you. They respect your husband. If you'll stand up beside me, maybe I can walk Caitrin into that prayer meeting and not get myself shot."

"Caitie?" Rosie asked. "Do you want this man to court you in public?"

"Aye. That I do, and very much."

"Well, then—" Rosie squared her shoulders—"I'll be pleased to serve as your chaperone for the prayer meeting Sunday night."

Jack broke into a grin that rivaled the sunrise. "Thank you, Mrs. Hunter," he said, grabbing her hand and pumping it up and down. "Thank you very much. I'll pick you up Sunday evening, then, Caitrin."

"Sunday," Caitrin said.

As the three wagons came to a stop before the mercantile, Jack turned and strode back toward his smithy. Rosie let out a little groan. "Seth Hunter is going to have a fit over this one."

CHAPTER 15

A CHAPERONE?" Sheena lay in bed, her hands folded over her middle, and stared at her younger sister. "Did Rosie really agree to that?"

"Aye," Caitrin said. "Jack Cornwall asked her, and she said she would."

"What do you suppose he wanted a chaperone for?"

Caitrin swallowed. Now was the moment she'd been praying about, yet she didn't feel a bit of peace. If her sister exploded in rage at the news, there was no telling what might result.

"Jack wants a chaperone," she said, "because he intends to start courting. He's planning to go to the prayer meeting with a woman."

"And I suppose that woman would be my own dear sister." Sheena took another sip of the rich broth Caitrin had brought her. "I'm not wrong, am I?"

"No," Caitrin said. "Jack has asked to court me."

"I don't know why he bothered asking permission. The man seems to do whatever he wants without noticing how others might feel about it. He certainly hasn't kept his distance from you."

"And why should he? I care for Jack, Sheena. He's built a fine smithy, and his work is valued in the community. He's hoping to put up a soddy soon. Jack wants to see to the welfare of his sister."

Sheena grunted. "Lunatic. The children are frightened of her, so they are. Lucy Cornwall ought to be locked up."

Caitrin folded her hands in her lap and sat in silence. How could she possibly respond to this irrational hatred? Could God be pleased that his people—the creation of his own hands—despised each other because of race or language or outlook? There were so many things that made people different from each other. Skin color, size, interests, fears, dreams. What made a short person better than a tall one? A white-skinned person better than a brown one? An Irishman better than a Cornishman?

Nothing. Caitrin knew God looked on the heart of each man, and by that, his standing was determined. There were so many things in Hope to take people's time and attention, yet they continued to focus on their petty differences. The only problem large enough to band the community together was the drought.

Caitrin wished it didn't have to take something so serious to turn the focus of Seth, Rolf, Jimmy, and most of the other townsfolk away from the traumatic incident between Sheena and Felicity. While not forgotten, it had been relegated to a back burner as everyone worked to fill barrels with creek water in preparation to irrigate the dry fields. St. Patrick's Day had come and gone, and the Cornwalls remained in their own small camp beside the creek.

Caitrin spoke with Jack briefly at least once a day when he brought tools to the mercantile to sell, but he had kept their conversation to a minimum. This was all right with Caitrin, for until this day she hadn't managed to work up the nerve to tell Sheena and Jimmy that Jack had asked to court her. Or that Rosie had agreed to chaperone.

"What does Seth say about Rosie's part in this grand scheme?" Sheena asked.

Caitrin lifted the broth bowl from her sister's hands. "I don't know yet, but I'm sure he won't mind. Seth has done his best to put the past behind him and see Jack as he really is."

"A Cornishman." Sheena clamped her lips shut as if that settled the matter.

"But he's more than that. Sure, he's a good man."

"A demon. How could he be else with that wicked mother of his?"

"That day in the smithy, Mrs. Cornwall let her anger get the better of her, Sheena. As did you."

"I was provoked."

"I can't understand why it happened at all."

"Cornish. Don't even let your thoughts dwell on those people, Caitie, my love. They're Cornish, and that's all you need to know." Sheena winced. "Oh, my head. At times it throbs so I can hardly bear it."

Caitrin tucked in the edge of the quilt that covered her sister. Poor Sheena. When she moved about much, her head ached or the cramping in her belly started again. She was hardly able to do her chores, and she still had months to wait before the baby's birth. If she were forced to stay in bed all that time, the O'Toole household likely would fall to ruin.

"Papa said the Cornish are all wicked," Sheena said with a sigh. "And wicked is as wicked does."

Caitrin considered this for a moment. "But Jack Cornwall is a Christian man, Sheena. He told me so himself. How can you call him wicked?"

"He's Cornish!"

"Do people always come to you in great batches like pickles, Sheena? These are the dill pickles, and they all taste sour. These are the bread-and-butter pickles, and they all taste sweet. These are the pickled green beans, these are the pickled watermelon rinds, these are the pickled pigs' feet—"

"What are you talking about?"

"People!"

"But you said pickles."

"'Tis the same thing with you, so it is. These are the Cornish people, and they're all wicked schemers and liars. These are the Italians. These are the Germans. These are the lunatics. You've put them into separate pickle jars, and you won't let each person stand on his own."

"Why should I?"

"Because I happen to know that Jack Cornwall is a man with a God-given talent. He can create beautiful tools from iron. He's a loyal son and brother. He's special and unique because he's *himself*."

"Jack Cornwall knocked me down, so he did."

Caitrin let out a hot breath. "He was trying to protect you, Sheena. Will you deny it?"

"Jimmy's furious with him."

"That's because Jimmy puts everybody into pickle jars, too. Jack Cornwall is a wonderful human being. And for all you know, Lucy may be a very nice young lady."

"Ha."

"Even though Lucy is deeply troubled, Christ taught us that he loves all people, not just the ones who behave as we'd like. In fact, the wickedest sinners and the most anguished souls need Christ the greatest. But if we shun them—"

"There you go again, Caitie. You'd change the whole world if you could."

"Aye, and why not?"

"Will you defend Jack Cornwall and his family even though they've treated us so ill?" Sheena elbowed herself up in the bed. "You believe I don't like the man purely because he's Cornish. Well, he's done nothing to prove himself any better than the worst scum of that lot. I cannot understand why you've allowed yourself to be swayed by his sweet words and bold kisses. Sure, I thought my own darling sister wiser than that. Jack Cornwall has tricked you, Caitie. He's nothing but a lying, bullying—"

"I won't hear this, Sheena."

"You will hear it, because someone has to talk truth to you." She paused. "Get the door, will you? It's one of the children. Tell them to run and play with Chipper."

Feeling hotter than the late-March afternoon would warrant, Caitrin marched to the door. "I don't believe people are pickles," she told her sister. "I think each person stands on his own, and each person should have the right to prove himself. Rosie said if you glue a label onto a jar of grubby tomatoes, you'll never be able to put strawberry jam into it."

"Wait a minute, I thought we were talking about pickles."

"We *are*, but . . ." Caitrin pulled open the door to the sight of Jack and Lucy Cornwall.

"Who is it?" Sheena called.

"Pickles," Caitrin said, ushering them inside. "Mr. Cornwall is here, and his sister Lucy. It looks as though they've brought a gift."

"It's cinnamon buns," Lucy said. She was holding a basket with her unchained hands, and her hair had been brushed into a rough knot at the nape of her neck. "I made them for you, Mrs. O'Toole. Jack told me you weren't well, and he helped me last night with the dough. I . . . I hope you'll like them."

Caitrin met Jack's eyes as Lucy walked shyly toward the bed. He shrugged. "Lucy's had three good days in a row," he said. "Matter of fact, she's been looking after Mama a fair bit."

"I'm happy to hear it." Caitrin was delighted to see the young woman calmly set the basket on the bed and then take the stool beside Sheena. She wore the blue dress Caitrin had given her, its hem now dusty and its sleeves frayed. But she looked lovely all the same.

"Mama tells me if I'll just stop thinking about myself all the time," Lucy said softly to Sheena, "I'll get better. I'm not sure she's right, Mrs. O'Toole. It's others who fill my thoughts, memories and worries going around . . . and around. And . . . and . . . all Mama and Jack could talk about was you and . . . and your baby . . ."

Lucy shuddered and fell silent. Caitrin glanced at Jack. He started toward his sister. At that moment Lucy spoke again.

"I . . . I just thought if I could help you out, Mrs. O'Toole," she said. "I might feel better . . . and you might, too."

Sheena stared at the young woman beside her. "You baked cinnamon buns for me?"

Lucy nodded. "Jack helped."

"Not much," he put in.

"And then I got to thinking," Lucy said, "if you need some . . . some washing done, I can do that. And I'm good with a broom."

"Glory be," Sheena murmured. She sat in silence so long, Caitrin began to think she'd gone into shock. Finally a look of resignation crept over her face. "Well, there's the broom then, girl. See what you can do with it."

Lucy leapt to her feet and grabbed the broom propped against the wall. "Do eat one of those buns, Mrs. O'Toole. I used extra cinnamon."

While Lucy swept the rough dirt floor, Caitrin took her place on the stool and divided one of the sticky buns with her sister. One hand jammed in his pocket, Jack accepted another bun. All three watched, mesmerized, chewing slowly as Lucy worked her way around the soddy brushing up a pile that included bread crusts, potato peelings, ashes, and wood chips.

"Sure has been dry lately," Jack said. "This drought is about to get the best of everybody. Didn't have much snow, and we could use some rain."

Sheena looked startled, as if she hadn't expected the man to speak in normal human tones. "Aye," she commented. "Jimmy says this is the driest spring he can remember."

"Dry, dry, dry," Jack said. "And not a cloud in the sky."

"Have we had a rain yet this year?"

"Not a drop."

Caitrin sank her teeth into a cinnamon bun. It wasn't much of a conversation, but at least they were talking. She wouldn't have interrupted if she'd been paid.

"Bluestem Creek is running mighty low," Jack said.

"Jimmy heard someone saying the Kansas River itself is down," Sheena added.

"Sure is hard for the boats to get through when the water is low like that."

"Aye. I expect we'll have showers in April."

"Hope so. I sure do." Jack licked a dollop of cinnamon goo off his thumb. "I'm not a farmer, but I know the rain keeps folks around here going. I'd hate to see anyone go belly-up."

"Thank heaven for the bridge tolls. They saved us last year after the grasshoppers passed through, so they did."

"Well, I'm finished with that job," Lucy said, coming back into the soddy after tossing out the rubbish she'd swept. "Would you like me to wash those dishes for you, Mrs. O'Toole?"

Caitrin watched a smile form on her sister's lips—a warm smile, a smile reserved for people Sheena favored. She smoothed a hand across the quilt. "Not today, but thank you kindly, my dear," she said. "Perhaps . . . perhaps you'll pop round and visit me another time?"

Lucy beamed. "Yes."

"Would you be willing to bake some of your cinnamon buns for us to sell in the mercantile, Lucy?" Caitrin asked. "I haven't had time to start up the restaurant, but more and more people are stopping to take their meals at the mercantile. 'Tis the fresh-baked bread and Sheena's pickles that draw them. But I know they'd adore your cinnamon buns. You could have all the money you earned from them."

"Really?" Her gray eyes lit up. "Oh, Jack, I . . . I . . ."

"Sure, Lucy. You could do that." He squared his shoulders. "And about that spit, Mrs. O'Toole. I made you a new one. We hope you'll accept it as a gift."

He stepped outside and reentered carrying a heavy spit rod with a sharpened skewer bolted near one end. He laid it across the hooks over Sheena's cooking fire and gave the handle a turn. The shiny metal glistened as it spun, and Caitrin could all but hear the sizzle of meat.

"Thank you, Mr. Cornwall," Sheena said in a low voice. "'Twas good of you."

"You're welcome, ma'am." He straightened and took his sister's hand. "We'll be going now."

"Good-bye," Lucy called as he led her out of the soddy. "Good-bye, Mrs. O'Toole."

The door shut behind them, and Caitrin felt her shoulders sag with relief. Sheena picked up another cinnamon bun. "These are quite tasty," she said. "Lucy should do well with them at the mercantile."

"She's a sweet girl."

"I suppose so." Sheena licked her lips. "Of course, you and I both know they did all that just to soften my heart so that Jack Cornwall could court you."

"Lucy said she was worried about your baby."

"So she did. I don't suppose she has the wits about her to lie."

"I believe she does care about your welfare."

"And he hopes to court you."

"He does, Sheena. I've said I'll go with him to the prayer meeting."

Sheena stopped chewing. "Caitie, my love. You mustn't go out in public with the Cornish."

"Pickles, Sheena," Caitrin said.

"At least take Jimmy with you."

"Jimmy needs to look out for you. Rosie will act as chaperone, and that means Seth will join us."

"Honestly, Caitrin—"

"I might just wear my green dress for Jack Cornwall."

"Oh, Caitie!"

"Pickles, Sheena," Caitrin warned again.

"I don't care if he did make me a new spit," she cried. "That man is a dill if ever there was one!"

>—

"We could color the eggs, Seth," Rosie was saying as Caitrin stepped out of her soddy into the evening. "Oh, hello, Caitie! We could paint them blue, pink, green, yellow—"

"Green eggs?" Seth asked. "Evening, Miss Murphy."

Caitrin walked toward Jack, who stood to the side, his hat in his hand. Glory be, but the man was a vision. Black coat, white shirt, a string tie at his neck, denim jeans, and a pair of boots . . . he wore clothing no more elegant than Seth's hand-sewn jacket, but a thrill ran up Caitrin's spine at the sight of him.

"Miss Murphy," he said. Thick and soft, his brown hair tumbled over his forehead as he gave her a little bow. "Good evening. You look lovely tonight."

Flushing with delight, Caitrin shook out the folds of her deep green skirt. "Papa bought this fabric for my sixteenth birthday, and Mama stitched it into a gown. This dress takes me all the way to the emerald sod of Ireland, so it does."

"What would it take to bring you back to the dry prairie of Kansas?" Jack asked, taking her hand and slipping it around the curve of his arm. As they followed Rosie and Seth down the narrow path toward the traveling camp, he whispered against her ear, "Would this do it?"

Bending over, he brushed a kiss on her cheek.

"Aye," Caitrin said, breathless. "I do believe I'm back."

"And cookies in the shape of rabbits," Rosie continued. "We could sprinkle sugar on top."

"I never have been crazy about rabbits," Seth mused. "If they get into your garden, that's the end of the lettuce, the beans, the carrots—you name it."

"I'm talking about rabbit *cookies*," Rosie protested. "It's for the spring celebration. Each child could eat a cookie after the hunt for the colored eggs."

"Green eggs," Seth repeated, his voice less than buoyant. "Somehow that doesn't sound too appetizing to me."

"Just the shells would be green, silly. Hard-boiled eggs with colored shells. Have you been listening to me at all, Seth Hunter?"

"Well—" he scratched the back of his neck—"I got sidetracked back when you started talking about those confounded rabbits."

Caitrin could hardly believe she was actually going to the prayer meeting with Jack Cornwall. Rosie had said she'd been all but tongue-tied when she started to speak to Seth about the notion of chaperoning. As it turned out, Seth already had made up his mind to see if he could get the Cornwalls over to the meeting. He thought a time of united prayer with the rest of the townsfolk might heal some of the trouble.

When Seth permitted Chipper to spend the evening with his Gram at the Cornwalls' camp down on Bluestem Creek, Caitrin all but smelled victory. God had somehow begun to heal some of the terrible rifts among the people in the little town. It was a miracle! Lucy was feeling well enough again to bake cinnamon buns. Sheena had not lost her baby after all, and she genuinely appreciated Lucy's offer of help. Chipper finally had been allowed to spend time with his beloved grandmother. And Seth had agreed to this outing with Jack. Caitrin's heart fairly sang.

"Tonight I'm going to ask Seth for permission to build a soddy," Jack told Caitrin in a low voice as they followed the Hunters. "I'll put it up next to the smithy. That way I'll be near Lucy in case she needs me."

"I think he'll agree to it."

"Mama's not keen on the idea. Ever since the trouble with Mrs. O'Toole, she won't even set foot outside our camp."

"I noticed she hadn't been up to the mercantile."

"She blames herself for the near loss of that baby, but she's turned her anger outward. Says everyone in Hope is dead set against us. Lucy bears the brunt of her temper, but I take my fair share, too. Mama's still talking to me about leaving."

"But you've just put up the forge."

"She doesn't feel welcome here. She reckons folks treat her worse than an old stray dog."

Caitrin could see the prayer meeting area clearly now. A wagon had been pulled over near the creek, and lanterns were hung on strings stretched from one tree to another. People were already gathering in the shadows. She knew her conversation with Jack would have to end in moments, and she could hardly bear it. This was the first time they'd been able to talk freely, man to woman, and with hardly a spark of tension between them.

"I don't like to think of you going away," she said. "I've been praying for the troubles here to end, but my thoughts keep turning to that dreadful Bill Hermann and his quest to take you back to the trial in Missouri."

Jack shook his head. "I won't go."

"How can you avoid it if he brings a subpoena?"

"There's nothing to pin on me." He slowed his steps. "Listen, Caitrin, don't tell folks about Bill Hermann and the Easton lynching, okay? That's my business."

"All right, Jack. Whatever you say."

They had stopped walking, and he was looking at her with those depthless gray eyes. She could hardly breathe as she gazed up at the man. The breeze toyed with the ends of his black string tie and feathered his thick hair. Lantern light gilded his high cheekbones. Moonlight silvered the bridge of his nose. Standing so close she could feel the heat of the forge still radiating from his skin, Caitrin prayed she would have the grace to behave like a lady this night.

The strongest urge poured through her veins to grab Jack's hand and race across the prairie grass until they came to a place that was completely free of strife. Completely silent. Completely alone. And there she would speak to him her every thought, listen to the music of his deep voice, and dance with him unattended by any but the cleansing wind and the presence of God himself.

"Do you want me to build a soddy here, Caitrin?" he asked, lifting a hand to her hair. "I'm asking you again. Do you want me to stay in Hope?"

She pressed her lips against his sleeve. "Aye," she said. "I do."

"I've always spoken what's on my mind, Caitrin. You've known that from the start."

"'Tis one reason I care for you as I do."

"Well, here's what I've been thinking. If I can get that soddy built, and if Lucy keeps on feeling good, and if the O'Tooles can come around to accepting us, and if Seth—"

"Are you two coming?" Rosie called. Turned sideways against the light, her silhouette clearly revealed the swell of the child within her. "Caitie, will you please explain to Seth about this spring party we're going to put on? He hasn't heard a word I've said past green eggs and rabbits. Oh, look at the crowd around the wagon! Is Rolf going to do all the preaching? I hope he's been practicing on some new subjects. I've about had my fill of *veeds*."

"Sure, he was speaking the word of the Lord that Sunday, Rosie." Caitrin walked beside Jack toward the wagon. "'Twas a message we all needed to hear."

"The weeds have grown up mighty high in town," Jack said. "Let's hope they don't try to choke us tonight."

"We'll be all right." The tension in Seth's voice belied his words. "You said Sheena's aware of this arrangement, didn't you, Miss Murphy?"

Caitrin nodded. "I've told my sister, but I'm not sure Jimmy knows."

"The Lord wants us to place ourselves in his trustworthy hands and rely on him for whatever lies ahead," Jack said. "The purpose of this meeting is to pray for rain, and I suspect Jimmy will honor that."

"Look, the O'Tooles are coming across the bridge, Caitie," Rosie said. "Is Sheena fit enough to walk?"

"A bit." Caitrin slipped her hand through the crook of Jack's arm again. "Jimmy's helping her. I don't think he's seen us."

The two couples spread a quilt near the brightly lit wagon. The crowd began to quiet, individuals taking their places on blankets and wooden chairs as Rolf Rustemeyer climbed up onto a platform erected on the wagon's bed. For a moment the big blond German didn't speak, instead holding up a Bible before the congregation.

"This is Word of Gott!" he cried out suddenly.

The crowd gasped.

"Gott says where two or three manners comen togedder in his name," Rolf continued, "there he is among them! Now, how many comen togedder tonight? Fifteen? Twenty? *Ja*, Gott is here tonight vit us!"

Jack gave a grunt as he sat down. "I reckon we might ought to hire ol' Rustemeyer for the preacher's job."

Seth and Rosie joined them as they settled on the quilt. "Rolf is a farmer," Rosie said. "He'll never be a preacher, but he certainly loves the Lord."

"Now is springtime," Rolf went on. "Gott gif us goot dirt, goot seed, goot plow, goot mule."

"And lots of *veeds*," Rosie murmured.

Caitrin tried to suppress a giggle. Relaxing a little, she realized this might turn out all right after all. Though she could see the O'Toole family seating themselves not far from their own party, they had given no evidence of the hostility everyone feared.

"Now need only one thing from Gott," Rolf said. "Vater!"

"*Vater*," Rosie whispered and nudged Caitrin, who bit her lip to keep from laughing out loud. She felt like a schoolgirl, silly and lighthearted for the first time in many months. Here she was with a handsome beau, a precious friend, and a wonderful town in which to live. God was indeed here among them, and rather than giggling at dear Rolf, who was doing his best, she ought to start singing the Lord's praises.

Rolf held the Bible high. "Time to pray for rain. Gott listen to us pray. Everybody pray for vater to come."

"That reminds me," Rosie whispered, turning to Jack. "There was a fellow in the mercantile this morning asking if I could sell him a new water canteen. He said he'd been on the road for months and was headed back to Missouri without laying eyes on what he'd been after. When he told me he'd been looking all over Kansas for *you*, I could hardly believe it! I said, glory be, Jack Cornwall works right across the street in the town smithy. You should have seen his face."

The muscle in Jack's arm went as rigid as steel. "Did you get the man's name?"

"Herman somebody," Rosie said. Then she frowned. "No, that wasn't quite it."

"Bill Hermann," Jack said.

"That's it! But instead of stopping by the smithy, he took off right away on his horse, headed for Topeka. Bill Hermann is an old friend of yours, isn't he?"

Jack swallowed. "You might say that," he said. "Or you might not."

CHAPTER 16

JACK felt his blood boil up inside his chest. So Bill Hermann had found him. No doubt the snake was now on his way to Topeka to fetch the law. By now he probably held papers of some kind, a warrant or a subpoena ordering Jack Cornwall back to Missouri to testify in the trial of his former gang members accused in the Easton lynching. The only way he could testify was to swear he was at the cabin the night of the murder—and implicate himself in the crime.

"Are you all right, Jack?" Caitrin asked.

He studied the fiery tumble of her hair and the sincere concern in her green eyes. "I'm not leaving," he said. "I told you I'd stay here, and I'm a man of my word."

"Can Bill Hermann make you go?"

"*Nothing* can make me go."

Jack felt like a wild dog on a chain. The links in the chain that bridled him—his newfound walk in Christ, his desire to make a peaceful life, his growing bond with Caitrin, his responsibility to Lucy and his mother—were strained to the limit. Could such a chain hold against the forces that pulled at him?

Jack clenched a fist. He'd like nothing better than to knock Bill Hermann's teeth right out the back side of his head. And as for the other members of the bunch, well, they could rot in prison for all he cared. All their idealistic talk about keeping the peace, bringing vigilante justice, and restoring the glory of the South hadn't done any of them a lick of good. In fact, they had all walked on the wrong side of the law about as often as their Yankee enemies.

It had been the most futile, empty time in Jack's life, and he was thankful it had ended without too much bloodshed and loss of life. Now he had given all he had to Christ, turned his back on the past, and was doing his best to be pure and blameless. He was done with the men he'd once called friends. They'd better not try to drag him back into their midst. He knew it was right to turn the other cheek, but he found living peaceably the hardest thing about being a Christian. If his old pals tried to pull him into their troubles, he had a bad feeling he'd jump right into the middle of them and make them remember why they'd valued his fists and gun.

"Now, manners and ladies," Rolf was saying, "who vill start the praying? Somebody comen up here onto vagon and pray, *ja?*"

The crowd murmured, and someone called out, "You pray, Rustemeyer. This meetin' was your idea."

"Okay, I am starting, but I not practice this part so much," Rolf said. He bowed his shaggy blond head. "Dear Gott, for goot land and goot peoples here, I say tank you. I say alleluia. For Jesus Christ love us and gif his life on cross for us, I say tank you. My heart is full to top vit happy for all you gif us, dear Gott. But one thing needed only, and that is rain. Please send rain here to Kansas so crops can grow. In name of Jesus, I pray this. Amen."

When Jack lifted his head, he saw that Seth was already climbing onto the wagon. "Dear God," the gentle farmer prayed, "you've given us so much, it seems a little prideful of us to come begging for more. I want to praise your name for the gift of my family. Little Chipper and the new baby we're expecting are precious to me. And Rosie . . ." Seth was silent a moment. When he spoke again, his voice was strained with emotion. "Lord, I thank you for my wife. Thank you for Rosie."

Jack swallowed and took Caitrin's hand. In the past, he hadn't given marriage much consideration, but the beautiful Irishwoman sure managed to slip into his thoughts about two hundred times a day. Jack knew he didn't have the right to a happy home, as many times as he and the bunch had stepped in and messed up the peace of others. But if the good Lord ever saw fit to forgive him enough to let him marry, Jack would do everything in his power to honor and respect his wife.

"Lord," Seth went on once he'd composed himself, "I sure don't like to think about anything bad happening to Rosie and our young'uns. So right here and now, I'm stepping up to ask you for rain. We need it bad, and we're counting on you to send it. Amen."

Seth moved to the side of the stage as Jimmy O'Toole stepped up onto the wagon. Jack had never thought of Jimmy as a religious man. The Irishman had resisted any plan to build the new church on his land, and he often was absent from the worship services held each Sunday morning in the mercantile. His green eyes sparkled as he took his place at the front of the stage. When he began to speak, his voice was filled with passion.

"I've not come up here to pray for rain," he said, "because I think rain has more to do with clouds and wind than with the Almighty. If he wants rain to fall, sure, there's naught we can do to stop it. And if there's goin' to be a drought, well then, all the prayin' in the world won't change that. But there is a matter we can change, and that's the presence of troublemakers among us."

"Jimmy," Seth called in a clearly audible whisper, "we're here to pray."

"I'll not stand about prayin' when my own wife and family are in danger from the Cornish ne'er-do-wells who've invaded our peace."

Jack took a deep breath and tried to calm himself as every eye in the gathering focused on him. Beside him, Caitrin went as still and cold as a stone. Rosie began fanning herself with a hand-kerchief.

"I say we run the vermin out of town!" Jimmy cried out. "The woman of the Cornwall family abused my wife and nearly robbed me of my own unborn child. She's a witch, so she is, a Cornish witch. She conked our Sheena in the head with a poker, and her son—right over there—threw the poor woman to the ground. Sure, the Cornwalls would have killed Sheena if they could!"

"Jimmy." Seth took a step toward the Irishman and laid a hand on his arm. "I said, this is a time for prayer. We'll handle the matter of the Cornwalls later on."

"Nay, we'll handle it now! I won't stand for another day of livin' in the same town with them Cornish devils. You've seen the daughter yourself, Seth, and she's a madwoman sure as I live and breathe. She's tried to drown herself in the creek, and she threw herself in front of the stagecoach. She's a danger, a blazin' danger, I say!"

Caitrin squeezed Jack's hand. "I'm so sorry," she whispered. "I had no idea Jimmy would do something like this."

"He'd better stop talking about Lucy," he growled, the blood racing in his veins. "I don't like it."

"That Cornish madwoman is going to hurt one of us," Jimmy continued, heedless of Seth's attempts to move him from the stage. "She's got a demon in her, so she does."

"That's enough, O'Toole!" Jack shouted, coming to his feet. "Get off the wagon before I throw you off."

"No, Jack," Caitrin croaked, tears squeezing from her eyes. "Please calm yourself!"

"I'll not get off the wagon until I've had my say, Cornish!" Jimmy cried. "'Tis you I'm talkin' about. 'Tis your mother has tried to kill our Sheena. 'Twas you yourself who knocked her to the ground and near cast the child from her belly. Now look at you there with our Caitrin!"

Jack glared as the man's face grew red. The crowd's murmuring intensified, and their rumblings of discontent filled the night air.

All around him, people were staring and muttering snatches of affirmation for Jimmy O'Toole's tirade. Jack didn't care if this was a prayer meeting and God himself stood among them, he wouldn't tolerate anyone talking poorly of his family. Felicity Cornwall was his mother, and Lucy was his sister . . . and he'd fight to the death before he'd let harm come to either of them.

"You've bewitched our Caitrin," the Irishman growled, "and now you're tryin' to work your evil on Seth and Rosie Hunter." He faced the crowd. "Let me tell you people about the Cornish. They're liars and cheaters and thieves, all of 'em. You saw how Jack Cornwall tried to steal Chipper right away from his own papa, didn't you?"

"Hold on, there, O'Toole!" Jack shouted, unable to contain his growing fury. "Get off the wagon!"

"Nay, I'll speak my mind to these good folk. Jack Cornwall frightened the ladies and smashed our parties into smithereens! He stole Seth's rifle right off his wall. He trespassed on my land, fed my good oats to his devil of a black horse, slept in my barn, and wooed my own wife's sister for his evil purposes."

"You leave Caitrin out of this!" Jack said, pulling away from her and heading for the wagon. "I've never done a thing to hurt that woman."

"Harmin' women is his favorite pastime," Jimmy told the crowd. "You can see my poor *donsie* wife there with her head in a bandage and her feet barely able to walk from the injuries of that Cornishman, can't you? And there's no tellin' what wickedness the man has done to his own sister. You've seen the lunatic driftin' in the creek in the middle of winter, tryin' to end her own life. You've seen her shriekin' and carryin' on at the dance when Rustemeyer kindly offered her a piece o' cake, haven't you? Aye, you've seen the demon that lives with her, and his name is Jack Cornwall!"

"Stop slandering my sister!" Jack roared, leaping up onto the stage. So much for peace and purity. He grabbed Jimmy O'Toole by the collar, took hold of the backside of his britches, gave a big heave-ho, and tossed the Irishman off the wagon.

The crowd's shock turned quickly to fury. With a howl of rage, men stormed onto the platform. The first one landed Jack a glancing blow to the jaw. The second hit him square in the stomach.

Anger poured through Jack's veins. With the strength of every muscle that had ever forged iron, he threw himself into the fray. Though he could hear Seth shouting at him to run, he slammed a fellow straight in the nose and felt the crunch of snapping cartilage. He knocked another man clear across the stage. He caught one attacker on the cheekbone, and he drove a fist into another's gut.

Somebody smashed a heavy black Bible over Jack's head. The world swam for a moment as his legs buckled. Another fellow rammed his fist into Jack's eye. Yet another man's chop to the stomach knocked him to his knees.

Coughing and spitting out blood, Jack lunged upward again, throwing a forearm into an assailant's chest and knocking him flat. Maybe he was a goner, Jack thought, but he wouldn't go down easy. Screams and shouts rang in his ears as he fought his way across the platform. He elbowed somebody out of his way and dodged a fist directed at his nose. A man shoved him from behind. He stumbled forward as a gun went off.

Searing, blinding pain tore into the back of his leg. He tumbled to the ground. A blow landed on his jaw, another on his temple. Someone kicked him in the stomach. He gasped twice, unable to breathe. And this time, the stars went out.

>-

"Let me go, Rosie!" Caitrin cried, trying to pull out of the woman's grasp. "Sure, they'll tear Jack to bits!"

"You can't go over there, Caitrin!" Rosie said. "Look, here's Seth."

Her husband raced up to the women, took them by the arms, and hauled them away from the meeting ground. "Come on, you two, let's get out of here."

"But I heard a gun, Seth." Caitrin strained toward the wagon. "I'm sure I did! What if Jack needs help? He's in terrible trouble!"

"Jack Cornwall makes his own trouble."

"This wasn't his fault! Jimmy provoked him." Caitrin struggled as Seth dragged her and Rosie up the road toward the mercantile. *Oh, God, dear God! Please help Jack! Help me! Help us all.*

"Look, there's Mrs. Cornwall coming out of one of the Cornwall tents!" Rosie said. "Seth, you must tell her what's happened."

"She shouldn't get messed up in that craziness," Seth barked. "She's liable to get herself killed."

"Mrs. Cornwall!" Caitrin cried, heedless of Seth's admonition.

"Miss Murphy?" she responded. "That was a short prayer meeting. I was just fetching Chipper a blanket from the other tent."

"Oh, Mrs. Cornwall, you must go after Jack," Caitrin said. "There's been a terrible fight. Sure, we've heard a gunshot."

"Gunshot!" Felicity glanced in the direction of the wagon and wrung her hands. "But I can't leave Chipper. And then there's Lucy! She's not doing well tonight. All day she's been dwelling on those Yankee soldiers and . . . and the things they did to her. She's troubled. Very troubled. I thought I might even need to fetch Jack back from the prayer meeting. Oh, heaven, what have those wicked O'Tooles done to my son? I told him I wouldn't have him marrying into that family, no matter how much he thinks he loves you. Now they've shot my boy, and I can't leave Lucy at a time like this!"

Breathing hard, Caitrin stared at Felicity Cornwall. What was the woman saying? Yankee soldiers had harmed Lucy . . . and Jack loved Caitrin. . . .

"Papa! Mama!" Chipper dashed out of one of the Cornwalls' tents and threw his arms around Rosie's skirt. "Aunt Lucy's scrubbin' herself raw in there!"

"Goodness gracious," Rosie said, kneeling and tucking the child into a warm hug. "How about if we head home and find you an oatmeal cookie and some fresh milk? Then you can tell your mama all about it, sweetie."

"You'd better stay here with Lucy," Seth told Mrs. Cornwall. "I'm going to take Miss Murphy to her house, and then I'll make sure my wife and son get home safe. If I know Rolf Rustemeyer at all, he'll be trying to settle the crowd and help out your son. Maybe by the time I get back to the wagon things will have calmed down enough that we can pull Jack away without getting ourselves killed in the process."

"Yes, Mr. Hunter," Felicity said. "Please help us!"

"What about Lucy?" Caitrin called, as Seth tugged her down the road toward her soddy. "Can I do anything?"

"She's scrubbing herself, Miss Murphy," Felicity answered, staring ahead hopelessly. "She gets to scrubbing sometimes . . . uses sandpaper and a horsehair brush . . . and nearly takes her own skin off."

"Dear God!" Caitrin whispered. "Help us all!"

Caitrin was on her knees beside her bed when a knock fell on the door. Her heart contracted, and she squeezed her hands together. *Please, Father, let Jack be all right! Oh, Lord, bring something good out of this terrible mess! Give us some reason to hope!*

"Caitrin Murphy? You in there?"

It was Jimmy O'Toole.

"I'm here," she said. "Just a moment."

She stood and hurried to the soddy door. After lifting the bar, she threw open the door on its leather hinges. Her brother-in-law stood outside as a huddled, blanket-shrouded figure cowered behind him.

"Is that Jack?" she whispered.

"Nay," Jimmy said. "Your not-so-secret beau is over at the mercantile getting the lead cut out of his leg by Seth Hunter. This here's your sister, who's so beside herself I daren't take her home to the *brablins*. Sheena's been weepin' like a blasted fountain, and I can't make her talk to me. Take her, if you will, Caitrin. She's mortal scared, so she is, and I know you'll have the words to comfort her."

"Sheena!" Caitrin clasped the woman in her arms and led her to a chair. "Are you all right? Is your baby well?"

The blanket fell back, and Sheena looked up, her great green eyes swimming with tears. Her red hair was topsy-turvy on her head, and her apron had fallen right off her dress. She sniffled and hugged herself around the middle.

"Sure, I'm well enough," she whispered. "But I can't stay here. I need to look after the wee ones."

"Nay, you won't," Jimmy barked. "You'll stay here with your sister until I've settled them into bed and all of us have had a good night's sleep."

"Oh, Jimmy, let Sheena go home," Caitrin said.

"And frighten the *brablins* with her weepin'?" Jimmy shook his head. "If there ever was a man put upon, 'tis me, I'll tell you that much. Them Cornish is the root of all the trouble. My poor Sheena's laid up thanks to that devil woman, Felicity Cornwall. And now we've had a row the size of which would flatten Topeka. Men runnin' this way and that. Ladies shriekin'. Cornwall himself is shot, and several others has lost teeth, broke noses, and got their jaws knocked outta joint. Leave it to a Cornishman to start up a fray like that one."

"Jack didn't start the trouble—"

"I ain't finished yet," Jimmy said, taking a step toward Caitrin. "I was on my way over to your soddy with my poor wife there, when who should come runnin' out of the Cornwall camp but that lunatic lass. She was naked as a frog and all scratched up and bleedin'. And after her came her own mother, chasin' her across the prairie. Now, I don't know what to make of *that*, Caitrin, but what they're both of them mad as hatters."

"I can explain, Jimmy."

"You'll explain it to the fairies, so you will. I'll not listen to your bold tongue nor be swayed by your stubborn ways. I'm not like Sheena, ready to overlook the sins of a blood relative. Sure *you*, Caitrin Murphy, have caused every bit as much trouble as them Cornish!"

"I have not!"

"Aye, you have. All I wanted in comin' to this land was a bit o' peace and quiet. I built my soddy and plowed my fields. I planned to take care of my *brablins* and my wee wife and give us all a good life. But glory be, now we've a mercantile and a post office and a church and a smithy and a confounded prayer meetin'. We've lunatics and lechers and poker-wieldin' grannies about. We've more people crossin' that blasted bridge in one day than I ever wanted to see in a lifetime. And you, my dear lass, have been nearly the death of your own sister—consortin' with Cornishmen and takin' lunatics into your own home. Well, I'll tell you this. I've had enough of it, so I have. I'm tellin' you now, as I've already told Sheena—you're goin' back to Ireland, lassie. The first stagecoach east tomorrow, you're on it. And good riddance to bad rummage."

Caitrin clenched her jaw, willing herself not to erupt. *Please, God give me the strength, the patience, the courage . . .*

"Out!" she shouted, her faith utterly failing her. "Get out of my soddy, Jimmy O'Toole, and don't come back until you've had the good grace to apologize."

"When hell freezes over," he snarled. "Until then, I'll leave you to look after my wife as a good sister should. 'Tis high time you chose whose family you belong to—us or the Cornwalls. And if you decide to join the dregs, Caitrin Murphy, that's exactly what you'll be."

Hair flaming red in the lamplight, Jimmy turned and stomped out of the soddy. He slammed the door behind him. One of the leather hinges snapped loose from the frame. The door swayed, tipped, and crashed to the ground in a pile of loose boards.

"I want to go home," Sheena said in a wavering voice.

Caitrin swung around to find her sister pulling her blanket up around her shoulders and standing to leave. "Wait," Caitrin said, holding out a hand. "Please don't mind Jimmy. He's worried about you, and he's hot about the Cornish. I've been praying for God to soften his heart, and praying that I can rein my tongue. But so far, I fear we've both a bit more surrendering to do."

A tear trickled from one of Sheena's green eyes. "Jimmy frightened me tonight, Caitie. I've never seen him so angry. Sure, he wasn't himself."

"Nay." Caitrin strode across the room and grasped her sister's hands. "Oh, Sheena, I never meant such trouble to come to Hope. My heart is bursting in two. How can I choose between my dear family and the man I love? You and Jimmy are all I have, so you are. I'll love you always. But Jack Cornwall . . . dear Sheena, he's a man like none other I've known."

"My poor Caitie." Sheena rubbed a hand under her damp eyes. "I . . . I don't know what to say."

"Say you'll stay with me this night. Sure, you've had a rough time of it, and you can use the rest. We'll hang a blanket over the door."

"Jimmy's furious with me, Caitie! After the fighting settled, I told him he was wrong to speak out against the Cornish at the town prayer meeting. I shouldn't have gone against him. I should have . . . should have honored my husband." Sheena bent over, sobbing. "I don't know what to do. I can't go on like this!"

"There now," Caitrin said softly, placing an arm around the woman's heaving shoulders. "A good cry is just the thing. I'm ready to join you myself, so I am. Never have I known such flames of hatred and fear and confusion in my life."

"Oh, Caitie, don't let's sit here and weep. Put the kettle on and make us a pot of tea."

Caitrin sniffled. "Aye, warm milk and a sugar will turn it that lovely caramel color and settle our nerves. As our dear mother used to say, there's nothing like a cup of hot tea for comfort."

Trembling, she headed for the fire. She had prepared the kettle earlier, hoping the two couples would take a moment after the prayer meeting to sit together and visit. How wonderful everything had seemed then. She had held great hopes that Seth and Jack would speak comfortably with each other, and then perhaps they could grow as true friends.

Was Jack all right? What if the bullet in his leg had done some terrible damage? Caitrin hung the kettle on the hook and stirred the fire. She couldn't leave Sheena alone to go and check on Jack. What if her sister's cramping started up again? But how could Caitrin bear to spend the night not knowing how Jack was? She ached to be near him, to hold and comfort him. And then there was Lucy . . .

The girl herself ran through the open doorway and into Caitrin's soddy. "I can't . . . I'm . . . I . . ."

"Lucy!" Felicity Cornwall was right behind her. "You'll be the death of me, girl!"

Caitrin gaped at the young woman. Lucy's flesh was raw and bleeding, and her hair hung in shaggy clumps. Coming to her senses, Caitrin grabbed a quilt from the bed and threw it over Lucy's shoulders. The girl shuddered and collapsed in a heap.

"Lucy!" Caitrin crouched beside her. "Lucy, 'tis Caitrin Murphy here. I'm going to hold you now. You'll be all right."

As she pulled the shivering woman into her arms, Felicity stood panting. "She was scrubbing herself with sandpaper, like I said," she told Caitrin between breaths, "and then she jumped up and ran off. I've been chasing her across the prairie for I don't know how long. She's right out of her head tonight. I never saw the poor child so bad!"

At that, Felicity sank down onto a stool and burst into tears.

"Now just calm down, Mrs. Cornwall." Caitrin tucked Lucy into the cradle of her lap, praying that God would settle the raving madness inside the young woman. "Lucy's going to be all right. She can stay here with me tonight. Sheena and I are just ready to have tea, and we'll welcome Lucy to join us."

Felicity glanced over at the chair where the Irishwoman sat. "Mrs. O'Toole," she said, and then she sobbed helplessly for a moment. "I'm so sorry! So . . . so sorry. I didn't mean to harm you that day, and . . . and your baby . . ."

"Nay, Mrs. Cornwall," Sheena whispered, blotting her own eyes. "'Twas I who came at you . . ."

"I struck you."

"I called you such vile things."

"Oh, whatever shall we do?"

"Mrs. Cornwall," Caitrin said, "I want you to go over to the mercantile and check on Jack. Please see that he's all right, and then come back and give me the news. If he needs me, I'll go to him at once. After that, you must make your way back to your camp and try to rest."

"Yes," Felicity said, dabbing a handkerchief on her cheeks. "I'll do that very thing."

As the older woman left, Caitrin held Lucy tightly and began to rock her. In a moment Sheena joined them on the floor. The three women slipped their arms around each other, and Caitrin thought of the despair and hopelessness that threatened. What hope of peace did any of them have?

And then she remembered. "The Lord is my rock and my salvation," she whispered. "Whom then shall I fear?"

Caitrin woke well past dawn the next morning. The blanket she had hung over the front door had fallen down in the night. Sunlight lit a golden rectangle on the bare earthen floor. Lucy lay nestled against Caitrin's left side, her sleep troubled and restless. Sheena slept soundly on the right. Caitrin stared up at the rough plank ceiling topped by blocks of heavy sod and thought of the time she had thrown a plate against the wall in frustration. As she recalled it, she'd been angry about grass roots burrowing into the house.

She hadn't known what trouble was.

Dear God, please protect Jack, she lifted up in silence. Felicity Cornwall had returned under cover of night to report that Seth had cut out the bullet, the wound looked clean, and her son was resting. Caitrin tried to feel relieved. *Father, what am I to do about that man? Why did you bring him into my life? I can't deny the stirrings of my heart for him. Jack is . . . he's so . . . what? He's interesting. He's dreadfully handsome. He's kind to children and to poor Lucy. He's intelligent. He's determined and hardworking. He loves you, Father, the best he can. But, Lord, he isn't altogether tame.*

She looked at Lucy lying beside her. Lucy wasn't tame, but God loved her all the same. She was his child. And Sheena? Caitrin turned her head to study her dear sister. Certainly she wasn't perfect, yet it appeared she was willing to leave past troubles with the Cornwalls behind.

Caitrin's thoughts again turned to the shattered plate. She herself was far from docile. She had a fiery temper. She argued vehemently. She stood up against her brother-in-law. Jack once had referred to her as stubborn and mouthy. Imperfect. Yet, God loved her, accepted her, gave his life for her. And his Spirit willingly lived in her heart.

Sheena's always scolding me, Father, about wanting to change the world. I do expect the best of everyone, including myself. But you loved us in the midst of our failures, didn't you? You loved us in spite of our sin. Is it all right with you if I love Jack Cornwall? He's not everything he could be or everything he will be in time. But, dear Father, may I have your permission to love the man?

Caitrin closed her eyes and hugged the two broken women beside her more tightly. "Beloved, let us love one another," the apostle John had written, "for love is of God; and every one that loveth is born of God, and knoweth God. He that loveth not knoweth not God; for God is love."

Though the sunshine crept across the soddy floor, Caitrin slept again, wrapped in an exhausted peace.

Dark clouds and an unexpected heat rolled across the prairie from the west. The promise of rain lifted Caitrin's heart as she hurried down the path worn in the creek bank. In spite of the town meeting's few prayers and violent battle, it appeared God had heard the people's plea and was sending water for their crops.

After feeding her two guests a late breakfast, changing the bandage on Sheena's forehead, and finding a complete set of clothing for Lucy, she convinced the younger woman to bathe. Never had Caitrin seen such a horrific sight as the self-inflicted scrapes and scratches that covered Lucy's pale skin. Sheena had gasped aloud, but she quickly took up a soft cloth and assisted Caitrin in the process.

When they finally had Lucy clean, dry, and dressed again, Sheena volunteered to brush out the tangled, matted hair. Though Caitrin's heart quaked at the trouble that might befall her two charges, she used the opportunity to leave them alone for a few minutes.

"Mrs. Cornwall?" she called outside one of the canvas tents. "Mrs. Cornwall, 'tis Caitrin Murphy, so it is."

Lightning flickered on the horizon. Within two hours, the rain should arrive. And it was about time. The long, dry prairie grass fairly stretched toward the heavens in a plea for water. Birds flocked around the wells hoping for a spare droplet spilled from a bucket. A child could ford Bluestem Creek without wetting his knees. The farmers would be thanking God at this very moment.

"Mrs. Cornwall?" she called again. "I've come to look in on Jack."

"Please go home, Miss Murphy." Felicity's voice grated like gravel. "I'll thank you to bring my daughter to me at once. After I've taken the horse and wagon to the smithy to load up Jack's tools, we'll be away by dusk."

Caitrin clasped her hands tightly. If Jack were too weak to resist, his mother could actually follow through on her plan. She might never lay eyes on him again.

"Please, Mrs. Cornwall, I've just come to see about your son. Is he all right?"

She listened to the silence from the tent. Finally she heard a groan. "Who's out there, Mama?"

"Jack!" Caitrin called. "'Tis I, Caitrin Murphy. Are you all right?"

"Come inside, Caitrin."

Fearing to incur Felicity's wrath after the previous night's fragile peace, Caitrin hesitated a moment. But her need to be with Jack overcame her concerns. Pushing aside the flap that blocked the entrance, she stepped into the shadowy tent. Felicity sat on a low stool near a pallet on the floor. She looked up from her knitting, her eyes swollen with crying.

Caitrin knelt beside the pallet and took Jack's hand. "Your mother told me the wound was clean. You'll be all right, won't you?"

"I reckon so." He reached up and touched a curly tendril of her hair. "You okay?"

"Aye. But worried."

"Listen, Caitrin." He winced as he elbowed himself upward. "About last night. I'm sorry for losing my head. I couldn't take Jimmy mean-mouthing my family, and I just—"

244

"Jack, you acted out of a right heart."

"A right heart maybe, but a reckless brain. Fact is, I didn't think. I just jumped up there and went after the fellow."

"And got a bullet for it," Felicity said. "That's the second time somebody in this wicked place has wounded my son."

"Now, listen here, Mama—"

"We're leaving, Jack, and don't argue with your mother. As soon as Miss Murphy brings Lucy to us, I'm going to load the wagons, and we'll be off. And none too soon."

Jack gazed at Caitrin. She could all but read the question in his eyes: *Do you want me to stay in Hope, Caitrin? Do you want me to stay?*

"Mrs. Cornwall," a man's voice called from outside the tent. "This is Seth Hunter. How's Jack?"

"Alive," she returned.

"I've come to give you a message. In light of what happened last night, the men around here feel it's important to discuss the future of the Cornwall family in Hope. We've called a meeting over at the mercantile one hour from now. Rustemeyer and I will keep order, and there'll be no guns and no fistfights. Jimmy O'Toole is coming to speak his piece in an orderly manner. We'd like you to come and stand up for yourselves."

"That won't be necessary," Felicity said. "We're leaving this wretched town."

Jack's gray eyes locked on Caitrin as if seeking strength and confirmation. "I'll be there," he told Seth. "I'll be at the mercantile in an hour."

CHAPTER 17

JACK hobbled into the mercantile at five that afternoon. His mother was busy packing up the tents and gathering the cooking gear and furniture they had used during their stay. Felicity had made up her mind to leave, and Lucy would go with her. The two women had no place to go in Missouri, and Jack knew he could not allow them to head off into the unknown. If he couldn't talk these stubborn townsfolk into letting them stay, he was going to have more trouble on his hands than he knew how to manage.

He eased himself down onto a bench and watched as the local homesteaders filed into the building. There was Casimir Laski, whose Polish hymns were a regular part of the Sunday services. Salvatore Rippeto entered the mercantile, glanced at Jack, and then turned away as if embarrassed. LeBlanc, the mill owner whose bevy of lovely daughters graced the community dances, followed Rippeto. Rolf Rustemeyer, Seth Hunter, and Jimmy O'Toole walked in, conferring in low tones. A handful of others, single young homesteaders—several of them sporting black eyes or swollen noses—took the benches around Jack.

"I reckon we ought to get started," Seth said, stepping up to the pulpit usually reserved for Sundays. "Some of you fellows have come a distance and need to get back before dark, so we'll try to make this quick. You all know Jack Cornwall here. Jack, would you mind coming up to the front here and taking this chair so we can all hear what you have to say?"

This was beginning to take on the aura of a courtroom trial, and Jack knew he didn't have much of a defense. All the same, he stood and hobbled painfully to the front of the room. As he turned to the chair, he saw Rose Hunter, Sheena O'Toole, and Caitrin Murphy enter the mercantile.

"Hold on a minute, ladies," Seth said. "This is men's business."

"Is that so?" Rosie returned, setting her hands on her hips and giving her husband a bold look. "It seems to me the Cornwall group is made up of one male and two females. That's more of us than you, by my calculation, and I think the women of this town deserve a say-so in the matter."

Some of the men chuckled as a flush crept up Seth's neck. "Now, Rosie, I don't need to tell you that women don't have any voice in the government of the state of Kansas. And since Hope is in Kansas—"

"We'll not vote then," Caitrin said. "But give us permission to listen to the proceedings. After all, we've done our part to make this a town."

"Suffragists," LeBlanc muttered. "I have a house full of them. You must be strong, Seth, or soon we will have women wearing trousers and putting their fingers into our politics."

"Aye," Jimmy agreed. "What are you doin' out of bed anyway, Sheena?"

"I'll be plucked for a goose if I won't watch this, Jimmy O'Toole! 'Tis my children who must grow up in this town, and I'll know what you men are about, so I will. Now will you kindly permit these ladies and me to sit down before we swoon in this unseasonable heat?"

Seth looked from Jimmy to Rolf, and then he surveyed the room for a reaction to the request. Jack noted that some of the farmers appeared more bemused than angry, but others looked downright irritated. "All right," Seth said. "You can stay and listen. But you're to keep quiet, and there'll be no female voting."

Jack watched a light of victory suffuse the women's faces. As glad as he was to see Caitrin, he wasn't too sure himself about letting ladies in on a matter like this. It was the men who would decide his fate.

"Back to business," Seth said. "There's two sides to the matter that has turned our town on its ear. On the one hand, we have a hardworking man in Jack Cornwall, a man who had the courage to put his past behind him and try to start a new life among us. He's built a fine smithy, and from what everyone tells me, he does good work. Matter of fact, I hear he's the best smithy from Topeka to Manhattan. Not only does the man do good work, but he stands up for his family. He has protected his widowed mother and his sister, and he has some loyal friends. I'd call myself Jack Cornwall's friend, despite some troubles we had in the past."

Jack shifted on the chair, trying to ease the pressure from his injured leg. He could see the thick black clouds moving closer across the horizon. Flickers of lightning licked the prairie. Puffs of dry dirt lifted into the air, spun around into dust devils, and danced away. That rain ought to be here before long, he thought, and a good thing. It would trap all the farmers inside the mercantile and give him time to argue his case. He had prayed for the chance to speak his mind. Maybe this rainstorm was God's answer.

"On the other hand," Seth said, "Jack Cornwall has brought with him quite a collection of troubles. Now as you all know, we gave him a month's grace here in Hope, and we've let him stay longer than that. But last night's ruckus over at the prayer meeting has brought us together to take a second look at the situation. Now let's consider that . . ."

Jack's attention wandered to Caitrin, and the hammering urge to defend himself with violence and revenge subsided. As long as he lived, Jack would never forget the night he met the red-haired

Irishwoman for the first time. *I love you,* she had told him. *You are precious to the Father, and I love you.* Because of those words, he had eventually surrendered his heart to Christ, given up his old reckless ways, and stepped onto a new path. He had left Missouri and the companions who had led him into trouble. He had done everything in his power to build a new life here on the prairie.

Love had always been a mystery to him, a word that had no real meaning, no definition. But through Caitrin, that word had become as bright, glowing, and real as the fire in his forge. By watching her example, he had come to understand that true love—for God and for people—couldn't just hide away in someone's heart like a cozy, personal secret. Love demanded an open demonstration in both words and actions.

Caitrin's love had led her to defend Jack, to believe the best of him, to trust him, and to honor him. In love, she stood by him with more than her words. She stepped out in active faith, taking his troubled sister into her home and helping Lucy find reason to hope. Caitrin respected his mother, in spite of Felicity's brusque ways and bitter tongue. Through love, Caitrin had stood tall against every flame of fire that threatened to consume her.

Faith, hope, and love, Jack thought, recalling the verse he'd read somewhere in the Bible. *The greatest of these is love.* He had learned how it felt to be loved. And Caitrin Murphy had taught him to love in return.

He loved her, he realized as he studied the woman across the room. He loved Caitrin Murphy with his whole heart. It was time she knew.

"I have something to say," he began, cutting into Seth Hunter's speech. He stood with difficulty and faced the congregated farmers. "I want to tell you why I came here to Hope and why I'm not leaving. It's Caitrin Murphy. I love her, and I'm—"

"Oh, Jack!" Caitrin cried, coming to her feet.

"You'd better shut your smush, Jack Cornwall," Jimmy O'Toole shouted, jumping up. "We're only halfway through the list of trials you've caused us, and you have no right to speak. And furthermore, Caitrin Murphy is my wife's sister, and she won't have you! We'll not allow it."

"You gentlemen better both sit down right now!" Seth ordered. "We've got a storm coming, and we need to get this over with so everybody can go home. Now, I already mentioned the problem with Miss Cornwall and her spells. Jack's sister has a passel of troubles, and those chains she wears don't help her a bit. But even though we all feel sorry for Miss Cornwall, a lot of you have confided to me that you don't like the notion of a grown woman throwing herself in front of stagecoaches, trying to drown herself in the Bluestem, and running around without her clothes on. She's scaring the children, and the women are complaining that they don't trust her not to hurt somebody."

Jack couldn't bring himself to sit. He didn't want to listen to a recitation of the trials that beset his family and in turn brought trouble on this community. Didn't *everyone* have troubles of one kind or another? And hadn't Jesus said something about bearing one another's burdens? Caitrin once told Jack that faith in Christ didn't take away the problems, but it gave a believer comfort and strength to bear them. Why couldn't these men just let him walk in that faith through the fires of his life? Why couldn't they support him with their concern and prayer. Was that too much to ask?

"And then there was that problem between Mrs. Cornwall and Mrs. O'Toole a while back," Seth continued. "We all know Sheena has been suffering for some time as a result of her fall on the creek bank. Now I certainly don't believe Mrs. Cornwall has the same notions as her daughter, but she's caused a good bit of trouble in her own right. Which brings us to last night at the prayer meeting."

"First, I'd like to speak to the matter of the trouble between

Felicity Cornwall and myself," Sheena said, rising. "I'll have you know—"

"Sit down, wife!" Jimmy commanded. "You're not to talk, lass, and I'll thank you to mind the rules Seth set out."

Coloring a bright red, Sheena sank back onto the bench as Seth went on. "Now, things were going along all right, until—"

A crack of thunder shook the mercantile. Jack glanced out the window. A rusty glow had joined the boiling black clouds moving toward the town. Dust blew against the glass windows. A loose shingle slapped on the roof.

"Anyway," Seth said, speaking quickly, "you all know what happened. Jack jumped up on the wagon and threw Jimmy over the side, a fight broke out, Jack got himself shot in the leg, and about half the men in this room wound up injured. So, now you know both sides of the matter, and it's time to vote."

"Both sides?" Jack spoke up. "You told me to sit up here at the front. Now it's my turn to speak for myself and my family."

"Your actions speak louder than words," Jimmy shouted. "You came to us with a bullet wound in your shoulder, and you'll leave with one in your leg. That tells us all we need to know about you. Let's vote, men! I've chickens to pen up."

At that moment Jack's old comrade, Bill Hermann, walked into the mercantile with a badge-wearing lawman at his side. Jack let out a groan as the farmers turned to stare. Caitrin gave a muffled cry.

"I think I can make this whole mess easy for you, gentlemen," Hermann announced. He turned to Jack. "I've been searchin' for you a long time, buddy. Seems you stir up a ruckus no matter where you go."

"This is none of your concern, Bill," Jack said. "You stay out of it. I'm going to work things out with these men, and then I'll talk to you outside."

"I don't believe there's any workin' out to do." Hermann held up a sheet of paper and unrolled it before his curious audience. "This here's a subpoena, gentlemen. Your friend, Jack Cornwall, is headin' back to Missouri."

"Now just a cotton-picking minute, Bill," Jack exploded.

"You gonna come peaceful?" the lawman spoke over the hubbub.

"Am I under arrest?"

"No, sir, but if you resist me, I can have you arrested sure as shootin'. This subpoena says you're to appear at a trial in Jefferson City to testify for the defense in the matter of the Easton lynchin'."

"I wasn't at the Easton lynching, and Bill Hermann knows it." Jack turned on his former companion. "Don't try to drag me into that mess, Bill. You know I wasn't there that night, and I'll be jiggered if—"

"You were there, Cornwall," Hermann interrupted. "Admit it. You were there. You saw everything that happened. You know exactly who done what, and you can get the fellers off the hook. Come on, Jack, stand up for the old bunch."

"I'd gone to Sedalia earlier that day. I was with . . . with somebody." Jack raked a hand through his hair. He knew he couldn't prove himself—not without causing more trouble than ever. "I never saw one thing that happened out at the Easton cabin. You expect me to get up there on the stand and lie, Bill?"

"I expect you to do whatever it takes to defend the men you once called brothers. Deputy, looks to me like he's resisting."

"Now hold on a minute," Seth Hunter said, holding up both hands. He turned on Bill Hermann. "Listen, sir. We're in the middle of a proceeding here. Whatever trouble happened between you and Jack Cornwall can be worked out later. We've got to get on with our vote before the storm hits."

"Then make it snappy," the lawman said as he took off his hat and scratched his head. "That rain's gonna make me miss my supper."

"All right, men," Seth said. "I'm going to give Jack five minutes to state his case."

"He's had more than a month to prove himself," Jimmy countered. "'Tis time to vote. How many think Jack Cornwall and his family ought to stay here in Hope? Raise your hand."

"I have a right to speak!" Jack roared. "This is my life you're messing with, O'Toole."

"I vote to keep the blacksmith," LeBlanc said, standing and lifting his hand. "I have many repairs on my mill. Maybe the man makes trouble, but he does good work."

"I'm for letting him stay," Seth said. "Jack had the guts to come back here and carve out a business. He may have a hot head, but there's not a man among us who wouldn't have to own up to a fault or two. Jack, you have my vote."

Rolf Rustemeyer stood up. "I, too, think is goot this Jack Cornwall to stay here," he said. "I haf chance to come from Germany and make my farm. Here Cornwall can haf chance. Here Cornwall can stay."

"That's three," Jimmy said. "Any others? All right, how many of you vote that we ask the Cornwalls to leave Hope?"

Rippeto's hand shot up, followed by Laski's and those of the other farmers. Jimmy counted the men and included himself in the tally. "That's three for staying and seven for leaving. I say it's clear—"

"What kind of justice is this?" Caitrin cried. "'Tis only fair that you give Jack Cornwall the chance to speak for himself."

"Sit down!" a chorus of men's voices erupted.

"More trouble!" Jimmy cried. "Now Cornwall has the women rising up against us, so he does. You're voted out, Jack Cornwall. And as for you, Caitrin Murphy, I'll say it again—good riddance to bad rummage! You'd better pack your trunks—"

"Enough with your blather, Jimmy O'Toole!" Sheena said, leaping up. "Caitrin is my sister, so she is, and you'll not put her on any boat to Ireland!"

Jack took a step forward and squared his shoulders. He'd have his say, blast it, and not a man would drive him out before. He glanced out the window. The rusty cloud had transformed into a creeping tide of flames that lit the sky and sent up the black billows of smoke everyone had mistaken for rain clouds.

"Fire!" he hollered. "Fire headed this way!"

Men raced to the windows. "Fire! Fire!"

Sheena began to scream. Rosie ran to Seth. Heart slamming against his chest, Jack climbed up onto the chair. "Listen up, men," he shouted. "I'm a blacksmith. In the army, I learned how to handle a runaway fire. I'll tell you what we've got to do."

The farmers quickly left the window and gathered around him.

"Hitch up your plows," Jack told them, "and run a half dozen or so fresh furrows around your houses and barns. A few yards of bare dirt can hold back a raging fire. The minute you're finished, grab all the grain sacks and buckets you can lay your hands on, and ride down here to the Bluestem."

"What about the women?" Seth asked.

"Take the smallest children across the bridge to the O'Tooles' house. The fire won't jump the creek. Then all the women and the older children meet on this side of the Bluestem and start soaking grain sacks and filling buckets. My leg won't let me do much against the fire, so I'll hitch my horse to a wagon and haul the sacks and buckets out to the front line."

"But what are we to do against such a blaze?" Jimmy asked. "Sure, I've never fought a fire in my life!"

"Some of you men take the wet sacks and beat out the flames. Others throw buckets of water. I'll start a backfire if I need to. The wind is driving the blaze this direction, and we don't want to lose the town. Let's go, everybody. And while you work—*pray!*"

Jack gritted his teeth against the pain as he stepped down from the chair. The farmers poured through the mercantile door. Jimmy huddled over Sheena, consoling her and begging her to stay abed in their soddy. Rosie gave Seth a quick embrace and started for the door, but he caught her hand and drew her close again. As they talked, Caitrin approached Jack.

"What about Bill Hermann?" she asked. "Jack, he says you know things about that murder."

"I wasn't at the Easton lynching," he said. "I told you that before. I may be hotheaded, but I'm no liar. Don't you believe me, Caitrin?"

He read the doubt in her green eyes and a fist knotted at the base of his stomach. He would fight the men of Hope to be allowed to stay here. He would battle Bill Hermann and the laws of Kansas and Missouri to be allowed to get his way. But if Caitrin lost faith in him . . .

"Oh, Jack," she said. "How has it come to this?"

He caught her by the waist and pulled her roughly against him. "What it's come to is that I love you, Caitrin Murphy. I love you, and I want you for my wife. I don't care what these rascals try to do to separate us, I won't leave you. I'll stand by you the rest of my life, and I'll make us a good home. A happy home. But I need to hear the words again, Caitrin. Those three words."

She stared up at him, her eyes filling with tears. "Jack—"

"Come on, Caitie!" Sheena cried out, grabbing her sister's hand. "Sure, the whole place is going to burn down around us if we don't get busy. Save your gabbin' for later."

Caitrin swallowed. "Be careful, Jack," she said.

He held his breath as she pulled away from him and ran out of the mercantile.

>-

"Lucy?" Caitrin sprinted into her soddy and looked around. "What are you doing here?"

The woman's head emerged from the hiding place she had made for herself. "I came back. I don't want to go away, Caitrin."

"Oh, Lucy, a prairie fire is coming. Sure, you must go back to your mother."

"I'll look after Lucy," Sheena said, entering the soddy. Her cheeks were flushed. "I'll take her to our soddy, and she can bake cinnamon buns for the *brablins*. 'Twill take our thoughts away from the fire."

The young woman rose from behind the bed. "Mrs. O'Toole . . . I . . ."

"Come with me, Lucy. Help me."

The young woman held her hand toward Sheena. "Tell me what to do, Mrs. O'Toole."

Embracing Lucy warmly, Sheena led her out of the soddy. Caitrin gathered grain sacks and towels and hurried away to defend her town.

>~

Black, pungent smoke clutched at Jack's throat as he drove Scratch down the line of men fighting the prairie fire. The horse tossed its head and neighed in terror of the flames, but Jack kept the creature moving parallel to the blaze. Dusk had settled as the fire crept ever forward, a bright, devouring glow that ate its way toward Hope.

Seth Hunter's new frame house stood directly in the fire's path. The shed would go first. Then the house would be consumed. Finally the new barn filled with the last winter hay would explode into flames. After that, it would be only a matter of time until the fire reached Caitrin's little home. The heavy prairie sod wouldn't burn, of course, but the smokehouse, the door, and the window frames would. The mercantile would be next—wood shingles, wood sign, new wood floor. All Caitrin's hard work would go up in flames. The new church would follow. Jack's smithy stood last in line before the Bluestem Creek would put a hissing stop to the crackle and flicker of this ravenous enemy.

"You'd better get the valuables out of your house," Jack called to

Seth as the homesteader unloaded a pile of dripping grain sacks. "Photographs, family treasures, that kind of thing."

Face blackened with soot, Seth stared up at Jack. "I spent all winter building that house. That's Rosie's . . ." The man looked away, fighting emotion. "That's Rosie's *home*."

"We'll do all we can to keep it safe, Seth. But I won't promise we can hold these flames at bay."

"Can you start a backfire?"

Jack studied the line of men, black silhouettes whipping at the tongues of orange flame and tossing bucket after bucket onto the conflagration. And still the wind pushed the fire ever forward. Behind the choking smoke, lightning flashed. The promise of rain. The hope of God's provision. But would it come in time? Would it be enough to stop the onslaught?

"Backfires are tricky," Jack said. "They can get away from you. If the wind takes this one the wrong direction—"

"It's worth a try. We're getting nowhere."

Jack tried to calm Scratch as he assessed the situation. "All right, but I'll need your help. We've got to keep fighting the big blaze until we can burn off a strip of grass a few yards away. Then we've got to get the men out of the way."

"We can do it," Seth said. "Help us, Jack."

They wouldn't have much time, and the wind was against them. But Jack pressed Scratch back toward the creek to alert the women and to pick up another load of sacks and buckets. Rosie had given out hours before and had joined Sheena and Lucy across the creek. With babies on the way, the women couldn't afford to push themselves too hard. But Jack was pleased to find Caitrin leading the others as they worked together at the creek.

Racing back to the fire, Jack prayed God would give him the wisdom to start the backfire in the right place. He prayed the wind would die down. He prayed the rain would fall. He prayed the homesteaders would have the stamina to keep fighting.

He could see the farmers now, gathering around Seth. Even Bill Hermann and the deputy had joined the effort. As the men divided into two groups, one to hold the big fire at bay and the other to manage the backfire, Jack climbed down from the wagon. He couldn't remember his shoulder ever hurting as much as his leg now burned. But there was no time to tend it.

"Stay near me," he told the group of men assigned to help him. "I'm going to light a line of fire. You fan it against the wind, keep it low, keep it safe. Once you've let the fire burn the grass for a couple of yards, beat it out and move to another place along the line. We can't let this thing get away from us."

As the men ranged out around him, Jack gathered a clump of dried prairie grass and lit it. Then he began moving slowly parallel to the encroaching fire and setting the grass aflame with his make-shift torch. The dry stems crackled like tinder, exploding as the sparks touched them. Alongside Jack, the men tended the back-fire, carefully fanning into the wind.

Once he had lit the backfire and it was successfully burning a barrier of charred grass between the prairie fire and the town, Jack made his way around the flames to the other men. "Seth!" he called. "Come on out now! It's time to let it go."

Dark shadows against the scarlet light, the exhausted farmers left their posts and hurried to escape the encroaching flames of the back-fire. As the men gathered in safety, they stood spellbound, watching the two lines of fire move ever closer toward each other.

"I think it'll work," Seth said. "I think we've got it licked."

"But fire can coming around?" Rolf asked, pointing to the vast stretch of prairie untouched by the backfire. "The big fire can coming this way around and still gif trouble?"

"Maybe," Jack said. "We'll keep an eye on it."

"Ja, goot." Rustemeyer clapped him on the back. "You helpen us. Now Jimmy O'Toole can see you are goot man. Where Jimmy is?"

Seth looked around, studying the soot-covered faces of the farmers. "Jimmy?" he called. "Jimmy?"

Jack scanned the flames. In a narrow patch of unburned grass between the prairie fire and the backfire, a lone silhouette whipped at the roaring blaze with a wet grain sack. Unhearing. Unseeing. Unaware of his peril.

It was Jimmy O'Toole.

CHAPTER 18

FOR AN INSTANT, Jack felt sure he was staring through the door of hell itself—and there stood Jimmy O'Toole, right in the middle of it. *Good riddance to bad rummage*, the Irishman had said to Caitrin. The words could just as easily be spoken to Jimmy himself. *Let him burn*, Jack thought. *He's a troublemaker—a spiteful, vengeful imp of a man without a redeeming bone in his skinny body.* With Jimmy out of the picture, Caitrin would have no reason to hold back. Would she?

But what kind of man was Jack to stand by and let another die? The words he himself had spoken came back to him. *Bear one another's burdens . . . Faith, hope, and love . . . the greatest of these is love.*

Love.

Grabbing a handful of wet sacks, Jack limped toward the fire. He could hear Seth shouting, ordering him not to go, but he picked up his pace. Rolf tried to catch his arm. The other farmers bellowed at him. "Too late," they cried. "It's too late!"

Jimmy turned now and saw the backfire creeping toward him. Eyes wide, face skeletal, he stared in helpless horror at the other men safe beyond the blaze. Jack edged forward across the blackened, smoking grass. Whipping at the flames that licked his trousers, he gritted his teeth and tried to ignore the pain that seared his injured leg. With agonizing slowness, he beat a path through the low-burning backfire.

"Cornwall!" Jimmy cried. Coughing, stripping away his shirt, the Irishman straggled back and forth on the narrow strip of un-burned grass, looking for a way out. "Cornwall, help me!"

"I'm coming," Jack called. He lashed at the fire, smothering flames, pushing forward. Smoke swirled around his head and filled his lungs. Choking, he paused and bent over to gasp for air.

Jimmy's voice came to him through the pall. "Cornwall, Cornwall!"

"Where are you?" Jack cried. "Where are you, O'Toole?"

Silence overwhelmed him as he stumbled onto the unburned patch. He could see nothing. Heat stung his skin. The crackle and snap of burning brush swirled around his ears.

"Jimmy O'Toole!"

A low cough caught his attention, and Jack fell to his knees beside the crumpled man. Lungs crying out in agony, he lifted the Irishman onto his shoulders. His leg might give out, Jack knew, but his arms were strong. With Jimmy's limp body sprawled over his back, Jack struggled to stand. *God, help me. Help me!*

Inching upward, he straightened. Which way? Which way out? He coughed, sure he would choke on the acrid smoke that filled his chest.

I am the way. Follow me.

Jack thought he heard the words, but he could see nothing. He staggered forward.

Follow me. Follow me.

Stumbling, aware of flames that caught the hems of his trousers and wreathed his ankles, Jack followed. Night cloaked him like a heavy, black blanket. His shoulders ached. His legs cramped. His lungs clamped down, strangling him.

Follow me.

Seth's face suddenly appeared and blessed arms gathered Jack in.

The weight lifted from his shoulders. He drifted upward, sure he was floating. *Out of hell and into heaven*, he thought.

Follow me.

Caitrin heaved the dripping bucket out of the creek and turned toward the fire. Across the moonlit prairie she spotted a cluster of men moving toward her like wraiths. Flames flickered behind them, smoke billowed above them. Whips of white lightning cracked through the air.

"Jack!" Caitrin knew immediately he was one of the men they carried among them. "Oh no, 'tis Jack!"

She dropped the heavy bucket, grabbed her skirts, and started running.

"Here is two manners," Rolf said, leaving the group and trotting toward the women. "Is Cornwall and O'Toole both."

"What about the fire?"

"Is stop."

"To my soddy then!" Caitrin cried. "Follow me!"

Unable to hold back her tears, she led the men through the night toward the low mound that formed the roof of her small house. They stepped over the boards of the broken door and carried their two comrades inside. Caitrin lit lamps as the men laid Jimmy and Jack side by side on the bed.

"They're neither one breathing!" Seth said. "One time a fellow in the army fell out of a tree, and the captain of our troop breathed the breath of life right back into him. You reckon we oughta try it, Miss Murphy?"

"Show me," she said, swiping the back of her hand across her damp cheek.

Seth leaned over Jimmy, clamped two fingers on the man's nose, and breathed deeply into the Irishman's mouth. Caitrin placed her lips over Jack's mouth, held his nose tightly, and forced a breath down into his lungs. She saw his chest rise. As it fell, the cloying scent of smoke escaped his lungs.

"I love you, Jack Cornwall," she whispered through trembling lips. "Sure, you're not a perfect man, but I love you all the same. No matter the consequences, I want to be your wife. Now breathe, Jack. Please, breathe!"

She bent over the man again and forced air down into his lungs.

Seth lifted away from Jimmy. "It worked on that soldier," he said. "I don't know what's wrong, Miss Murphy."

She drank in another deep breath. When she leaned toward Jack's mouth, his arms slipped around her, drawing her close. "Caitrin," he mumbled.

"Thank God!" Letting out the breath, she sank onto Jack's shoulder and sobbed. His hands moved up her back, his fingers slid into her hair, and he heaved a deep sigh. Beside him, Jimmy began coughing, shaking the whole bed, as Rolf and the other men gathered around with words of encouragement.

"Jimmy? Jimmy?" Sheena cried as she appeared in the doorway. Behind her were Rosie, Lucy, Felicity Cornwall, and the other women and children. At the sight of her husband sitting up and wiping the soot from his eyes, Sheena stopped. "Oh, Jimmy, are you alive?"

"Aye, but barely." Jimmy stretched out his arms. "Come here to me, Sheena, my love. I need a hug."

Bursting into tears, Sheena elbowed her way to the bed and threw her arms around her husband. Caitrin held Jack so tightly she was afraid she might suffocate him all over again. But she couldn't let go. Not now. Not ever.

"Caitrin?" Jack's voice was husky. "Say the words again."

"I love you," she said softly, knowing what he needed to hear. "'Tis those three words that will bond us forever. You are precious to the Father, and with his love I love you. But you are precious to me, too, Jack Cornwall, and with my whole heart I love you."

He let out a rattling breath and drew her closer.

"Pretty words and a happy scene," Bill Hermann said as he appeared at the door of the soddy and attempted to push through the crowd, "but I ain't got time for sweetness. Jack, let's go."

"You'll not take this man anywhere!" Caitrin cried, looking daggers at the rascal. "Sure, he's a *donsie* thing, barely alive, and you want to cart him off to Missouri? You'll do no such thing!"

"I got a subpoena."

"I don't care if you've a letter from the president himself. Get out of my house!" She jumped to her feet and shook a finger in the man's face. "Out, villain! Out!"

"Listen, ma'am," the deputy said over Hermann's shoulder. "This ain't exactly somethin' I enjoy, but I've got my duty. This here subpoena means Jack Cornwall has to go back to Missouri to testify about that lynchin'."

"I wasn't there," Jack said.

"He's telling the truth," Lucy whispered. "My brother was in Sedalia with . . . with me the night of that lynchin'."

All eyes turned to the frail young woman. "Ma'am, you may be tellin' the truth, but a sister's word ain't gonna be worth nothin' in a court of law."

"It's okay, Lucy," Jack said, elbowing himself up. He coughed and then spoke in a raspy voice. "Listen, Deputy, I've got a blacksmithing business to run here. Can't you just take a sworn testimony that I wasn't at the Easton cabin that night?"

"Nope. Says right here, you got to testify in person."

"He wasn't there," Lucy repeated softly. "Jack was . . . he was in town. He was with me. We were . . . we were—"

"That's enough, Lucy!" Felicity Cornwall said. "We don't tell our family business in public."

"Mama, please . . ."

"It's okay, Lucy." Jack studied his blackened hands. "Bill Hermann, you know if I lie for you, I'm going to land in jail myself.

If I tell a court of law that I was at the Easton cabin, I'm implicating myself in the crime. You expect me to do that for the bunch?"

"Don't you care about us no more, Jack?" Bill Hermann asked. "We was your family there toward the end of the war. We gave you a place to stay, food to eat, a cause to fight for. We loved you, Jack."

Jack lifted his head and eyed his former comrade. "You don't know the meaning of love, my friend," he said. He looked at Caitrin. "But I do. I understand love. It's more than just words. It's stepping out on a limb for someone, even if they don't deserve it—the way Christ laid down his life for me, bad as I've been." Turning back to Bill Hermann, Jack squared his shoulders. "So I'll go to Missouri with you."

"No!" Caitrin cried.

"Come on then," Bill said, reaching for Jack. "We'll get a wagon and—"

"He was with me!" Lucy elbowed her way around the bed toward the deputy. "Jack was with me. I can prove it."

"Don't do this, Lucy," Jack said. "Don't—"

"I know about love, too, Jack," Lucy said softly, her gray eyes huge and luminous. "I can . . . I can walk on limbs as good as the next person." She drew a locket from around her neck, pried it open, and pulled out a small piece of folded paper. "Here, Deputy. I carry this with me everywhere."

"Oh, Lucy, how could you!" Felicity cried and fled the soddy.

The deputy took the paper and opened it. "This here paper is signed by Mr. Cornwall, Miss Cornwall, and by a Sedalia lawyer, too. It looks like a document turnin' over a baby for adoption."

Caitrin slipped her arm around Lucy's shoulders as she spoke in a voice barely audible. "The Yankee soldiers," Lucy said. "They came to our farm and . . . robbed and . . . and burned . . . and . . ."

"Lucy," Jack said, reaching for his sister.

"After they . . . they hurt me . . . I was carrying a baby. Mama didn't want the shame. The shame . . ."

"Aw, Luce, you don't have to do this."

"I loved my baby," Lucy continued in the hush of the room. "But Mama said . . . said it was a good family . . . and Jack took me to Sedalia to sign the paper. It has the date and time stamped on it." With a trembling finger, she pointed to the document in the deputy's hand.

The man scratched his head. "Yep, that's the day of the Easton lynching, and the time is six in the evenin'. That Easton feller was swingin' by a rope at six o'clock that night."

One arm still around Lucy, Caitrin gripped Jack's hand. Confused, hopeful, and terrified all at once, she waited for the man's response.

The deputy looked down at the paper in his hands. "This lawyer a feller I can find in Sedalia?"

"Yes," Lucy whispered.

"You reckon he'd swear he signed this document?"

"Yes, sir."

The deputy folded the document and stuffed it into his own shirt pocket. "I'm hungry," he said. "I'm hungry, and I missed my supper fightin' that confounded prairie fire out here in the middle of nowhere. And now I find out this subpoena can't hold no more water than a leaky bucket. Bill Hermann, you better wangle up another witness, 'cause Jack Cornwall just got himself an alibi."

"You're not taking Jack back to Missouri?" Caitrin asked, scarcely able to form the words.

"I'm not haulin' any of you folks nowhere. I'm goin' home to my wife and my supper."

As the deputy exited and Bill Hermann stomped out of the soddy behind him, Caitrin clapped her hands over her mouth. A whoop of joy went up around the room. Rosie grabbed Lucy's hands and started dancing around in circles.

"Will wonders never cease?" Sheena said over the racket. Standing, she crossed her arms and surveyed the scene. As the group quieted, she lifted her chin. "An Irishman in bed with a Cornishman? And the pair of you as black as midnight and smelling like chimneys. Well, isn't this as cozy as two lumps of sugar in a teacup?"

"Aye," Jimmy said. With a grunt, he sat up. "And 'tis a cup of tea as sweet as any ever tasted. When I saw Jack Cornwall comin' through the flames, Sheena, he was no Cornishman to me. He was an angel of God himself. This man carried me out of that fire on his own two shoulders, and he saved my life. I'm an Irishman, tough as the sod and unforgiving as a winter wind, but my own sin is standing right before my eyes, and I'll not ignore it any longer."

Jimmy turned to the man beside him. "Forgive me, Jack Cornwall."

"And me," Sheena whispered. "Thank you for saving my Jimmy's life."

"Done," Jack said, shaking the Irishman's hand.

"Well," Felicity Cornwall said, stepping back into the soddy. "This is quite a sight. My son abed with an Irishman and in love with an Irishwoman. My daughter's shame spread into the open air for everyone to see. My husband dead . . . dead and buried, unable to . . . to defend his family . . ."

"Mrs. Cornwall," Sheena said, "there's naught to defend, for there's no longer an enemy."

Felicity set her hands on her hips and studied the faces around the room. "I don't understand this," she said. "I don't understand it."

"It's love, Mama," Jack said. "Accept it."

"Well," Felicity said. "Well, I never."

"I never either, Mama, but it's about time we did."

"You are precious to the Father, Mrs. Cornwall," Caitrin murmured, taking Felicity's hand. "And I love you."

"Well," Felicity said again. She swallowed hard. "Thank you,

268

Miss Murphy. And, Mrs. O'Toole . . . thank you for . . . I'm sorry for . . ."

"La, Mrs. Cornwall," Sheena said, wrapping the older woman in a hug, "all's forgiven."

"Time for another vote!" Seth called out. "How many in favor of letting the Cornwall family stay in Hope?"

A roar of response filled the soddy as every hand in the room shot toward the ceiling. "Welcome to Hope, Mrs. Cornwall, Jack, Lucy," Seth said. "Now let's go check on that fire, men!"

His words were followed by a crack of lightning, a boom of thunder, and a wall of rain that raced over the soddy's roof like a bag of spilled marbles. Laughter filled the air at the knowledge that the town called Hope had been spared, that the creek would run high again, and that crops would flourish. Fathers lifted their sons onto their backs and headed into the downpour. Mothers took their daughters' hands and skipped outside to dance in the puddles.

Seth tugged a quilt around Rosie, grabbed Chipper, and headed for home, Stubby barking at their heels. Felicity took Lucy's hand and hurried her toward their camp to unroll canvases and cover the half-filled wagons. Jimmy hobbled out of bed, gave Jack a friendly squeeze on the shoulder, gathered his wife and his *brablins*, and made for the bridge.

Jack stood slowly, his arm around Caitrin's shoulders for support. Together they stepped out of the soddy into the night and let the cool water pour over them, washing away pain and fear along with the soot.

"The fire nearly got us," Jack said, holding Caitrin close.

"'Twas not a killing fire, as we feared," Caitrin answered softly. "'Twas the heavenly Refiner's fire, melting away the dross and impurities in our lives and welding us together with a golden bond that will never break."

"You know something, Caitrin Murphy?" Jack asked. "You're going to make some blacksmith a mighty fine wife."

"Aye," she said with a laugh. "And all because of three little words."

Their lips met, and a love beyond any she had ever imagined welled in Caitrin's heart as they melted into the Father's precious baptism of hope, grace, and peace.

Prairie Fire

DISCUSSION QUESTIONS

1. Why does Caitrin extend kindness in word and deed to Jack Cornwall? What effect does this have on him?
2. What causes Jack's change of heart? How does God draw Jack to himself?
3. Why does Rosie stand up for Jack and convince Seth to give him a chance?
4. In chapter 6, Sheena tells Caitrin, "That's the trouble with you. You see things for what they could be, not for what they are." Caitrin points out that that kind of thinking is what causes transformation. Who is right, in your opinion? Is Sheena right when she says one can't change people? that you have to accept them as they are?
5. At one point, Caitrin is so frustrated with her circumstances that she throws a plate against the wall as she complains to God. Is it okay to be mad at God for one's lot in life? Why or why not?
6. Jack says that Caitrin was sent to him by God to show him what God and love are like. This scares Caitrin, who tells him not to look to her, an imperfect person, to understand God. Who is right? How does God use imperfect people to show who he is and what he is like?
7. What is the real cause of Lucy's mental problems? Does the way her brother and mother treat her help her or hurt her? What finally sets her free?

8. Jack thinks he knows what God wants of his people. What is it? Is he right? How does the story prove it?
9. Fire is a recurring theme in this book. Discuss how this image of fire plays out in Jack's and Caitrin's personalities, in their relationship, and in the plot.
10. The town of Hope prays for the rain they so desperately need. What does God send? Does he answer their prayer?
11. In this story, what is the source of prejudice? What is the result of prejudice? How is it overcome?

ABOUT THE AUTHOR

CATHERINE PALMER lives in Atlanta with her husband, Tim, where they serve as missionaries in a refugee community. They have two grown sons. Catherine is a graduate of Southwest Baptist University and holds a master's degree in English from Baylor University. Her first book was published in 1988. Since then she has published more than fifty novels, many of them national best sellers. Catherine has won numerous awards for her writing, including the Christy Award, the highest honor in Christian fiction. In 2004, she was given the Career Achievement Award for Inspirational Romance by *Romantic Times BOOKreviews* magazine. More than 2 million copies of Catherine's novels are currently in print.

With her compelling characters and strong message of Christian faith, Catherine is known for writing fiction that "touches the hearts and souls of readers." Her many collections include A Town Called Hope, Treasures of the Heart, Finders Keepers, English Ivy, and the Miss Pickworth series. Catherine also recently coauthored the Four Seasons fiction series with Gary Chapman, the *New York Times* best-selling author of *The Five Love Languages*.

Visit catherinepalmer.com for more information on future releases. To learn more about her work as a missionary to refugees, visit palmermissions.blogspot.com.

Available now

Dogwood
Chris Fabry

The Moment Between
Nicole Baart

Fireflies in December
Jennifer Erin Valent

My Sister Dilly
Maureen Lang

Vanish
Tom Pawlik

Out of Her Hands
Megan DiMaria

www.tyndalefiction.com

*For more information, check online
or at your local retailer*

CP0225

have you visited
tyndalefiction.com
lately?

Only there can you find:

- ⟩ books hot off the press
- ⟩ first chapter excerpts
- ⟩ inside scoops on your favorite authors
- ⟩ author interviews
- ⟩ contests
- ⟩ fun facts
- ⟩ and much more!

Sign up for your **free** newsletter!

Visit us today at: **tyndalefiction.com**

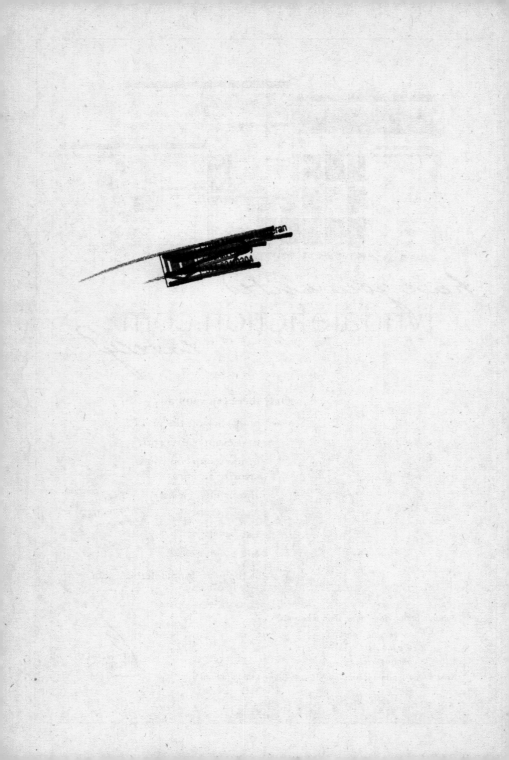